The Loner:
TRAIL OF BLOOD

The Loner:
TRAIL OF BLOOD

J. A. Johnstone

PINNACLE BOOKS
Kensington Publishing Corp.
www.kensingtonbooks.com

PINNACLE BOOKS are published by

Kensington Publishing Corp.
119 West 40th Street
New York, NY 10018

All Kensington titles, imprints, and distributed lines are available at special quantity discounts for bulk purchases for sales promotions, premiums, fund-raising, educational, or institutional use. Special book excerpts or customized printings can also be created to fit specific needs. For details, write or phone the office of the Kensington special sales manager: Kensington Publishing Corp., 119 West 40th Street, New York, NY 10018, attn: Special Sales Department; phone 1-800-221-2647.

ISBN-13: 978-0-7860-2616-6
ISBN-10: 0-7860-2616-2

First printing: February 2011

10 9 8 7 6 5 4 3 2 1

Printed in the United States of America

Chapter 1

The men boarded the train at different stops as it rolled through West Texas: three at Sweet Apple, four at Sierra Blanca, the final pair at Pecos. Each group gave no sign they knew the others.

Yet those who were familiar with the signs could tell the men were cut from the same cloth, whether they were acquainted or not. They had the same hard, watchful eyes, the same air of tension about them that was mindful of a coiled spring. Their hands never strayed far from the guns on their hips.

Nearing the dawn of a new, modern century, fewer men packed iron than had twenty years earlier, and fewer still did so openly. Since the men were spread out on the train, no one really paid much attention to them despite the guns.

That is, until one of the men in the second of two passenger cars stood up, balanced himself against the slight swaying and rocking of the coach, and reached up with his left hand to yank on the emergency cord. Passengers were flung forward in their seats, some tumbled to the floor and most cried out in sudden fear as the engineer up in the cab of the smoke-spewing locomotive threw on the brakes. Outside, sparks flew in the air as drivers locked and skidded on the steel rails.

The man who pulled the cord braced himself for the jolt by grabbing the back of the bench seat beside him. He was still on his feet when he lifted the bandanna around his neck up over the lower half of his face. He drew the Colt from its holster on his hip and yelled over the hubbub, "Nobody move! Do what you're told and nobody gets killed!"

The menacing revolver drew more screams and shouts. A male passenger, red-faced with anger, leaped up and yelled, "By God, you can't—"

The man with the gun shot him.

The Colt's roar was deafeningly loud in the close confines of the railroad car. The slug smashed into the red-faced man's shoulder, slewing him halfway around. Crying thinly in agony, he slumped against one of the seats as blood welled from the wound.

"I said, nobody move!" the gunman repeated.

"Is-is this a holdup?" a woman asked in a quavering voice.

Under the bandanna, the outlaw grinned. "Yes, ma'am, it sure is, so you might as well go ahead and fork over that fancy bracelet you're wearin', along with any other jewelry you got."

A similar scene was playing out in the first

passenger car, although none of the passengers had been foolish enough to leave their seats and threaten the gunman who had taken over that car. The outlaws began collecting watches, wallets, jewelry, and anything else of value they could find.

Up at the engine, two members of the gang had scrambled over the coal tender and invaded the cab as soon as the train jolted to a halt. They covered the engineer and the fireman to make sure the train didn't move again until they were gone. One man was in the caboose, keeping his gun on the conductor and the two brakemen. That left two men to loot the express car and two more to take over the private car that had been added to the train between the express car and the caboose.

"Who do you think this fancy rig belongs to?" one of the outlaws asked the other as they paused in the private car's vestibule with their guns drawn. "The president of the line, maybe?"

"Who else would be rich enough to have his own railroad car?" the second man asked. "This is a real stroke of luck. I knew there was money in the express car, but I didn't figure on bein' able to grab somebody we can hold for ransom!"

They made sure the bandanna masks were secure over their faces. It wasn't their first train robbery, but so far the law didn't have good descriptions of any of them. They boarded the trains at different places, they didn't bunch up so as to create suspicion, and when the time came to strike, they moved with practiced ease and efficiency.

As they liked to congratulate themselves when they were holed up in their hideout, celebrating their most recent holdup, ol' Jesse James didn't have anything on them.

One of the outlaws threw open the door leading into the fancy car. Holding their guns tightly, thrust out in front of them, they charged into the car and found themselves in a sitting room with a thick rug on the floor, an overstuffed divan, several armchairs, a writing desk, and a hardwood bar. Everything was richly appointed, and the car itself was trimmed with gleaming brass. A door on the other end of the sitting room led into a short corridor with a sleeping compartment on either side.

The man standing at the bar smiled and said calmly, "When the train made an unscheduled stop, I thought someone might be coming to call. Would you gentlemen care for a drink before we get on with the business at hand?"

The outlaws stared at him. His reaction wasn't at all what they had been expecting. Usually folks either screamed or begged for mercy. Often they did both. They didn't stand around offering drinks.

The man was tall and broad-shouldered. He wore an expensive but not ostentatious black suit with a dark gray vest and white shirt. Black boots and a string tie gave him a Western look, although his voice wasn't a Western drawl. His sandy hair was longish, his tanned features rugged enough to be handsome but not pretty. He had to be rich, sure enough.

He held a wide-belled glass in one hand, a bottle of cognac in the other. He cocked an eyebrow quizzically as he lifted both items and held them out toward the robbers as if offering them.

"Damn it, we don't want a drink!" one of the gunmen burst out. "You're comin' with us. I bet your family will pay plenty to get you back in one piece!"

The man's easy smile went away as his face hardened. "You're going to kidnap me and hold me for ransom?"

"That's right, you fancy-pants son of a bitch!" the second gunman said.

"I don't like that. I've been kidnapped by outlaws before, and it wasn't a pleasant experience at all."

"Stop flappin' your jaw!" the first outlaw said. "Put that booze down and give us anything you got on you right now!"

"If you insist." The man dropped the glass and the bottle.

The eyes of the two outlaws instinctively followed them as they fell. Before the delicate crystal shattered as it struck the floor, the man crossed his arms, sweeping aside the tails of his coat to grip the butts of the two short-barreled revolvers the garment had concealed. Faster than the eye could follow, he drew both weapons and fired. Flame spat from the muzzles, the shots shockingly loud. Despite the relatively small size of the guns, each packed a .38 caliber punch.

The two outlaws were taken completely by surprise. The first pair of slugs drove into their chests and knocked them back a step. Their guns sagged as pain coursed through them. As they tried to lift the weapons again, the man fired a second time. One of the outlaws dropped with a bullet in his brain, the other reeled to the side as he clutched at his blood-spouting throat. He collapsed after a couple steps, pitching forward onto his face. Blood began to pool around his head, soaking into the thick rug.

"That rug's going to have to be replaced. On the other hand, this new cross-draw rig worked very well." The man holstered his left-hand gun, sliding it butt-forward into the leather on his right hip, but kept the other gun in his right hand as he checked on the two outlaws, making sure they were dead. Then he turned and called through the open door, "You can come out now, Arturo. It's safe."

A slender, pale man in his thirties emerged from one of the sleeping compartments and stepped into the sitting room. He wore an expression of disapproval as he looked at the two corpses sprawled on the floor. "Really, sir, was that completely necessary?"

"Yes," said Conrad Browning, "I think it was."

He took a couple of cartridges from the loops on his gunbelt and replaced the rounds he had fired from the Colt Lightning still in his hand. As he reloaded the other gun, he went on, "I'm certain these two didn't stop the train all by themselves. I think I'll go have a look for their friends."

"Sir, are you sure you should—"

Conrad snapped the gun's cylinder closed. "Yes. I am."

Chapter 2

The gang would have taken over the caboose, too, Conrad figured, so he might as well start there. He stepped around Arturo, leaving the nervous-looking valet in the car with the two dead outlaws. Knowing the man—or men—in the caboose probably heard the shots from the private car, and would be alert for trouble, Conrad swung down from the private car's rear platform instead of stepping across to the caboose. He dropped lithely to the ground with one of the .38 Lightning double-action revolvers in his right hand. Crouching low, well below the level of the windows, he ran to the rear of the train.

Silently, he climbed onto the caboose's rear platform and put an ear against the closed door. What he heard reminded him of why he hated outlaws so much.

Years earlier, as a young man, he had been kidnapped by lawless men with a grudge against his father to go along with their greed, leaving him with a mutilated ear—a permanent reminder of the pain and terror he had endured. He wore his hair long enough to cover it, and most of the time it didn't hurt anymore, but he had never forgotten what had happened.

Of course, he had suffered much greater pain since then, and that tended to dull the old aches.

As Conrad listened, he heard a man's loud, angry voice inside the caboose—one of the outlaws yelling at the conductor and the brakemen. He waited until he had a pretty good idea of where the man was standing, then wrapped his left hand around the doorknob and threw the door open.

Instantly, his keen eyes took in the scene. The conductor was sitting at his desk, off to the left, and the two brakemen stood near him, their hands lifted in the air as a single outlaw menaced them with a drawn six-gun.

The train robber wore a bandanna over the lower half of his face like the two men Conrad had killed in his private car. The man's head jerked toward the door where Conrad had made his unexpected entrance. The eyes above the bandanna bulged in surprise. He tried to shift his aim and bring his gun to bear on the newcomer.

Conrad's gun blasted twice. The first slug punched into the outlaw's gut, doubling him over. The second bullet caught him in the center of the forehead. It left behind a neat black hole as it bored into his brain. The train robber crumpled into a lifeless heap.

"Mr. Browning!" the conductor exclaimed as he recognized their unlikely savior. "How—"

"Was there just one of them?" Conrad asked sharply, interrupting the conductor's question.

"Yeah, just one man came in here, right after somebody pulled the emergency cord. I tried to get my gun out, but the bastard winged me."

Conrad noticed for the first time the conductor's left hand clutched a bloodstained right arm. "He won't hurt anybody else. Do you know how many more of them there are?"

The conductor shook his head. "No idea."

"All right. Stay here."

The conductor started to stand up as he protested, "This is my train, damn it—"

"And I own a considerable amount of stock in this railroad," Conrad pointed out, "which means you work for me. You're wounded. Stay here." He added to the brakemen, "See if you can patch up that arm for him."

Confident that his orders would be carried out, Conrad stepped onto the rear platform again. He checked along both sides of the train and didn't see anyone moving around. Filling his left hand with the other .38 he dropped to the ground, and ran forward toward the engine.

Two masked men carrying canvas bags leaped from the open door of the express car, obviously not expecting any trouble, though their guns were still drawn. Spotting Conrad right away they swiveled toward him, but both his guns roared as he instinctively veered to the side to avoid any possible lead flying at him.

One of his shots ripped a bloody furrow along an outlaw's forearm, making the man cry out in pain and drop his gun. The other bullet shattered the right elbow of the second train robber. He dropped to his knees, whimpering in agony. The bags of loot lay on the ground where they'd been dropped when bullets started to fly.

The first outlaw was still on his feet. Using his left arm he jerked a knife from his belt and lunged at Conrad, raising the knife and driving it down in a killing stroke.

Too close to the man to avoid his charge Conrad squeezed off another shot that missed as he ducked and twisted. The deadly blade whipped over his back, slicing a gash in his coat and shirt, leaving a burning trail along his skin. The two men collided and went down in a tangle of arms and legs.

In close quarters, the outlaw's knife was more dangerous than Conrad's guns. He threw himself aside as the cold steel swiped within a couple inches of his face. He rolled, trying to put some distance between himself and the outlaw, but the man threw himself after him, slashing back and forth with the knife.

Conrad thrust his right-hand gun up to block the blade. Steel rang against steel. At the same time, he saw an opening and his left-hand gun flashed up. Jamming the muzzle under the outlaw's chin, he pulled the trigger.

The bullet smashed upward through the man's brain and exploded out the top of his head in a grisly pink spray of blood, gray matter, and shattered skull. The man's eyes nearly popped from their sockets. Grimacing, Conrad shoved the corpse aside and rolled away.

A bullet kicked up dust in front of his face, spraying grit into his eyes and blinding him.

"You son of a bitch!" a man yelled.

Unable to see much of anything, Conrad blinked furiously and scrambled toward the roadbed underneath the express car figuring the voice belonged to one of the outlaws who'd been robbing the passengers. Another slug spanged off the steel rail on the side of the train. Rocks chewed into Conrad's hands and shredded the knees of his trousers as he dived forward into the shade underneath the car.

He blinked rapidly, suppressing the urge to paw at his eyes. Grinding the dirt into his eyeballs would do more damage. Better to let his eyes water and wash the grit out.

"He's under the train! The bastard's under the train!" The harsh shout was followed by the rapid thud of footsteps.

Conrad shook his head from side to side, his vision starting to clear. Spotting a pair of boots running alongside the train, he aimed at them and squeezed off a couple shots.

The man howled in pain and fell hard in an out of control sprawl as one of the bullets busted an ankle. He came to a stop staring at the space underneath the express car.

Conrad shot him between the eyes, turning the outlaw's face into a crimson smear.

"Move the train!" a man yelled. "Move the train!"

Conrad bit back a curse as he rolled onto his back and jammed both guns into their holsters. He could hear the train engine rumble and feel the vibration in the roadbed beneath him. It still had steam up. With a clash and clatter, the drivers engaged. Conrad reached up, grabbed one of the iron rods that ran underneath the car, and wrapped his legs around it. He lifted himself from the roadbed a scant second before the train lurched into motion.

It didn't go very far, just far enough he would have been revealed had he stayed where he was. When the train jolted to a halt again, he dropped to the ground and rolled out the far side, hoping the remaining outlaws wouldn't expect him to be there.

Surging to his feet he drew his guns again. He had lost track of how many men he had killed and had no idea how many more outlaws there were. Obviously some of them were up in the cab, or they wouldn't have been able to force the engineer to move the train. Conrad sprinted for the locomotive.

"Over there!" a man shouted from the other side of the train. "He's headed for the engine!"

A man leaned out of the cab and drew a bead on him. Before Conrad could react, someone jumped the outlaw from behind, tackling him and knocking him out of the cab. Both men fell to the ground. Conrad knew from the clothes of the man who had pitched in to help that he was the fireman.

The outlaw rolled over and swung his gun toward the fireman. Conrad got there first and launched a kick that slammed into the outlaw's head and drove it far to the side. The man's neck broke with a sharp crack like that of a snapping branch. The gun went off as his finger involuntarily jerked the trigger, but the bullet screamed off harmlessly into the vast West Texas sky.

Conrad holstered his left-hand gun and grabbed the fireman's arm to haul him to his feet. "Are you all right?"

"Yeah." The man stared at him. "Good Lord! Ain't you Mr. Browning?"

Conrad didn't waste time answering him. "Do you know how many more of them there are?"

"At least two."

From the corner of his eye, Conrad spotted a cloud of dust boiling up a couple hundred yards from the train. As it came closer, he realized the outlaws would have had at least one member of the gang bring their horses. The odds were about to get worse . . . and he had already overcome more than any man, by rights, should have been able to.

But not every man was the son of Frank Morgan.

"Get back in the cab," Conrad snapped. "Tell the engineer to get the train moving again. Open it up. I want us rolling away from here before the rest of the gang shows up."

The fireman jerked his head in a nod. "Sure thing, Mr. Browning." As he climbed back into the cab, he called to the wide-eyed engineer, "Full throttle, Asa! Mr. Browning says we're gettin' the hell outta here!"

Conrad hurried along the tracks. The train was a relatively short string: a couple freights, the two passengers, the baggage and express cars, Conrad's private car, and the caboose. By the time he reached the first passenger car, smoke was billowing from the locomotive's diamond-shaped stack and the train was moving again.

He reached up for a grab iron and swung himself onto the steps, hoping the rolling train would take the gang members still alive by surprise and they wouldn't have time to get back on board. Screams came from inside the car as he lunged onto the platform.

Conrad could tell the engineer had the throttle wide open. The train began to rattle and sway as it picked up speed. He paused on the platform long enough to thumb fresh rounds into both guns, then threw the door open and dived inside.

He slid to a stop on one knee with both guns leveled. At the far end of the car, one of the outlaws had an arm around the neck of a female passenger, dragging her backward as he held a gun pressed into her side. The other passengers in the car were hunkered on the seats, trying to stay out of the line of fire.

The robber's bandanna had slipped down to reveal a hard, heavy-jawed face with dark beard stubble on it. "Stay back, mister!" he yelled at Conrad. "I'll blow a hole right through her!"

"If you do, you'll be dead a second later,"

Conrad said. "You know that. You might as well drop the gun and save your life."

A savage grin twisted the outlaw's face. "You can go to hell!" he cried. "You can't shoot me without hittin' her!"

That wasn't strictly true. Conrad could see enough of the man's face looking over the woman's shoulder that he thought he could put a bullet in the outlaw's eye. But it was chancy, and he couldn't guarantee the hostage wouldn't be hurt. He held his fire for the moment, as the outlaw continued to back up with his hostage in tow until they reached the vestibule and were almost to the platform.

Conrad glanced through the window to his left. Though much of the West Texas landscape was featureless, making it difficult to know exactly where they were, there were a few landmarks. One of them flashed past as he looked out the window.

As a major stockholder in the line, Conrad had ridden the route a number of times, and he recognized the elevated water tank they had just passed. Normally, the train would have stopped there to take on water, but the engineer still had it barreling along the tracks.

In less than a mile, the tracks angled sharply to go around a mesa. Knowing that put an idea in Conrad's head. "Let the woman go," he called to the outlaw. "If you do, I give you my word you won't be killed."

"What'll you do? Send me to prison for twenty years? No thanks. I'd rather take a chance on a bullet."

"If anything happens to that woman, it'll be a hang rope, not prison," Conrad promised. "I'll see to that."

"Who in blazes *are* you, mister?"

"My name is Conrad Browning. I own this railroad."

That was a stretch. He actually owned only part of it. But his father owned another block of stock, and between them they had almost a controlling interest.

The train robber didn't believe it. He laughed harshly as he backed onto the platform. "That's a damned lie. You're a gambler or a gunfighter. No damn railroad tycoon could ever handle a gun like you!"

Conrad smiled thinly as he approached, both guns still in his hands. "It's true."

"Stay back!" the robber snapped. "Send word to the engine to stop this damn train so my pards with the horses can catch up."

Conrad shook his head. The train was almost at the bend. "Give up now, while you've still got a chance."

A snarl curled the outlaw's lips. He spat, "Go to hell—"

The train hit the bend.

At that high rate of speed, the turn was almost too much. But the engineer knew his train, knew it would stay on the rails. The sudden lurch was violent enough it threw the outlaw on the platform off balance. He yelled in surprise, staggering toward the edge. His gun fell away from the hostage as he windmilled his arm in an attempt to keep from falling off the train.

It was what Conrad had been waiting for. His right-hand gun snapped up and blasted. His shot drilled the man's forearm and sent the gun flying away.

The outlaw howled in pain, let go of the woman, and stumbled backward. Conrad leaped forward, grabbed the woman, and practically threw her behind him. He reached for the wounded outlaw next, but he was too late. The man had staggered too close to the opening in the railing around the platform. With a shriek of terror, he toppled backward through it, landing on the coupling between the cars and sliding off to wind up underneath the wheels. His scream ended abruptly as those flashing wheels chopped him to pieces.

Conrad caught hold of the woman's shoulder as she sobbed in relief. "Are there any more of them?"

She shook her head. Tears rolled down her cheeks. "I . . . I don't know!"

Conrad pushed her into the car, then turned toward the second passenger car.

It might not be over yet.

Chapter 3

But it was, Conrad discovered a moment later. He met the wounded conductor and the two brakemen coming forward through the second passenger car, and they reported the surviving pair of train robbers had been left behind, along with the other outlaws who had tried to rendezvous with them.

"We got a Winchester back there in the caboose," one of the brakies said. "I threw some lead at those varmints as the train was pullin' away, but I don't know if I hit any of 'em or not."

"It's all right if you didn't," Conrad told the man while he reloaded the round he had expended on the robber who had fallen underneath the train. "You discouraged them from coming after us, anyway."

"Asa's got this thing flying," the conductor said. He had a makeshift bandage tied around his arm. "Somebody better get up to the engine and tell him it's all right to slow down."

"We passed the water stop at Yucca Flats," Conrad pointed out. "Can we make it to Monahans without taking on more water?" He didn't particularly want the train to have to back up to the water tank, not with several owlhoots still roaming around the area.

"I'll check with the engineer, but I'm pretty sure we can," the conductor said. "Especially if he slows down." The man looked at Conrad and shook his head in awe. "I never saw anybody take on a whole gang of killers and nearly wipe them out. How'd you learn to shoot like that, Mr. Browning?"

"It's a knack."

In truth, it was an ability inherited from his father, a natural talent he had never known he possessed until great tragedy had forced him to pick up a gun and become an avenger. Since then he had worked diligently to improve his gun-handling skill.

Normally he didn't go out of his way to demonstrate it and wouldn't have displayed it if circumstances hadn't forced him to. Not many people knew that Conrad Browning, businessman, financier, stockholder in mines, railroad lines, shipping concerns, banks, and numerous other enterprises, was the son of Frank Morgan, the Drifter, last of the fast guns.

Or perhaps next to last. When pushed to it, Conrad could almost match his father's blazing speed with a Colt.

The conductor said, "Maybe you'd better go talk to that butler fella who works for you and let him know you're all right. He was so worried he was about to have a fit when we came through your private car a minute ago."

Conrad pouched both irons in the cross-draw rig and smiled a little. Arturo was the high-strung sort, all right.

The conductor and the brakemen continued on toward the engine while Conrad left the passenger car and headed for the caboose. He had to climb onto the top of the baggage car and the express car to reach the rear of the string. That was the way the trainmen had come, but they were experienced at navigating the top of a swaying car. It was trickier for Conrad, but his sense of balance and superb reflexes enabled him to manage it without any trouble.

He climbed down to the platform of the private car and went inside. As he stepped into the sitting room, he found Arturo pacing back and forth restlessly. The valet stopped short, stared at him for a second, and exclaimed, "You're alive!"

"And relatively unharmed," Conrad said, holding up his gravel-scratched hands.

For a moment he thought Arturo was going to hug him, but of course that would have been much too great a breach of decorum. Instead, Arturo looked down at Conrad's knees and frowned. "You've ruined those trousers, in addition to getting blood all over the rug."

"You knew you were going to work for a barbarous American when you took this job," Conrad pointed out.

"Yes, I did, but I didn't know you were going to

wreak this much havoc before we even reached our destination."

Conrad's smile disapeared and was replaced by a tight, grim mask. "Believe me, Arturo . . . I've just started wreaking havoc."

Arturo hesitated, then as the train began to slow, he said, "Why don't you allow me to tend to those cuts on your hands, sir, and then you can don clean raiment. I'm sure the, ah, train workers will come and dispose of the, ah . . ."

"Corpses."

"Yes, the corpses you left in your wake."

Conrad relaxed and let the valet clean the minor damage to his hands. None of the scrapes were bad enough to require a bandage.

Arturo was an Italian by birth, although he spoke perfect English, without a trace of an accent. He had been educated not only in his homeland but also in England. Coming from a long line of servants, at one time he had worked for a deadly enemy of the notorious gunfighter known as Kid Morgan . . . who was, in reality, Conrad Browning.

A few years earlier, Conrad had been rich, successful, and happily married to a beautiful young woman named Rebel. His life had been close to perfect.

But in nature, perfection is always short-lived. So it was with Conrad Browning. His wife had been murdered, his life turned upside down. Since it had appeared he had died in a related outburst of violence, for a while Conrad had allowed everyone to believe he was dead. During that time, he recuperated from his injuries and taught himself how to be a cold, ruthless killer. He came up with a new identity, Kid Morgan, taking the name from his famous father, so Rebel's murderers wouldn't know Conrad Browning was actually alive and on their trail.

One by one, Kid Morgan had tracked down the men he was after and had his vengeance on them. Eventually the trail had led The Kid to the person behind his wife's death: Pamela Tarleton, who had once been engaged to Conrad Browning. Her twisted nature had brought about her own accidental death, completing Kid Morgan's quest.

That had left The Kid facing a heartbreaking revelation. All the blood, all the death, had not brought Rebel back. The emptiness caused by her loss was still inside him. Knowing that he could not return to his life as Conrad Browning while he felt that way, he chose to remain Kid Morgan, a loner riding through the West, drifting in and out of an assortment of dangers. His essential nature, no matter what he called himself, would not allow him to turn his back on people in trouble.

It was during one of those adventures that he had run up against Arturo's former employer, an Italian count willing to kill anyone in his way to get what he wanted. Tangling with Kid Morgan had not turned out well for the count, and Arturo had wound up without a job when Fortunato died in the New Mexico wasteland known as the *Jornada del Muerto*.

By that time, the lawyers representing Conrad Browning's business interests knew he was still alive, as did his father Frank Morgan. Having developed a liking for Arturo, The Kid had sent him to San Francisco, where Conrad's lawyers had no trouble finding a job for him. He had remained in that position until recently.

Kid Morgan had resumed drifting, until a case of mistaken identity had landed him in New Mexico's Hell Gate Prison. Through a series of harrowing adventures, he had escaped and believed he had cleared his name.

Being captured by ruthless bounty hunters proved him wrong. Again he had escaped with his life, but in the process The Kid had discovered he had a shadowy enemy, pulling the strings behind the scenes to make his life a living hell. In order to deal with that threat, he had put aside his identity as Kid Morgan and fully resumed the mantle of Conrad Browning. Things had come full circle . . . in more ways than one.

A showdown in Santa Fe had revealed the mastermind behind The Kid's troubles to be Roger Tarleton, Pamela's cousin. The Tarleton family was still seeking vengeance on Conrad, and Pamela herself had reached out from the grave to drive one final knife into his heart.

He didn't have to reread the letter from her that Roger Tarleton's lawyer had delivered to him. Every word of it was etched into his soul.

Conrad,
If you're reading this, it means I'm dead. I'm entrusting this letter to my beloved cousin Roger with instructions that he should make certain

*you receive it, should my efforts to avenge my
father's life and my own honor go unrewarded.
There is something I want you to know.*

*As I am sure you recall, you and I were
intimate before your marriage, Conrad.
Committing those words to paper should shame
me deeply, but I am beyond shame. What you did
not know is that when you broke our engagement,
I was with child by you.*

*Yes, Conrad, you are a father . . . not once,
but twice. I gave birth to twins, your children,
not long after you married that other woman.
They were healthy, happy infants, and now they
are hidden away where you will never find them,
somewhere in the vast frontier for which you
deserted me.*

*You are a father, Conrad, but you will never
know your children and they will never know you.*

And this . . . is my final revenge on you.

That staggering discovery might have been
more than some men could stand. But the man
who was both Conrad Browning and Kid Morgan
had been forged in a crucible of tragedy and
grief, and though he was broken, that unholy
fire had fused him together again, leaving him
stronger than before. After reading that letter,
he had allowed himself a moment of horror and
sadness . . .

And then he started making plans for how he
would find his lost children.

One thing was certain. Conrad would have to

take up the trail first, not The Kid. He knew better than to trust *anything* Pamela had written in that letter. She had indicated the twins were hidden away somewhere in the West, but that was likely not true. After he had broken their engagement, she had remained in Boston, where both of them had lived at the time. He was confident that was where she would have given birth to the children.

So that was where the trail would start. Conrad Browning was much better suited to dealing with the East than The Kid was, so it was Conrad that had boarded a train in Santa Fe and set off on the journey that would take him back to Boston.

He hadn't boarded the train alone, however. If he was going to fully assume the identity of Conrad Browning again, he needed a servant. Conrad wouldn't travel without a valet. That was what his friends and associates back East would expect.

He'd thought of Arturo and sent him a telegram, offering him the job. Arturo was more than happy to leave his current employer and accept the offer. True, Arturo was eccentric and set in his ways, but he was also loyal and intelligent, two qualities Conrad expected might come in handy before he found what he was looking for.

"There," Arturo said when he finished cleaning the scrapes and cuts on Conrad's hands. "I think you'll be fine until the next time you attempt to exterminate every owlhoot and gunman west of the Mississippi."

"Well, I've sort of got a cut on my back, too,

where one of those train robbers tried to stab
me . . ."

Arturo rolled his eyes. "Turn around and let me
see. Of course. The coat is ruined, too. It's a good
thing you're filthy rich, sir, the way you go
through clothes. Trouble just lies in wait for you,
doesn't it?"

"Seems that way," Conrad muttered. "It was just
a coincidence those men attempted to hold up
the train we're on."

"Coincidence, sir . . . or the universe attempt-
ing to tell you something?"

"Like I'm jinxed?"

"I don't believe in superstition. But you must
admit, it seems as if you can't go anywhere without
someone shooting at you and trying to kill you."

Conrad chuckled. "Then I guess it's a good
thing I can afford plenty of bullets, too."

Chapter 4

Three days later, Conrad and Arturo disembarked from a train in Boston. Arturo fussed around, supervising the unloading of their baggage, while Conrad leaned on the silver-headed walking stick he carried at times. His leg had been injured while dealing with the threat of the bounty hunters in New Mexico, and every now and then it twinged a little. The exertion of stopping the train robbery in Texas had left it aching.

"I've engaged a carriage for us and a wagon for our bags, sir," Arturo reported. "I just need to tell the drivers our destination."

Conrad nodded and gave him the address of the mansion on Beacon Hill. The big house had belonged to his mother Vivian and her husband, and later Conrad and Rebel had begun their married life there before moving to Carson City, Nevada. Since then the house had been closed up and vacant, dust settling on the covers over the furniture.

Conrad wasn't looking forward to returning to his childhood home. It contained a lot of memories, memories he didn't necessarily want to stir up again. If it proved to be too much to deal with, he could always pack up and move to one of the opulent hotels downtown, he told himself.

"Have you been to Boston before, Arturo?" he asked the valet as they left the train station in the rented carriage.

"Yes, sir, on several occasions with Count Fortunato. It's one of the more civilized cities here in America, isn't it?"

"I suppose so," Conrad replied with a smile. "Of course, I'm not as fond of civilization as I once was. I've gotten used to the frontier. Life out there is more honest, more open, more direct."

"More dangerous and barbaric."

Conrad inclined his head. "Depends on how you look at it, I suppose."

Arturo regarded him shrewdly. "I must say, sir, you've changed a great deal since the first time I saw you. Back then, you were wearing that horrible fringed jacket and that big hat, carrying enough weapons to be a walking arsenal! Now you appear to be a fine gentleman of culture and breeding."

"But appearances are deceptive, eh?" Conrad asked, chuckling.

"That's not what I meant at all. But you must admit, sir, you are a rather complicated individual."

"Most folks are, when you get down to it."

"Not I, sir. I am exactly who I appear to be."

"Well, I suppose we need a few things in the world we can count on."

Conrad felt a twinge of apprehension when the carriage drew up in front of the mansion. It was a big house of red brick with a gabled roof, but it seemed to be some sort of monster, squatting there waiting for him to come close enough so it could spring on him and devour him. With his heart pounding, he said, "Wait, Arturo. Have the driver take us to a hotel instead."

"Are you sure, sir? This is your family home."

The only family he had left was Frank Morgan, and Frank had nothing to do with that monstrosity of a house. Frank was somewhere out west, roaming the high country, or the deserts, or the forests.

The twins, he reminded himself. He didn't know where they were, but it was a foregone conclusion they had never been at that house. "I'm certain," he said firmly. "We'll be more comfortable in a hotel suite."

"As you wish, sir."

Arturo swung the carriage door open and stepped out to talk to the driver. When he got back in, they started off again, leaving Beacon Hill behind.

A short time later, they were ensconced in the best suite in the most expensive and luxurious hotel in Boston. Conrad said, "As soon as we've unpacked, I want you to put on your secretary's hat, Arturo, and send notes to a list of people I'll give you, letting them know I'm back in Boston. I expect that'll generate a number of invitations to dinner and whatever parties are being held in the near future."

Arturo frowned. "But I don't *have* a secretary's hat, sir, only my bowler."

Conrad laughed. "It's just an expression. I'm surprised you haven't heard it before. Don't be so literal-minded, Arturo."

"The mind is a literal thing, sir. At least mine is."

"I'll keep that in, uh, mind," Conrad said dryly. Not surprisingly, Arturo rolled his eyes.

Conrad dined that evening in the hotel dining room. He wanted to be seen. Many people from the upper crust of Boston society went there, not just guests in the hotel. The word would get around quickly that he was back in Boston, and the notes sent out by Arturo would make it clear he wanted to resume his former place as one of the city's elite.

But as he ate the fine food and sipped the finer wine, surrounded by elegance, he compared it to meals of biscuits and bacon, washed down by a tin cup of Arbuckle's, that he'd had in camps alongside many a lonely trail, and he knew he'd been happier on the trail than he was in the city. He hadn't realized how much he had changed over the past few years until he'd come back to Boston.

That was where Pamela would have given birth to his children, he told himself. It was where the trail had to begin. There was no way of knowing where it would lead.

"Conrad?" a man's voice asked as he was sipping an after-dinner brandy. "Conrad Browning? Is that really you?"

Conrad turned with a smile and saw a well-dressed couple wearing expressions of surprise. He recognized them instantly, although it took him a second to recall their names.

He stood up and extended a hand. "Joseph! So good to see you again." After he had shaken hands with the man, he hugged the woman. Delicately, of course, because she was one of those elegant blondes who gave off an air of fragility. "And Celeste, as beautiful as ever! It's wonderful to see you both again."

"What are you doing back in Boston?" Joseph Demarest asked. His father owned one of Boston's oldest and most prestigious banks, and he was a vice-president of the institution. "I thought you had moved west for good."

His wife touched his arm and said in a soft, chiding tone, "Joseph."

Realization dawned on him. "Oh, that's right." Soberly, he put a hand on Conrad's shoulder. "We were so sorry to hear about your loss, old man. Such a terrible, terrible tragedy."

"So sorry," Celeste echoed.

Conrad nodded. He was going to have to get used to that, he told himself.

"Thank you," he murmured. "It's been more than a year now, but the wound is still very fresh."

"I'm sure it is," she said.

"You know," Demarest said, "we heard this wild rumor that you . . . well, that you had passed away, too. Something about a fire at your house in Nevada or wherever it was . . ."

"Carson City," Conrad said. "Yes, I don't know

how those rumors got started, but as you can see, they were false. I'm standing here right in front of you, as hale and hearty as ever."

"Yes," Celeste said, "I can see that."

Something in her voice and the way her pale blue eyes frankly appraised him reminded Conrad that on more than one occasion when he had lived there, Celeste Demarest had subtly let him know she might not be opposed to a little dalliance with him. Conrad had never pursued the matter, of course, because he'd been happily married to Rebel at the time and she was plenty of woman for him.

He had no interest in Celeste, except for the fact that she was a notorious gossip and would help spread the word that he was back.

All the people he had known in Boston had also known Pamela. The two of them had been a couple for several years and had been engaged for part of that time. Her father had been a wealthy man. Someone in their mutual circle of acquaintances would have seen Pamela following the end of their engagement.

Someone would know something about the children she had borne.

That was Conrad's hope, anyway. There were other ways of approaching the search, but he was going to start with his society friends.

"What brings you back to Boston?" Demarest asked. "Business?" He had a slightly hopeful tone in his voice. If he could bring some of the deposits of the Browning business empire to his father's bank, it would be a nice feather in his cap.

Conrad shook his head and said, "Pleasure." He noted the brief flash of disappointment in his old friend's eyes. "I want to see everyone again and renew all my old acquaintances."

"You'll have no trouble doing that!" Celeste said with a merry laugh. "There's a round of parties and balls coming up. I'm sure once everyone knows you're back, you'll have more invitations than you can handle."

"That sounds good." Conrad took her hand and squeezed it lightly. "Can I count on you to act as my ambassador, Celeste?"

"Of course! Come to tea tomorrow, and we'll discuss it."

"An excellent idea," her husband agreed. "I'll be at the bank, of course, but I'm sure Celeste will entertain you and take good care of you."

Conrad wondered if Demarest was really as thick as he sounded, or if the man simply didn't mind if his wife hoisted her skirts for the Browning financial empire. Either way, it didn't matter. Conrad didn't intend to take advantage of the offer. "I'll have to see what I can do."

"Of course," Celeste said. "Telephone me and let me know."

Conrad nodded. Having spent so much time in the West, he tended to forget how prevalent telephone lines were in eastern cities. After all, Alexander Graham Bell had invented the contraption right there in Boston, a little more than twenty years earlier. Conrad owned a considerable amount of stock in a telephone company that had proven to be a good investment.

The Demarests went on their way, and Conrad resumed his seat. He smiled to himself as he swirled the brandy in the snifter. He'd completed the first move in what might prove to be a long game, but so far it was looking like a successful one.

Despite that, despite all the elegance and comfort surrounding him, for a moment he wished he could hear the lonely hoot of an owl in the night and look up to see the western stars spread across the sky.

Chapter 5

The next morning, Conrad telephoned the Demarest house and informed one of the servants that he wouldn't be able to accept Mrs. Demarest's kind invitation to tea. He asked the woman to tender his regrets to Celeste and had just hung up the instrument when a knock sounded on the door of the suite's sitting room.

He started to open it himself, but Arturo got there first. As the valet swung the door open, a man's voice said, "I'm here to see Browning."

"*Mister* Browning may or may not be available," Arturo replied archly. "I shall have to tell him who is calling."

The man looked over Arturo's shoulder, pointed, and said, "He's standing right there, and I can see he's not doing anything but drinking coffee."

Arturo waited, his posture indicating he wouldn't budge though the visitor outweighed him by at least a hundred pounds.

"All right," the man growled after a moment. "Tell him Jack Mallory is here."

"Very well." Arturo turned toward Conrad. "Sir, a Mister Mallory to see you."

"Send him in." Conrad tried not to smile.

"Please come in," Arturo told Mallory as he moved aside and gestured for the visitor to enter.

With an impatient shake of his head, Mallory stepped into the room. He was tall and brawny, with heavy shoulders and long arms. He carried himself like a prizefighter, Conrad thought. His gray suit didn't fit him very well. Rusty stubble sprouted on a belligerent jaw despite the early hour. His rumpled thatch of hair was the same shade. He carried a hat in one big-knuckled hand.

"I'm Conrad Browning." Conrad introduced himself and shook hands with Mallory. "Would you like some coffee?"

"Sure. If you want to splash a little cognac in there, I wouldn't complain."

Conrad raised an eyebrow in surprise. He would have figured Mallory for more of a straight whiskey drinker.

"I'm afraid we don't have any cognac."

Mallory shrugged. "Black will be fine, then."

Conrad nodded to Arturo, who poured coffee from the pot on the sideboard into a fine china cup. Mallory took it, handling the cup with more deftness than Conrad would have expected from such a big, rough-looking man.

"I'm told you're the best detective in Boston, Mr. Mallory," Conrad said. "It's strange. I used to live here, and I don't recall ever hearing your name."

"Not that strange," Mallory said with a shake of his head. "I've only been here about a year. If you've been gone longer than that, you never would have heard of me."

"Where were you before that?"

"Down in Mexico, working for a mining company that was having trouble getting their ore shipments out. Before that I was in Central America, seeing to it that a bunch of guerrillas didn't keep a railroad from getting built."

"And before that?"

"Knocking around here and there. I worked for the Pinks, off and on."

"But you're not a Pinkerton operative at the moment?"

Mallory shook his head. "I have my own office."

"You've spent time in some rough places. What made you decide to settle in Boston?"

"I never said I was settling here. There are parts of Boston where you can get killed quicker than in any Central American jungle."

Conrad nodded. "I suppose that's true."

Mallory drank some of the hot, strong coffee. "You sent word for me to come here and talk with you for a reason, Mr. Browning. Why don't you tell me what that reason is, and we'll see whether or not we can do business."

"Of course." Conrad wasn't comfortable with a lot of small talk, either. He appreciated the detective's bluntness. "I want to hire you to find a woman."

Mallory frowned. "Let me guess. You want to be reunited with some long-lost love."

"Not hardly," Conrad snapped. "This woman is dead, and if hate wasn't such a useless emotion, I think I would probably hate her with every fiber of my being."

Mallory's bushy red eyebrows rose a little as he tugged at his right earlobe. "That sounds a little more interesting. Why don't you tell me about it?"

Conrad explained about his history with Pamela Tarleton and the posthumous letter he had received from her a couple weeks earlier. He hated to open up and reveal his pain to the stranger, but if Mallory was going to help him, the detective had to know the background.

The two of them had sat down while Conrad was talking. When he finished the story, Mallory asked, "What is it you want me to do?"

"I think it's quite likely Pamela gave birth to the children at some private hospital or sanitarium in this area. If she did, it's possible she might have shared some of the details of her plan with someone there, a doctor or a nurse, maybe. I want you to find out if that's true." Conrad leaned forward in the comfortable armchair and clasped his hands together. "But that's not all. To be completely honest with you, Mr. Mallory, I don't believe Pamela Tarleton was quite sane. She blamed me not only for ending our engagement but also for her father's death."

"It's none of my business, but did you have anything to do with that?"

Conrad shook his head. "Clark Tarleton was

killed by an assassin hired by one of his crooked business partners. Pamela never really accepted that. I suppose it was easier for her to blame me."

"So she was loco, as they say down in Mexico," Mallory replied. "What's your point?"

"I've been going on the assumption that what Pamela said in the letter about the twins is true, although I'm not fully convinced she's hidden them somewhere on the frontier. It seems to me it would have been much easier for her to conceal them somewhere here in the East, where she's more accustomed to things. However . . . everything Pamela said has to be doubted on some level."

Mallory tugged at his earlobe again and slowly nodded in understanding. "You don't know for sure there really *are* any twins."

"That's right." Conrad stood up, put his hands behind his back, and began to pace. "It's possible the entire thing is nothing but a vicious hoax, intended to cause me more pain."

"That would do it, all right," the detective mused. "Tell a man he has children he doesn't know about, send him on a wild goose chase looking for them, and then he's crushed when he finally finds out they don't exist."

Conrad stopped his pacing and jerked his head in a nod. "Exactly. That's just the sort of warped cruelty that might have occurred to Pamela."

"So you want me to find out where she had the kids not just to help you locate them, but to prove that they actually exist."

"Yes. Will you do it? Your fee and expenses will be no object."

Mallory got to his feet and held out his hand. "I won't soak you." He gripped Conrad's hand. "You strike me as a decent sort of gent, Browning. I'll do what I can to help you."

"Thank you. I'll have my secretary write you a bank draft before you leave. Just tell Arturo how much you need."

"What'll you do in the meantime?" Mallory wanted to know. "You don't seem to me like a man who sits back and waits for somebody else to do all his work for him."

Conrad smiled. "I have my own avenues of investigation to explore. Consider it a race if you like, Mr. Mallory . . . a race for the truth."

One of those avenues of investigation opened up that afternoon. A messenger arrived at the hotel with a note for Conrad. When he broke the seal on it and unfolded it, the scent of expensive perfume rose from the paper.

Arturo had taken the note from the messenger and handed it to Conrad. He cocked a quizzical eyebrow but didn't come right out and ask what it was about.

Conrad told him anyway. "This is an invitation to dinner tonight, Arturo. At Mrs. Beatrice Garrison's house. She apologizes for the lateness of the invitation but says she only heard today that I'm back in Boston."

"I'm afraid the name means nothing to me, sir, although it clearly does to you."

"The late Mr. Wilbur Garrison owned textile mills, a shipping line, and everything else he could get his fat, greedy hands on. When his heart gave out in his mistress's bed, his wife inherited everything and became one of the wealthiest women in the Northeast. She's a prominent figure in Boston society."

"Ah, then I take it no one else knows about the amorous activities that cost her late husband his life."

"On the contrary." Conrad smiled. "Practically everyone knows about them. But members of high society never allow the truth to interfere with their illusions. I know what I'm talking about, because for a long time I was the same way."

"Having seen you in action, sir, I find that difficult to believe."

"Believe it. There was a time when I was the most pompous, priggish stuffed shirt you could ever hope to see. My mother, rest her soul, tried to help me grow up, but it took a couple of other people to finally accomplish that."

A couple people named Frank Morgan and Rebel Callahan.

Conrad put away the thoughts of his father and his late wife and went on. "It's short notice to get a tuxedo fitted and altered in time for dinner this evening, so we'd better get busy. The jacket is going to be especially tricky."

"Why is that, sir?"

"It'll have to be cut so you can't see the guns."

Chapter 6

When attending a dinner party in one of Boston's most elegant Beacon Hill mansions, most people wouldn't have felt the need to go armed with anything more than a gracious smile, a quick wit, and good manners. But Conrad felt naked when he wasn't packing iron.

The alterations on the tuxedo had been hurried but expert. The price he'd paid insured that. When he climbed out of the carriage in front of Mrs. Beatrice Garrison's house that evening, no one could tell he carried a .38 caliber revolver under each arm. The holsters had been removed from the cross-draw rig he'd worn during the train trip and attached to a special shoulder harness that was invisible under his clothes. Being armed like that wasn't particularly comfortable, but the weight of the guns was certainly reassuring. Conrad didn't expect any trouble at Mrs. Garrison's party, especially the kind that required hot lead, but he was ready just in case.

A servant met him at the door and took his hat and walking stick. Conrad vaguely recognized the old butler. "So good to see you again, Mr. Browning," the man murmured. "Welcome back to Boston."

"Thank you, Charles," Conrad said, coming up with the butler's name. "I trust that Mrs. Garrison is well?"

"Very well, sir. She and the guests who have already arrived are in the solarium. Do you remember your way?"

"Yes, I do, thank you." Conrad started along a richly carpeted hallway lined with sober portraits of generations of wealthy Garrisons, thinking of the many dinners and balls he, his mother, and stepfather had attended at that house.

The solarium was a high-ceilinged room with numerous tall windows. Boston wasn't blessed with the sunniest climate in the world—those people wouldn't know what hot sunlight was until they'd been through the *Jornada del Muerto*. During the day the room took advantage of what sunlight there was, but the curtains had been drawn against the dark night.

A servant handed Conrad a drink as soon as he stepped into the room. He sipped the champagne and moved toward the cluster of people around a short, stout, white-haired figure in a glittering dress and an abundance of brilliant jewelry.

"Conrad Browning!" the woman cried happily when she spotted him. "Dear boy! I thought you had deserted us forever."

The beautifully dressed crowd parted to let

him through. He took the hand Mrs. Garrison extended to him, bent over it, and pressed his lips to the back.

"How wonderful to see you again," she went on. "We won't stand on ceremony. Come here and give your Aunt Beatrice a hug."

She wasn't really his aunt, of course, but she and his mother had been close friends. Conrad hugged her, being careful not to spill his drink, and kissed her rouged and powdered cheek.

Her blue eyes sparkled as she looked up at him. "You should be ashamed of yourself."

"Why?" he asked, smiling.

"First of all, for taking that charming wife of yours and abandoning Boston in the first place." She grew serious as she placed a beringed hand on his arm. "I was so sorry to hear about Rebel. She was . . . very different from the sort of woman to whom we're accustomed around here, but I could tell she was very good for you, my boy. I liked her a great deal."

"She liked you, too," Conrad said softly. Although two women couldn't have been more different than Rebel and Mrs. Garrison, they both had a streak of honesty a mile wide. Mrs. Garrison had known perfectly well her late husband was a pirate and a lech. She had chosen to deal with it by not dealing with it.

"And you let all of us believe for the longest time that you were dead! Didn't it ever occur to you to let your old friends know you were alive?"

"I've been . . . busy."

That was an understatement. Every time

Conrad had turned around, he had been mixed up in some gun ruckus or another. He had fought outlaws, land grabbers, and bounty hunters. He had come within a whisker of dying more times than he liked to think about. He had slept on the hard ground, gone hungry, and been tortured. Thoughts of Boston society hadn't really entered his mind.

"Well, now you're back, hopefully for good," Mrs. Garrison went on. "I won't monopolize your time. I'm sure everyone here wants to speak to you."

Conrad didn't tell her he wasn't planning to stay in Boston a minute longer than he had to and spent the next half hour exchanging greetings, small talk, and pleasantries with the other guests, with all of whom he was acquainted. Joseph and Celeste Demarest were there. Celeste pouted a little as she said, "I was so disappointed you couldn't come to tea this afternoon, Conrad."

"I had to get ready for this evening." He lowered his voice. "Can't disappoint Mrs. Garrison, you know. And I was sure I'd see you and Joseph here."

"Of course," Joseph said. "Conrad, you and I really should have lunch sometime while you're here. I know you said you weren't in Boston to do business, but it never hurts to consider your options."

"I'll think about it," Conrad promised, which was an utter lie.

What would these people do, he asked himself, if they knew that only a few months ago, he had been locked up in Hell Gate Prison, a beaten, half-starved wretch? What would they think of all the men he had killed? How would they react if he told them about gunning down the bastards who had murdered his wife?

Ignoring his thoughts he smiled and chatted, and none of it meant a damned thing. The party was just an ordeal to be endured until he found out what he needed to know.

No one had mentioned Pamela Tarleton or her father by the time everyone was called into the dining room. They had to be curious, but Conrad knew they were avoiding the subject—like they always avoided talking about anything unpleasant. He was willing to bide his time.

After dinner the guests moved into the ballroom for dancing. Conrad tried to plead a stiff leg, but Celeste Demarest dragged him onto the floor anyway. As they circled the room to the music of a string quartet, Celeste said, "You must be terribly lonely these days, Conrad. I don't mean to remind you of your loss, but I worry about you."

He doubted if she had spared a thought for him until he showed up unexpectedly in Boston again, but he didn't let that show on his face. "I try to keep myself busy. It helps not to think about things, you know."

"Well, if you ever need someone to talk to, or simply a soft shoulder on which to rest your head for a while, you know where to find me."

"Indeed I do," he said, making her flush with pleasure. "Things have certainly changed in the past few years. Five years ago, it would have been Pamela in my arms."

"Pamela . . ." Celeste repeated. For a second her face hardened. "That was a dreadful thing, you know."

He thought she meant how Pamela had died from a gunman's bullet in a tiny New Mexico settlement, but then Celeste went on. "The way she shut herself up in her house was just tragic. She never saw anyone for months at a time, at least no one in our circle. I assume she saw her servants."

"She isolated herself?"

"Because she was too ashamed to show her face after . . . Oh, Conrad, don't get me wrong. No one blames you for breaking off the engagement. I don't know what actually happened. It was all shrouded in some sort of cloak of mystery, but I'm sure you had perfectly good reasons for doing what you did, probably more than one reason. Pamela was always rather . . . rather . . ."

Celeste couldn't find the words. Conrad could have supplied them.

Vicious. Scheming. Insane.

"It was a terrible time for all of us," he murmured.

"Oh, I'm sure it was! Such a shame, such a shame."

"So she never saw anyone?"

"Not that I'm aware of."

That made sense. Pamela hadn't wanted anyone to know she was pregnant.

"And then after a year or so, she went away again," Celeste continued. "No one knew where.

We heard later that she had been killed in some sort of accident out West somewhere." A shudder went through her delicate frame. "What a dreadful place to die."

Before either of them could say anything else, Joseph Demarest tapped Conrad on the shoulder. "Could I trouble you for my wife back?" he asked with a smile.

"Of course," Conrad said as he handed over Celeste, who didn't bother hiding her disappointment at having to dance with her husband.

Conrad walked over to Mrs. Garrison, who was watching the dancers with a faint smile on her face. "A lovely evening, as always," he said.

"Thank you, dear boy." She linked her arm with his. "How are you holding up? The losses you've suffered, first your wife and then Pamela—"

"Pamela was nothing to me," he said bluntly.

Mrs. Garrison's lips tightened in disapproval. "The two of you were once engaged to be married."

"That was a long time ago."

"You would have been a good match."

"I don't think so."

Mrs. Garrison waved her other hand. "Oh, not as good as you and Rebel, of course, but still, it's a shame that things didn't work out."

"I heard that she shut herself up in her house, and stayed there for a year."

"Indeed. I suppose she was in mourning for what she had lost when you broke your engagement to her."

"With all due respect, Aunt Beatrice, I don't intend to explain myself."

"I'm not asking you to. What happened between the two of you can remain between the two of you as far as I'm concerned. Anyway, it's obvious. You met Rebel, and that was the end for Pamela."

"Do you know where she went when she left Boston after that?"

The old woman shook her head. "I'm afraid not. There's a rumor she was killed."

"It's true," Conrad said with a nod. He didn't mention that he'd been there when it happened.

"A terrible shame. First Clark and then her. But these things happen, I suppose."

"I'd like to know more about what she did during those days."

Mrs. Garrison frowned up at him. "I thought you washed your hands of the poor girl."

"That's true, but I'm curious. Do you think you could ask around for me?"

Her eyes narrowed. "You want me to be a gossipmonger for you, is that it?"

"Not exactly." He sighed. "I'd just like to get everything straight in my mind at last, so I can put it all behind me and get on with the rest of my life."

Her expression relented a little. "I suppose I can understand that. I felt the same way when Wilbur passed on. Sometimes the knowledge is bitter, but it's better for us to go ahead and swallow it and be done with it."

"That's true."

"All right. I'll see what I can find out." She squeezed his arm. "I knew you must still be in pain when I heard that you couldn't bring yourself to go back to your mother's house and were staying in a hotel. I'll do what I can to help you, Conrad."

He kissed her cheek. "Thank you."

"I warn you, though . . . sometimes when we look for the truth, we find out things we would have rather not known."

She didn't know how well acquainted with that idea he already was. He and the bitter truth were already old friends.

Chapter 7

Conrad was a little surprised at how much relief he felt when he left the Garrison mansion later that evening. He paused before climbing into his carriage and drew in a deep breath. The air was full of the various unpleasant odors of the city, but it wasn't as stifling as the hothouse atmosphere of stratified society inside the mansion.

Someday, he thought, he would once again breathe in the clean, crisp air of the mountain desert country that had become his real home.

But first he had a job to do.

The driver he had hired was a burly, middle-aged Irishman named Clancy. He turned around on the seat and asked, "Where to, Mr. Browning?"

"Back to the hotel, I suppose. Where else would I go?"

Clancy grinned at him. "Well, there's this little pub I know where ye could indulge in some good Irish whiskey and a song or two."

"Do you really think I'd leave a dinner party at a mansion such as this and go to some pub?"

"Beggin' yer pardon, sir, but ye strike me as a diff'rent sort of gent than most o' these stuffed shirts."

Conrad returned the grin. "And thank God for that! Sure, Clancy. The idea sounds like a good one to me."

After spending the evening with all those swells, it would be nice to be around some real people again, he thought as he climbed into the carriage. To forget about everything for a while and just enjoy himself.

Clancy got the team in motion and sent the carriage rolling through the cobblestoned streets. Conrad leaned back against the comfortable, cushioned seat.

They left Beacon Hill behind for a more working class neighborhood. The gas streetlights were fewer and farther between, and as a result, there were some dark stretches of road.

They were on one such stretch when several men on horseback suddenly rode up alongside the carriage. Conrad heard the hoofbeats pass and saw the dark shapes looming at the carriage windows. Instinct warned him, so he wasn't completely surprised when Clancy called out, "Here now, you scoundrels! Leave those horses alone!"

"Shut up, old man, or I'll put a bullet in ye! Now pull up, I tell you! Pull up!"

"Go to hell!" Clancy roared.

The sudden jolt of the coach picking up speed

threw Conrad back against the seat. Clancy yelled at the horses. His whip popped.

A gun blasted, followed by a groan from the burly Irishman. The carriage slewed to the side. Conrad knew Clancy must have been wounded and dropped the reins.

His hands went under the coat of his tuxedo and came out filled with the twin Colt Lightnings. As the carriage lurched to a halt, Conrad kicked the door open and leaped out. A couple men in long coats and derby hats had grabbed the team's harness, one on either side, and forced the horses to stop against a curb. Two more riders dressed the same way brandished revolvers. The barrels swung toward Conrad as one of the men yelled, "Drop them little guns, Fancy Dan! This is just a holdup. We don't want to kill you!"

"Unlucky for you I don't feel the same way," Conrad said as he tilted the barrels of the Lightnings up and blazed fire.

In the dimness of the street, Conrad couldn't tell where he had hit them, but the cries of pain from both men told him his bullets had hit their marks. One of the men got a shot off, but the slug whined off a cobblestone.

The other two let go of the harness and tried to drag guns from under their coats. Wounded or not, Clancy left the carriage seat in a dive that sent him crashing into one of the men. The impact knocked the would-be thief out of the saddle.

The last man thought better of continuing the debacle. He wheeled his horse around and kicked it into a gallop. Conrad started to send a slug after him, but stopped before he squeezed the trigger. If he missed, there was no telling where the bullet would wind up. Brownstones lined the street closely on both sides. A stray shot could hurt someone who didn't deserve it.

The next instant, he leaped aside as one of the men he had wounded tried to ride him down. The horse's body clipped Conrad's shoulder with enough force to send him spinning off his feet. He landed next to a carriage wheel.

The two men fled on horseback in the other direction from their companion. Conrad held his fire as he stood up. The narrow streets of Boston were no place for a gunfight.

"A little help here, sir, if ye don't mind!" Clancy had the man he had tackled on the ground, struggling with him. One of his hamlike fists rose, then fell, landing on the robber's jaw with a sound like an ax splitting wood. "Ah, never mind, sir. The rascal seems to have gone to sleep."

As Conrad hurried toward them he heard whistles shrilling in the distance. "That's the police, isn't it? Someone reported those shots."

"Aye, that'd be the coppers. Do ye want to talk to them?"

"I'd just as soon we didn't."

"My thinkin', exactly. Should we leave this'un here for 'em to find?"

An idea occurred to Conrad. "No, let's put him in the carriage. I'd like to have a talk with him."

From all appearances, the incident was just an attempted robbery that had gone very wrong for the would-be criminals. But Conrad had learned not to trust appearances. He wanted to ask the robber a few questions when the man regained consciousness.

"Let me give you a hand," he said to Clancy. "How bad are you hurt?"

"'Tis nothin' to worry about, sir. A mere scratch on me arm."

Conrad wasn't so sure about that. Clancy seemed to be having trouble using his left arm as together they lifted the unconscious man and piled him into the carriage.

"Can you handle the reins?"

"Aye."

"Do you know a place we can take this man where we won't be disturbed?"

Clancy frowned and scratched his head before he put on the plug hat that had fallen off when he tackled the robber. "Aye, but just what did ye have in mind? I won't be a party to cold-blooded murder."

Conrad laughed, but the sound didn't have much genuine humor in it. "If I wanted him dead, he'd already be dead."

"Somehow I'm not doubtin' that," Clancy muttered.

"I just want to talk to him. Really."

"All right. Best keep them guns handy in case he wakes up while we're goin'." The big Irishman paused. "You're the first tuxedo-wearin' gentleman I've hauled around who carries a couple o' six-guns. I don't know ye, sir, but I got the feelin' you ain't much like the other swells in Boston."

Conrad's chuckle was real, as he said, "Let's go, if you're sure you're all right."

"Aye. Them coppers'll be here in a minute."

The carriage got underway, leaving the scene of the attempted holdup. Conrad holstered one of the Lightnings but kept the other gun in his hand, covering the man who slumped on the carriage's front, backward-facing seat.

It was a good thing he had Clancy along to find their way out of the warren of narrow streets and alleys through which the vehicle rolled, Conrad thought. He had grown up in Boston, but wasn't sure exactly where they were, not having spent much time in those neighborhoods as a boy and a young man.

Clancy finally drew up at the closed double doors of a big, barnlike structure. "Gallagher!" he called. "Gallagher, 'tis me, Clancy. Let us in, that's a good lad."

A smaller door next to the big doors opened a little, leaving a crack big enough for the twin barrels of a shotgun to thrust through it. "Clancy? What're ye doin' here in the middle of the night? You're drunk, right?"

"Nary a drop has passed me lips this evenin'," Clancy insisted. "I've had a spot of trouble and could use your assistance." He paused. "It'll be worth your while."

"Well, why didn't ye say so? Hold on."

The shotgun disappeared, the narrow door closed, and a moment later the big ones began to swing open with a creaking of hinges.

Inside the carriage, the robber stirred. He grated a curse as he started to sit up.

"Take it easy." Conrad pointed the Lightning at the man. If he'd had a single-action revolver, he would have cocked it, to reinforce the threat behind the order. Since it was too dark to see much inside the vehicle, he added, "I've got a .38 aimed at you. At this range it'll blow a nice-sized hole in you if you try anything."

"What the hell?" the man whined. "Who're you?"

"The man you tried to rob," Conrad said coldly.

The carriage rolled into the barn, and the big doors closed with a firm slam behind it.

"Mister, take it easy," the man said with fear edging into his voice. "We didn't mean to hurt you. We just wanted your wallet."

Outside the carriage, someone struck a match and held it to a lantern's wick. As the glow washed outward, some of it spilled through the carriage window and showed Conrad the scared, ratlike face of his prisoner. Clancy opened the door.

Conrad gestured slightly with the Colt's barrel and ordered, "Get out."

"I'm goin', I'm goin'. Just don't shoot." The man climbed out.

Conrad followed, assuming the small, wiry man holding the lantern was Gallagher. The light revealed the bloodstain on the left sleeve of Clancy's coat.

"You need to get that wound tended to," Conrad said with sudden concern. "It looks like more than a scratch to me. We'll find a doctor—"

"Who'll tell the coppers about me comin' to him with a bullet hole in me arm." Clancy shook his head. "No need to do that, sir. Gallagher here can clean and patch up a wound as good as any sawbones. We got plenty of experience at such chores, fightin' the Rebs from Chickamauga to Richmond."

"Aye," Gallagher agreed. He had a small brush of a gray mustache on his upper lip.

"All right, if you're sure." Conrad looked around. The barn had several stalls on each side of the center aisle. He spotted a short, three-legged stool and told the prisoner, "Go over there and sit down."

"What're you gonna do to me?" the man asked in a surly voice as he did what Conrad told him.

"Nothing, as long as you give me straight answers." Conrad held the .38 revolver straight out in front of him, pointing at the prisoner's forehead. "But if you lie to me, I'll blow your brains out."

The man's eyes widened, his face took on a frightened pallor, and his prominent Adam's apple bobbed as he swallowed hard.

"So tell me, did someone hire you to kill me tonight?"

Chapter 8

In the tense silence that followed the question, Clancy cleared his throat. "Beggin' your pardon, sir, but I said I wouldn't be a party to cold-blooded murder."

"Killing a rat isn't murder," Conrad said, his eyes never leaving the prisoner's terrified face. "Well, how about it? The truth, now. This is a double-action revolver, and it doesn't take much pressure on the trigger to make it go off."

The robber lifted trembling hands. "Please, Mr. Browning, don't kill me. It was just a robbery, I swear. We seen the coach and knew whoever was inside it was likely to have some money and jewels on them."

Conrad's nostrils flared as he drew in a deep breath. The self-declared robber had just made a critical mistake without being aware of it.

"Coming from vermin like you, I might be inclined to believe your story . . . if you hadn't just called me by name. How did you know that unless someone *sent* you after me?"

The man's eyes bulged with the realization of what he had done. He tried to recover, stammering, "I-I heard the driver say your name—"

"He didn't," Conrad cut in. "You were *told* who I am. The question is, who did the telling?" He moved a step closer. "Are you going to answer me, or am I going to—"

He didn't get the chance to complete the threat he wouldn't have carried out anyway. At least, he didn't think he would have pulled the trigger and killed the man in cold blood.

Sheer desperation sent the man falling over backward as he upset the stool and kicked at Conrad's gun hand. The toe of his shoe struck Conrad's wrist and sent the revolver flying.

Conrad bit back a curse and leaped after the man, who twisted around onto his hands and knees as he hit the floor. He headed for the doors, trying to scramble away. Fear had the ratlike little gunman moving fast.

"I'll cut him off," Clancy bellowed as he broke into a run. The Irishman was so big it was more of a lumbering trot.

Conrad's right hand throbbed from the kick. Reaching across with his left he drew the other Lightning.

Clancy had almost caught up with the escaping prisoner. He reached down to grab the man, saying, "C'mere, ye little—"

The man snatched up a pitchfork leaning against a post and whirled around to slash at Clancy with the razor-sharp tines. He let out a startled yell and jerked back just in time to avoid having his belly ripped open. One of the tines tore his coat.

Clancy was in the line of fire as Conrad tried to draw a bead on the robber and knock a leg out from under him with a well-placed shot. Conrad couldn't risk firing.

The hijacker jabbed the fork at Clancy again, forcing the Irishman to give ground. "Leave me alone, you big damn lummox!" the man yelled.

"Clancy, get down!" Conrad called.

The robber or would-be assassin or whatever he was slashed back and forth with the pitchfork. As Clancy backed up, he stumbled and his balance deserted him. He fell heavily to the hard-packed dirt floor. The man lifted the pitchfork, ready to plunge the tines into Clancy's body.

Conrad drilled the thief's right thigh with a slug from the .38.

Yelping in pain the man dropped the pitchfork as his wounded leg gave out and folded up underneath him.

Then he screamed as he fell on the pitchfork and the tines speared deep into his body.

"Son of a bitch!" Conrad leaped forward. He still wanted to question the man. Cold steel buried in the man's gut. Blood was already welling around the tines as the man lay on his side, curled up around them in agony.

Conrad didn't try to move him. Kneeling beside the man he said, "Who sent you after me? Who?"

The man gave a gurgling groan. He turned his

head enough to look up at Conrad, who saw the pain and hate in the man's beady eyes.

"You can . . . go to hell . . ." the man gasped. Cords stood out prominently in his throat and he bared his teeth in a grotesque grimace as a fresh spasm of pain wracked him. His expression smoothed out abruptly. A long, rattling sigh came from him.

Conrad had seen and heard those signs too often in the past. Life began to fade from the man's eyes as Conrad grabbed his shoulder and shook him. "Damn it, who hired you? Who sent you after me?"

"I don't think he's gonna answer ye, sir," Clancy said from behind him.

"I know it," Conrad said bitterly. He stood up. "He's gone." He turned to look at Clancy. "He didn't get you with that pitchfork, did he?"

"No, but it wasn't for lack of tryin', the little scut."

Gallagher came over to join them. "Now that I take a better look at the fella, I think I recognize him."

"Do you know his name?" Conrad asked.

"Albie, Alfie, somethin' like that." Gallagher shook his head. "It don't really matter. What's important is that I know who he works for. He hangs around with Eddie Murtagh at a tavern not far from here. Hung around, I guess I could say, because he ain't gonna be doin' it no more."

"Who's Eddie Murtagh?"

"A bad man," Clancy answered with a solemn frown. "He'd throw his own ma down a flight o' stairs if ye paid him enough to do it."

"That sounds like the sort of man you'd hire to get rid of somebody you wanted gotten rid of."

Clancy said, "You sure *ain't* like any of the other society swells I ever saw."

"What's the name of this tavern where I'll find Murtagh?"

Gallagher said, "It's called Serrano's. Run by a Eye-talian fella."

Conrad smiled faintly. "I didn't think the Irish and the Italians got along that well."

"We don't." Gallagher snorted contemptuously. "But Serrano sells cheap booze and cheaper women. I don't go there, myself."

"And you shouldn't, either, sir," Clancy added. "I don't know what's goin' on here, but ye'd be better off steerin' well clear o' Eddie Murtagh."

"We'll see." Conrad looked at the bloody corpse. "Right now we have a more pressing problem."

Gallagher shook his head. "No, I can get rid of that body, don't ye worry. Nobody will ever find it and ask any inconvenient questions."

"What about that gunshot?"

"Also nothin' to worry about. Since it was just one shot, anybody who heard it will figure somebody was shootin' at a rat or some such." Gallagher frowned at the corpse. "They wouldn't be far wrong, at that."

"Tend to Clancy's wound first," Conrad told him. "Then we'll get out of here." He took some bills from his pocket and pressed them into Gallagher's hand. "For your trouble."

"Gettin' rid o' gutter scum like this is no trouble. It's more along the lines of a pleasure."

Gallagher got Clancy's bloody coat and shirt off him, revealing the wound in the big Irishman's arm to be a fairly deep furrow where a bullet had creased him. It had bled a lot and probably hurt like hell, but Conrad didn't think the injury was serious. Gallagher used some whiskey to clean it, leading to bitter complaints from Clancy about a waste of perfectly good booze. Then the smaller man bandaged the wound.

"I can get back to the hotel alone if you're not up to driving," Conrad offered.

"Oh? Ye think you could find your way back, do ye?"

Conrad smiled. "Well . . . not really."

"Never you mind. I'm fine to drive, now that Gallagher here has finished tendin' to me arm."

"There's a bonus in this for you, too. I know you didn't expect gunplay when you hired on to drive me tonight."

"'Tis not necessary . . . but I'll not be turnin' it down."

Conrad asked Gallagher, "Is there anything else you can tell me about this man"—he nodded toward the dead man—"or about Murtagh?"

Gallagher shook his head. "I have as little as possible to do with their sort. Men like Murtagh been runnin' gangs in this town for a long time. They're used to killin' anybody who gets in their way. I still think it'd be best for you to stay away from Serrano's. Hell, if somebody wants you dead bad enough to hire Murtagh, maybe you ought to get outta Boston entirely!"

"That wouldn't do any good," Conrad said.

"Whoever it is would just come after me, or send someone like Murtagh after me. I'd rather meet the trouble head-on."

"May the saints be watchin' over ye, then," Gallagher said, "because you're likely to need all the help ye can get!"

Chapter 9

Arturo knew something had happened as soon as Conrad came into the hotel suite. "You're rumpled and dusty and positively disreputable, sir. What have you been doing, rolling around in the street?"

"As a matter of fact, yes. A horse knocked me down."

"I thought I smelled something. I take it this incident did *not* occur at Mrs. Garrison's dinner party?"

"No, some men stopped the carriage on the way back here." Conrad left out the fact that he and Clancy had actually been on their way to an Irish pub, not to the hotel. "They tried to make it look like a robbery, but I'm convinced their actual goal was to kill me."

"Let me guess," Arturo said. "You killed them instead."

"Well, I wounded a couple of them, but they got away. I don't know how bad they were hit. One of the others . . . well, he wound up with a pitchfork in his belly, but that wasn't completely my doing."

Despite his attempt at an unflappable demeanor, Arturo looked a little shocked. "Are you injured or just disheveled, sir?"

"I'm all right," Conrad assured him. "I'd appreciate it if you'd have this tuxedo cleaned and pressed. I might need it again while I'm here."

"Of course. Is there a chance the night's activities are going to result in a visit from the authorities?"

"Not likely. I don't think anybody knows what happened except you, me, and Clancy . . . and the men who tried to kill me, along with the man they work for."

"Do you know who that is?" Arturo asked.

Conrad smiled. "I have a pretty good idea."

"So I suppose you'll be paying him a visit, as well?"

"Yes, but not tonight." Conrad pulled his tie off. "I think I'm done for the night."

Despite that comment, he had a lot to think about. After he turned in, he found himself lying in bed, staring up at the ceiling as the wheels of his brain revolved.

It had been a hunch on his part the apparent robbery was more than that. Once it was confirmed, it left him with another, more compelling question. Who wanted him dead badly enough to hire Eddie Murtagh to see to it?

Pamela's cousin and lover, Roger Tarleton, had been behind Conrad's recent troubles, but Roger was locked up in New Mexico. Some other Tarleton relative could have taken up the family legacy of twisted vengeance.

Another possibility occurred to Conrad. Pamela had gone to a lot of trouble in her efforts to make his life miserable. He wondered if she could have made some sort of arrangement with Murtagh before she left Boston with the twins. She could have paid him to arrange to have Conrad killed if he ever showed up in the city again, whether she was still alive or not. That was just the sort of diabolical thing she might have done.

The good thing about all this, Conrad told himself, was that he didn't have to wonder.

All he had to do was ask Eddie Murtagh.

Conrad didn't plan to venture out to Serrano's until the next night, thinking he would have more luck finding Murtagh then. He slept late and was having breakfast in the sitting room when a knock came on the door.

He didn't think Murtagh would come after him in the hotel, but he slipped his hand into the pocket of his dressing gown and closed it around the butt of the small .32 caliber pistol he had placed there before he nodded to Arturo to answer the door.

"Who's there?" the valet called.

"Jack Mallory."

Conrad nodded again. Arturo opened the door to admit the private detective. Mallory came in and handed Arturo his hat.

Conrad asked, "Would you like some coffee?"

"Sure."

"I didn't expect to see you again so soon," Conrad said as Arturo poured the coffee.

"You didn't say how often you wanted reports from me. Since I had some information I thought I'd go ahead and give it to you."

Conrad leaned forward eagerly. "What have you found out?"

"I have contacts in most of the hospitals in the city. Pamela Tarleton wasn't admitted to any of them in the past four years, at least not under her own name."

Conrad shook his head. "I expected that. I've believed all along that she gave birth in a private hospital or sanitarium."

Mallory took the cup from Arturo and nodded his thanks. "Here's the thing. Some of the nurses I know have also worked for doctors in private hospitals. I was able to spread the word, including Miss Tarleton's description, and I found a girl who remembers a patient who might have been her."

Conrad came to his feet. "That was fast work."

"I haven't determined yet if the patient actually *was* Miss Tarleton," Mallory said with a shrug. "I can continue to investigate, but I'm not sure how far I'll get. The doctor who runs this place has a lot of rich patients, so I'm sure he's in the habit of being discreet. He's not going to want to talk to a detective."

"What's his name?"

"Dr. Vernon Futrelle."

The name was familiar to Conrad. Dr. Futrelle operated a sanitarium across the river in Cambridge that catered to the wealthy and powerful members of Boston's elite. It was just the sort of place where a woman such as Pamela, who found herself with child and without a husband, could go to give birth without anyone knowing about it. Conrad suspected that plenty of daughters from rich families had done exactly that. It was easier than sailing off to Europe for a year, another time-honored method of dealing with that particular problem. Futrelle also numbered among his patients women who were too fond of alcohol or opium, things like that.

Mallory was right about one thing: Dr. Futrelle would never reveal his patients' secrets willingly. Discretion was as important as his medical skill, if not more so.

He might be more inclined to talk to a member of Boston society, however.

"Tell me what else you know," Conrad said as a plan began to formulate in his mind. "When was this mysterious patient who might have been Miss Tarleton at Dr. Futrelle's sanitarium?"

Mallory shook his head. "The girl I talked to couldn't remember for sure. Somewhere between three and four years ago. That was as much as she could narrow it down."

"How long was she there?"

"Several months. She had a private suite, of course. Her and the maid she brought with her."

"Maid?"

"Yeah, she had a servant with her."

"Did the nurse you talked to remember anything about the maid?" Conrad thought it might be productive to track the woman down.

But Mallory shook his head again. "I'm afraid not. Who pays attention to servants?"

Unfortunately, that was true. Pamela and her father had had numerous servants working for them, and despite the fact that Conrad had been in the Tarleton house a great deal while he and Pamela were engaged, he couldn't remember any of them. Of course, he had been a pompous jackass back then, he reminded himself.

"All right. That's good work, Mr. Mallory. Excellent work. I'll speak to Dr. Futrelle myself and see if I can find out anything."

"That might be your best bet," Mallory agreed.

"Do you have anything else to report?"

"No, that's all I've learned so far. You want me to continue with the investigation?"

"Of course. This business with Dr. Futrelle might not pan out at all." Conrad paused. "There's something else I'd like to ask you. Are you familiar with a man named Eddie Murtagh?"

Mallory's bushy red brows drew down in a puzzled frown. "Murtagh's the leader of one of the gangs you can find in the worst part of town. He's a killer, even though the law's never been able to get anything on him. Everybody in that neighborhood is too scared of him to ever testify against him. Why do you want to know about Eddie Murtagh?"

"I understand he can be found at a tavern called Serrano's. I'll go see Dr. Futrelle this afternoon, but I thought I might pay Murtagh a visit tonight."

Mallory grimaced. "No offense, Mr. Browning, but that's a crazy idea."

"I expressed the same opinion," Arturo put in. "Although in more civilized terms."

"Why do you want to get yourself killed poking around Murtagh's business?" Mallory asked.

"Because *he* started poking around *my* business," Conrad replied. "Or rather some of the men who work for him did. They tried to kill me last night."

The detective grunted in surprise. "You've got to tell me about this, if you don't mind."

"Not at all." Conrad explained the events of the night before.

Mallory listened with rapt attention, his coffee forgotten. "If you go waltzing into Serrano's and start asking questions of Murtagh, you won't make it out of there alive."

"I don't intend to walk up to the man and introduce myself as Conrad Browning. I thought I'd be a bit more subtle than that."

"You don't think you'll stick out like a sore thumb in the place?"

Conrad glanced down at the silk dressing gown he wore. "I don't plan to wear this, you know. I can change my appearance and pretend to be someone I'm not."

Mallory could ask the notorious gunfighter Kid Morgan about that if he didn't believe it.

"You need somebody with you who knows what it's like down there," Mallory said.

"Are you volunteering for the job?"

"Hell, no!" A grin spread across Mallory's rugged

face. "I'm not volunteering. It'll cost you. More than you're paying me to go around and ask questions at hospitals. In fact, if we're lucky, that's where we'll wind up, in a hospital."

"And if we're not lucky?"

"The morgue," Mallory said, then added with a shrug, "Or the Charles River."

Chapter 10

They made arrangements to meet at the hotel at seven o'clock that evening. In the meantime, Conrad would pay a visit to Dr. Vernon Futrelle's sanitarium in Cambridge.

Conrad put in a call to the boarding house where Clancy lived, which was equipped with a telephone, and got him on the line. He asked the big Irishman to meet him at the hotel at two o'clock, then added, "That is, if you're able to handle a team. How's your arm today?"

"A bit stiff and sore, but fine other than that. Gallagher did a fine job of patchin' it up, although I still hate to think of all that whiskey goin' for medicinal purposes."

Conrad chuckled. "Stick with me, my friend, and you'll be able to afford plenty of whiskey."

"I'm your man, Mr. Browning. I'll be there."

After Conrad ended the call, Arturo said, "It sounds to me as if you'll be leaping right from one danger into another, sir."

"Are you talking about going to the sanitarium?"

Conrad asked with a frown. "I shouldn't be in any danger there. Now, Serrano's will be a different story tonight."

"I don't like sanitariums," Arturo said. "There's an air of madness about them, and it's too easy for one to be locked up in such a place."

Conrad shook his head. "This isn't that sort of sanitarium. Dr. Futrelle handles different kinds of ailments."

Yet there might be something to what Arturo said, Conrad mused. When Futrelle's patients were drying out from booze or trying to get away from opium or other drugs, there might well be times when they would have to be locked up, perhaps even restrained, as lunatics were in asylums. In order to do that, Futrelle would have to have some tough, burly orderlies working for him.

"But don't worry, Arturo, I'll be careful." Conrad's face and voice grew grim. "These probably won't be the last risks I'll have to run before I find my children."

The valet couldn't argue with that. He inclined his head in acknowledgment that for Conrad Browning, there were more important considerations than his personal safety.

Clancy arrived with the carriage at the appointed time. A slight bulkiness under the left sleeve of his coat where the bandage was wrapped around his arm was the only sign of his injury. He thumbed his plug hat back on his head and asked, "Where is it we're headed this afternoon, sir?"

"A private sanitarium in Cambridge, Clancy."

The big Irishman frowned. "Are ye havin'

medical problems, sir? I hope you're not thinkin' about havin' this arm o' mine looked at. 'Tis not necessary."

"No, I'm just looking for information," Conrad assured him.

They crossed the Charles River on the West Boston Bridge and rolled into Cambridge, where Conrad had attended Harvard. He saw a lot of familiar sights from those days but felt no particular nostalgia for them. When he was in college, he had thought he knew everything there was to know. It had taken life itself to teach him how ignorant he truly was.

The Futrelle Sanitarium and Private Hospital was located behind a high stone wall lined with hedges. When the carriage pulled up to a pair of massive wrought-iron gates, Conrad looked between the bars and saw a squarish, three-story building of brown brick squatting in the middle of a landscaped lawn that covered several acres. The grounds were fairly attractive, with plenty of green grass, trees, and flower beds with flagstone walks winding between them. The sanitarium itself was plain and ugly.

A stocky guard in a blue uniform and black cap that made him look a little like a police officer stepped out of a guardhouse next to the gates. He carried a single-barreled shotgun tucked under his arm and regarded Clancy with narrow, suspicious eyes. "What can I do for you?"

Conrad had told Clancy what to say. "Mr. Conrad Browning to see Dr. Futrelle, if ye don't mind."

"Wait there." The guard ducked back into the little building and was gone for a minute or so. When he came back, he shook his head and said, "Mr. Browning isn't on the list of the doctor's appointments. Sorry, you can't come in."

Conrad opened the carriage door and stepped down to the ground. He smiled at the guard. "I know I don't have an appointment, but I won't take up much of the doctor's time. He and I have a number of mutual friends."

"You need to see him about a medical matter?" the guard asked.

"That's right."

Working there, the man would know wealth when he saw it. He thought it over for a second, then said, "If you can wait a minute, Mr. Browning, I'll check with the doctor's secretary."

"Thank you. I appreciate that."

They had some way of communicating between the guardhouse and the main building, Conrad thought. Either a telephone line or some sort of speaking tube. He filed the information away in his mind. You never knew when such a thing might come in handy.

The wait was longer, but when the guard came back out, he said, "Dr. Futrelle will see you for a few minutes." He shoved a lever that sent the gates rumbling back. "Drive straight to the main building and someone will meet you."

"Thank you." Conrad climbed back into the carriage.

By the time they reached the main building, a

woman in a starched white dress and light blue apron and cap was waiting for them. "Mr. Browning?" she asked as Conrad climbed down from the carriage. "I'm Lois Fielding, one of the nurses here. If you'll come with me, I'll take you to Dr. Futrelle's office." She glanced at Clancy. "Your driver will have to wait here."

"That's fine. Don't wander off, Clancy."

"Oh, no, sir. I'll be right here."

Having spent so much time in the more egalitarian West the past few years, Conrad found the nurse's condescending tone when she spoke about Clancy bothersome. He didn't show his annoyance. As a rich Bostonian, he was supposed to feel the same way.

Conrad noted the heavy locks on the front door and the bars on the windows as he went inside the sanitarium with the nurse. She led him through a small reception area and down a corridor to a set of double doors. He had a feeling it was all offices on the ground floor, with the patients being housed on the upper floors. The iron bars on the windows ought to keep them in, but the height served as an extra deterrent to escape. Somebody who really wanted a drink might go to almost any lengths to get one.

Nurse Fielding knocked on one of the double doors. A man's voice called from the other side. "Come in."

The nurse opened the door and said, "Mr. Browning, Doctor." She stepped back.

Conrad entered and found himself in a large, book-lined room that obviously served as both office and library for Dr. Vernon Futrelle. The window behind the desk looked out over the grounds and relieved some of the grim atmosphere engendered by the rank upon rank of thick volumes mostly bound in black or dark brown leather.

The man who came out from behind the desk and walked toward Conrad with his hand extended was familiar. He realized he had seen the doctor at various social functions in the past. Futrelle was short and thick-bodied, with a prominent paunch over which a gold watch chain draped. He had a bulldog face, spectacles, and a brush of graying red hair that stuck up straight from his head. His grip was strong as he shook hands with Conrad.

"Mr. Browning," he said. "I believe we've met before. I knew your mother and your father, certainly."

The way he phrased it made it sound as though he wasn't aware that Frank Morgan was really Conrad's father, which was certainly possible. Vivian Browning had never done anything to publicize that fact, and neither had Conrad while he lived in Boston.

"It's good to see you again, Doctor."

Futrelle waved him into a comfortable leather armchair in front of the desk. "Sit down, my boy. What can I do for you? You're not having medical problems, are you? I must say, you look as healthy as a horse! Healthier than some horses I've seen, in fact."

"No, I'm fine," Conrad said as he sat down and

crossed his legs. He rested his hat on his knee. "I'm here about someone else. A . . . friend of mine."

Futrelle settled back in his chair and clasped his hands over his stomach. "Not one of those hypothetical friends that are really you, I hope."

Conrad laughed and shook his head. "No chance of that. This lady had a condition that's quite impossible for me to attain."

Futrelle raised his eyebrows. "A lady, eh? Are we speaking of a . . . delicate condition?"

"Precisely," Conrad said.

"Well, that's troubling," Futrelle said. "I suppose that discretion is an absolute necessity, eh?"

"Yes, I'm afraid so."

Futrelle nodded slowly, wisely. Conrad knew exactly what he was thinking. The doctor believed Conrad had gotten some girl pregnant, probably a servant, and wanted the situation dealt with as efficiently as possible, with no fuss. In cases such as that, the gentleman involved would pay for the girl to stay at the sanitarium until the baby was born, and then a discreet adoption would be arranged. The whole process was expensive, but well worth it for a man who valued his privacy.

"I believe we can assist you, Mr. Browning," Futrelle said. "What's the young lady's name?"

"Pamela," Conrad said.

Futrelle raised his eyebrows again. He was surprised, and though he tried to control the reaction, he didn't quite succeed.

"Pamela Tarleton," Conrad went on.

There was a flash of genuine fear in Futrelle's

eyes, and Conrad knew he had come to the right place.

Anger replaced the fear as Futrelle snapped, "This isn't amusing, Mr. Browning. I know very well that Miss Tarleton was your fiancée at one time. I also know that she's dead. If she ever was a patient here, and I'm not saying she was, I'd be honor bound not to reveal anything about her stay with us."

"You don't have to reveal anything, Doctor," Conrad said in a tone as sharp as Futrelle's. He played the rest of his cards. "I already know she came here to give birth, and that's exactly what she did. She bore two children, twins. What I want to know is what happened to those children."

Futrelle reached for a bell push on the desk. "This is none of your business, sir—"

In a motion almost too swift for the eye to follow, Conrad was on his feet. His hand shot out and closed around Futrelle's wrist, stopping the doctor from reaching the bell.

"It is every bit my business," Conrad said in a low, dangerous voice. "Those were my children, Doctor. You're going to tell me what happened to them and where they are now."

Futrelle's eyes looked wild and panicky behind the thick lenses of his spectacles. "You're insane! I don't know what you're talking about. None of this ever happened—"

"Show me the records, Doctor," Conrad grated. If he found out what he needed to know at the sanitarium, he wouldn't have to go to Serrano's. "Show me the records, or my lawyers will be in court first thing tomorrow morning filing motions."

"You can't force me to do such a thing! It's not legal."

"Maybe not, but it certainly wouldn't be a good thing for your business to be dragged into the light of a courtroom, would it?"

"But . . . but . . . I can't show you the records! There *aren't* any records!"

Conrad's grip on the doctor's arm tightened. "Are you trying to tell me that Pamela wasn't here?"

Futrelle shook his head. "No . . . No, she was here . . . but she took all the records with her. When she left with . . . with the children . . . there were some men with her. I don't know who they were, but they were very . . . threatening."

Conrad drew in a deep breath. He didn't doubt that Pamela had hired some thugs to make Futrelle turn over all the records. She had hired gunmen to kidnap and murder Rebel and then later to try to kill him. He wondered suddenly if Eddie Murtagh had been working for her even back then.

The main thing filling his mind at the moment was Futrelle's admission that Pamela had left with the children. It was the first direct evidence Conrad had found that the children even existed.

"The twins," he said softly. "They were twins?"

Futrelle jerked his head in a nod. "That's right."

"Boys? Girls?"

"One of each," the doctor said.

A powerful sensation, almost like a physical

blow, coursed through Conrad. He was a father. He had a son and a daughter. Even though he had read Pamela's hateful letter dozens of times, even though he'd heard Mallory's report about a patient at the sanitarium who might have been Pamela and who might have given birth to twins, he finally had proof. It was a world-changing revelation that went right to his very core.

He let go of Futrelle's arm and stepped back. His hands covered his face for a moment. He felt stunned. But he was alert enough to realize he'd made a mistake.

Futrelle lunged forward and slapped his hand down on the bell push. "You won't get away with coming in here and threatening me like this," Futrelle gloated. "Now you'll see that in this sanitarium, my word is law!"

The doors behind Conrad burst open. In answer to Futrelle's summons, three big, heavily-muscled orderlies rushed in, obviously ready for trouble.

Futrelle pointed at Conrad and ordered, "Grab this man! He's unstable and needs to be locked up!"

Chapter 11

Conrad instantly grasped what Futrelle was trying to do. The doctor didn't want any kind of scandal to threaten his lucrative business. By claiming Conrad was insane, Futrelle could get away with locking him up and keeping him a prisoner in the sanitarium, perhaps forever. He knew Conrad no longer had any relatives in Boston to dispute the claim.

As he whirled around to face the three orderlies, Conrad was aware he was fighting not only for his freedom but for his very life. Once he was a "patient" there, it would be easy for Futrelle to dispose of him without anyone knowing about it.

As the orderlies lunged at him, Conrad's hands flashed underneath his coat and came out filled with the Lightnings. "Stay where you are!"

The men came to awkward, skidding halts as they looked down the barrels of those revolvers.

Conrad heard movement behind him and looked around. Futrelle was coming at him, swinging a heavy glass ashtray he had snatched up from the desk. The doctor had quite a bit of strength in his short, stocky body, and smashed the ashtray against the side of Conrad's head with stunning force. He went down on one knee.

One of the orderlies leaped forward and grabbed his right arm, wrenching the gun aside. Another man went for his left arm. Pain shot through Conrad's shoulder as the orderly tried to twist the arm out of its socket. The third orderly closed in from the front.

The way the three of them moved in tandem told Conrad they had plenty of experience at dealing with violent patients. Unless he broke free quickly, they would overpower him and all would be lost.

He would never find his children.

He let his weight sag so the two men who had seized him were holding him up. Pulling both legs up, he snapped them out in a savage double kick that sunk the heels of his boots deep into the belly of the third orderly. The man grunted in pain, doubled over, and blundered right into his companion who was holding Conrad's right arm.

That loosened the man's grip enough for Conrad to pull free. He twisted his body and hooked a foot behind the knee of the man holding his left arm. A quick jerk upset that man, and suddenly everyone in the office was on the floor except for Dr. Futrelle, who danced around nervously, still holding the ashtray as if he wanted to hit Conrad with it again.

Conrad surged to his knees. One of the orderlies tried to grapple with him again. From the corner of his eye, Conrad saw Futrelle rush in and swing the ashtray at him. He jerked his head aside. Futrelle's momentum carried him forward, and the blow smashed into the orderly's face, crushing the man's nose and shattering cheek bones. Blood spurted as the orderly howled in pain and fell backward, clutching at his ruined face.

The man Conrad had kicked in the stomach was lying curled up on his side, mewling in agony at the damage done to his gut. The one with the broken nose was hurting too much to worry about anything else. That left just one orderly and Dr. Futrelle for Conrad to deal with.

He rolled to his feet and realized he still had the guns in his hands. As the remaining orderly tried to scramble up, Conrad pointed one of the Lightnings at his face and said, "Don't." He leveled the other .38 at Futrelle, who had backed off and stood against one of the bookshelves, his face pale and his chest heaving with fear.

"Don't . . . don't shoot me!" the doctor babbled. "Please, don't kill me! I . . . I'm sorry about the children!"

"I reckon you've figured out by now that I don't have a whole lot left to lose, Doc." Conrad didn't realize until later how much that sounded like something Kid Morgan would say. "Were you telling me the truth about the twins?"

"Yes! Yes, I swear it."

The orderly asked, "What twins?"

"That's none of your business," Futrelle snapped at the man, some of his imperious attitude coming back now that he was talking to an underling.

"And the records?" Conrad asked.

"I already told you. Miss Tarleton took them with her when she left with her maid and those . . . those men."

"The man who was in charge, do you remember what he looked like?"

"Not . . . not that well. It was years ago. You have to understand. All I recall is that he . . . he had dark hair, and he wasn't very big. But he was frightening. I looked in his eyes, and I felt like a . . . a bug on the sidewalk, like he could step on me and crush the life out of me and never feel a thing about it." Futrelle swallowed. "His eyes . . . I remember now . . . They were a very pale blue-gray, like the color of ice."

Conrad nodded. "Pamela didn't call him by name?"

"Never. Not that I heard."

Conrad was convinced Futrelle was telling the truth. The man was too scared to lie. Conrad nodded and backed toward the open double doors. He holstered the left-hand gun and picked up his hat, which had fallen on the floor. The two injured men continued to groan. The other orderly looked like he wanted to tear Conrad's head off, but he was smart enough to know he would get a bullet for his trouble if he tried.

"Here's what you're going to do, Futrelle," Conrad went on. "You're going to take excellent care of those men, because it's your fault they're hurt. They can stay here in your hospital for as long as they need to, at your expense. You understand?"

The doctor bobbed his head. "Of . . . of course."

"If I hear otherwise—and I *will* hear about it if you don't do what I tell you—I'll be back. You don't want that."

Wordlessly, Futrelle shook his head.

"You're not going to say anything to the police about what's happened here and you'll make sure your staff doesn't say anything." Conrad glanced at the third orderly. "By the way, I'm not insane, and I'm not just saying that because it's what a lunatic would say. Your boss wanted me locked up because he didn't want me going around talking about what really goes on in here."

Futrelle managed to lift his chin in a show of defiance and anger. "I've broken no laws," he insisted. "Everything I've ever done in this institution has been perfectly legal."

"Sometimes there's a difference between legal and right, and you know it," Conrad snapped. "Anyway, I don't have any interest in putting you out of business, Futrelle. I came here for information, that's all. We're finished, you and I, as long as you do what I've told you. Let's keep it that way."

Futrelle swallowed again and nodded. "Yes. Yes, I agree."

"Don't push any more buttons or have your staff try to stop me on my way out of here."

Futrelle waved a hand. "Just go," he said bitterly. "No one will try to stop you."

Conrad gave him a curt nod and backed through the doorway. As he turned to walk quickly along the corridor toward the entrance, he put the hand holding the gun under his coat, but he didn't holster the .38. Not until he was outside in the sunlight again.

Clancy was waiting for him, leaning against the carriage. The big Irishman straightened. A frown creased his broad forehead as he said, "Ye look a wee bit rumpled, sir. Trouble inside?"

"A little," Conrad admitted. "But I found out what I wanted to know. Let's get back to the hotel."

Clancy opened the carriage door. "Aye. To tell ye the truth, I'll be glad to get away from this place. I was just standin' here lookin' at the bars on the windows, and I got to admit it made me a mite nervous. Like standin' outside a prison."

Conrad looked at the building and realized just how close it had come to being exactly that for him. "You're not far wrong," he murmured. "Let's go, Clancy."

Chapter 12

Back at the hotel, Conrad filled Arturo in on what he had discovered at the sanitarium. "It was a close call," he concluded. "Futrelle could have claimed I was crazy and kept me locked up there from now on."

"Doubtful, sir," Arturo said. "For one thing, *I* know you're sane, and so does Mr. Mallory. We would have taken action on your behalf."

"No offense, Arturo, but I'm not sure the word of a valet and a shamus would carry enough weight against a man like Futrelle to do any good."

"None taken, sir. In that case, I would have simply gotten in touch with your father and told him you had disappeared. Even though I've never met Frank Morgan, I suspect he would not have allowed the situation to go unchallenged."

Conrad grinned at the thought. Frank Morgan had come to Boston once before to right a wrong, and Conrad had no doubt Frank would have answered Arturo's summons, much to the regret of Dr. Vernon Futrelle.

"We don't have to worry about that," Conrad said. "Futrelle has enough sense to keep his mouth shut."

"What if he tries to make sure *your* mouth is shut . . . permanently?"

"You mean if he hires somebody to kill me?" Conrad shrugged. "Wouldn't be the first time, now would it? I'm pretty hard to kill."

He hoped that continued to be true.

By the time evening rolled around, Conrad was dressed in clothes he had sent Arturo out to buy at a second-hand shop. The gray tweed suit was threadbare, and Conrad preferred not to think about the origin of the stains on it here and there. Under it he wore a dingy work shirt and no tie. Brogans with holes in the soles were on his feet. Arturo handed him a workingman's cap and watched critically as Conrad pulled it down on his sandy hair.

"Sir, you look positively disreputable."

Conrad smiled. "Good. Maybe I won't look too out of place at Serrano's."

"You wouldn't look out of place in the back of a police wagon, either. What is it they call them? Black Marias?"

"Something like that."

He was only going to carry one Lightning, since the coat wasn't cut to conceal either the shoulder harness or the cross-draw rig that belted around his waist. He checked the revolver, made sure the hammer was resting on the lone empty chamber, and tucked it behind his belt at the small of his back.

A knock sounded on the door of the suite. Conrad said quietly, "You can answer that while I get out of sight in case it's not Mallory."

He stepped into his bedroom while Arturo went to the door. A moment later the valet called through the open doorway, "It's all right, sir, it's the gentleman you were expecting."

Mallory wore a buttoned-up overcoat despite the season not warranting it, and he had a neatly creased fedora on his head. He took off the overcoat to reveal that he was dressed in old, well-worn clothes like Conrad. He brought a flattened derby from under his coat and punched it into shape. It looked like it had been knocked off and stepped on in numerous barroom brawls. If he had worn the garb openly into the hotel's lobby, he never would have been allowed upstairs.

The two men nodded in approval of each other's outfit.

"Nobody'll pay much attention to us in a dive like Serrano's," Mallory said.

Conrad asked, "Are you armed?"

Mallory reached into one pocket and brought out a heavy black sap. Another pocket produced a pair of brass knuckles. "And if that's not enough"—the detective stowed those items away—"I've got this, too." He brought out a razor that he opened with a flick of his wrist. The obviously keen blade glittered in the lamplight.

"Excellent," Conrad said with a nod. "I have a .38."

"I hope we won't need it. We don't want to get in a shootout with Murtagh and his boys. They'll outnumber us, and they're lads who don't shoot to wound." Mallory paused. "What is it you intend to do, anyway? You can't just ask Murtagh who hired him to kill you."

"I don't know," Conrad admitted. "I'll figure that out when we get there."

Mallory sighed. "I ought to have my head examined for going along with a crazy scheme like this."

"I know a place where you could have that done," Conrad told him, smiling. "Dr. Futrelle's sanitarium. Once he got you in there, though, he might not let you out again."

Mallory frowned. "What do you mean by that? What happened over there this afternoon?"

Conrad told him about the conversation in Futrelle's office and the violence that had resulted. When he was finished, Mallory said, "Somebody needs to take that man down a notch or two."

"I promised to leave him alone if he went along with what I said."

Mallory rubbed his angular jaw. "Yeah, but I didn't. I'll be keeping an eye on him from now on."

"I don't think that would hurt a thing."

A short time later, they were ready to go. Before they left the hotel room, Arturo asked, "Would it do any good to tell you to be careful?"

"Probably not," Conrad said.

He and Mallory waited until the hotel corridor was clear of guests and staff, then walked quickly to a set of service stairs and went down, leaving the hotel through a rear entrance used by employees. Once they were outside, they caught a streetcar that took them to the North End of Boston, within walking distance of the dangerous neighborhood where Serrano's tavern was located.

"Keep your wits about you," Mallory warned as he and Conrad walked along the narrow streets. "The Eyeties aren't that fond of Micks like me, and they'll likely take you for one, too."

"How does Murtagh get away with making Serrano's his headquarters?"

"He's always surrounded by plenty of tough boyos who can shoot fast and straight. And Eddie Murtagh *likes* living dangerously. He and Serrano have a truce, but it's a delicate one."

Conrad was aware of hostile stares and glances directed toward him and Mallory by the people they passed on the street, but no one tried to stop them. A few minutes later they came to Serrano's, an old frame building with large, dingy front windows covered by heavy curtains. When they went in, they found themselves in a foyer where two large men lounged, passing a jug of some sort of liquor back and forth. They were obviously guards, and came to their feet as Conrad and Mallory entered.

"What do you want here, Irish?" one of the men asked as he thrust his jaw belligerently at Mallory.

Conrad answered, "We're looking for Eddie Murtagh."

"No Micks here," the other guard snapped. "Go back to the south side."

Conrad shrugged. "All right, but Murtagh won't be happy when he finds out you cost him some money."

"What sort of money?"

"The sort you can spend."

The man moved closer to him, hands clenching into fists. "I don't like funny Irishmen. They ain't funny."

"Just go tell Murtagh that Futrelle sent us," Conrad said.

"Who the hell is Futrelle?"

"He'll know."

Conrad had no idea if Murtagh knew who Dr. Futrelle was, but it seemed like a worthwhile gamble. If Murtagh was connected somehow with Pamela, he might know where she had gone to give birth to the twins.

The guards thought it over. They looked at each other, and one of them shrugged. The other nodded and turned to go through a closed door on the other side of the foyer. During the moment it was open, Conrad heard piano music coming from inside, along with talk and laughter.

The guard who was left slipped a hand into a coat pocket. Conrad was pretty sure the man was gripping a gun.

The other man came back a couple minutes later. "Serrano says let them in," he reported. "But if they cause any problems, out they go on their Irish asses."

"Fair enough," Conrad said.

He and Mallory went on through the foyer into

the tavern's main room. It was dim and smoky, an eastern version of the sort of squalid western saloon Conrad had seen more than once. A man wearing an apron over his vest and trousers got in their path. His nose was big and impressive, and his dark eyes sparkled with menace.

"I'm Serrano," he growled. "What do you want with Eddie Murtagh?"

"I have a business deal I want to offer him," Conrad said.

Serrano was every bit as big and brawny as Mallory. He looked like he could break most men in half without really trying. He jerked his head toward a door. "In there. But tell Murtagh I don't like him doing business here. He can come here and drink, but he needs to keep his business elsewhere."

Conrad nodded. "I'll tell him."

"I'll go first. Otherwise you're liable to get shot, and it's hard enough keeping this place clean without a lot of blood on the floor."

Serrano led them to the door and knocked on it. A rough voice from the other side of the panel asked, "Who is it?"

"Serrano. Murtagh has visitors."

The door opened a little.

"No shooting, got it?" Serrano said.

"Come on in, laddies," the voice said, and something about it reminded Conrad of death. It was like being invited into a grave.

He and Mallory stepped into a room lit by a couple of lamps that had been turned down low.

Four men were in the room. The one who had answered the door was as cadaverous as his voice. Two men sat at a table with glasses and a half-empty bottle of wine in front of them. The fourth man was stretched out on a sofa, his ankles crossed and a lit cigarette dangling from his mouth. He held a huge revolver on his chest that looked like a miniature cannon.

One of the men at the table was smoking, too. He said around the cigarette between his lips, "Thanks, Serrano."

The tavern owner lifted a finger. "No trouble."

"No trouble," the man at the table promised. His voice was soft . . . but so was the hiss of a snake, Conrad thought. As the door closed behind Serrano, the man looked at the two visitors and asked, "What can I do for you lads?"

"Dr. Futrelle sent us." Conrad moved a step closer to the table.

The gaunt man who had let them into the room slid a hand out from under his coat, revealing a big revolver. It looked heavy enough that the weight seemed to be more than his spindly arms ought to be able to support, but he handled the weapon like it was a toy.

Conrad was close enough to see the eyes of the man at the table. They were a very pale bluish-gray, like chips of ice. And the man's hair, which was brushed back thickly from his forehead, was as black as midnight. He was Eddie Murtagh, Conrad thought.

And Murtagh was the man who had been with

Pamela when she left the sanitarium with the children.

His children, Conrad thought, putting more steel in his spine.

"Who's Futrelle?" Murtagh asked.

"You know who he is," Conrad answered confidently. "And you have something that belongs to him. He wants those records back that Miss Tarleton took with her."

Slowly, Murtagh shook his head. "What makes you think I know anything about any records? And who's Miss Tarleton?"

"You know perfectly well who she is. She's the one who paid you, three years ago, to get rid of anyone who showed up looking for her, especially her ex-fiancé, Conrad Browning."

"I still don't know what you're talking about," Murtagh insisted, "and you're beginning to bore me. Not to mention you've worried my friend Serrano. I think you should leave now."

"Not without those records you took from Futrelle's sanitarium. Unless Miss Tarleton destroyed them . . . ?"

Murtagh didn't respond to that. He poured wine from the bottle into his glass and said to the other man at the table, "Get them out of here. If they give you any trouble, kill them."

The man put his hands on the table and started to heave himself to his feet. Mallory was starting to look pretty worried.

He was about to get even more worried, Conrad thought. Before Murtagh's companion could get up, Conrad's hand swept his coat back, pulled the .38 from behind his belt, and lined it up on Eddie Murtagh's face. "Those were my children, you bastard, and unless you tell me what happened to them, I don't care if I walk out of here alive."

Chapter 13

"So that was your plan?" Mallory said bitterly into the stunned silence that followed Conrad's pronouncement. "Walk in here, behave like a total lunatic, and get us both killed?"

Conrad smiled. "He's not going to have us killed. He can see my finger on the trigger. Those gunmen of his can't shoot me fast enough to keep me from blowing his brains out."

Ever so slowly and carefully, Murtagh raised his hand and took the cigarette out of his mouth. "Liam, Patrick, put them guns away."

"But, Eddie, this is him!" the man on the sofa protested. He had sat up and swung his feet to the floor. The heavy revolver in his hand pointed toward Conrad. "This is the fella from the carriage last night. Ask him what happened to Dennis!"

That would be the unfortunate fellow who had wound up with the pitchfork in his belly, Conrad thought.

"Dennis got himself caught, so whatever happened to him is on his own head," Murtagh said with a snarl in his voice. "But is it true, mister? You're Conrad Browning?"

"That's right."

"You don't handle a gun like any rich man I ever saw."

"I'm not like any rich man you ever saw."

Murtagh leaned back slightly in his chair and smiled to himself. "She told me you were just a weak-kneed pansy. I see the bitch lied about *that*, too."

"What do you mean?" Conrad snapped.

"Just that she made promises she never delivered on."

"Then why are you still honoring the bargain you made with her years ago?"

Murtagh gave a lazy shrug. "She paid well, and besides, she's dead. It's a good thing to honor the wishes of the dead, innit?"

Conrad didn't answer. "Where did she take the children?"

"You think she shared all her plans with me? She hired me to convince that quack doctor to hand over all the records he had on her, and to make sure anyone who came lookin' for her would run into a dead end . . . literally. Especially if it was you, Browning."

"Where did you last see her?"

Murtagh took a drag on his cigarette. "At the train station. She and that maid of hers, who was more of a nanny by then, were boardin' a train."

"Westbound?" Conrad asked tensely.

"Bound for Chicago." Murtagh's shoulders rose and fell slightly again. "Where she was headed after that, I have no idea."

Conrad studied the man's face for a second. "You're lying."

"What would it profit me to do that now?"

"I don't know, but I'm convinced of it. You know more than you're telling."

Murtagh laughed. "Why wouldn't I tell you the truth? You're going to be dead in a few minutes anyway."

"That won't matter to you if you're dead first."

The other man at the table said, "Eddie, you can't let this son of a bitch talk to you like that!"

Murtagh nodded slightly. "You're right, Chris. But he says he's going to shoot me."

"Then stop him!"

"Aye. I think I should."

Murtagh's hand flashed out, grabbed the other man's collar, and dragged him across the table. Conrad held off on the trigger as he saw Murtagh throw himself behind his startled companion, using the man as a human shield.

"Kill 'em!" Murtagh yelled as he hit the floor.

Conrad pivoted toward the man standing in front of the sofa. He and the cadaverous gunman were clawing their guns out again with blinding speed. The Lightning in Conrad's hand blasted as the killer's revolver tipped toward him and roared. Flames licked from both barrels, so close they almost crossed.

Conrad felt more than heard the hum of the slug pass his ear. The bullet from his .38 struck the man in the chest and knocked him back on the sofa but didn't make him drop his gun.

Conrad fired again, driving a .38 round into the

man's forehead. Blood and brains sprayed across the cushions behind him as he flopped back lifelessly.

Mallory had gone into action as well, scooping the wine bottle from the table and flinging it at the tall, gaunt gunman. The bottle crashed into the man's face as he pulled the trigger, the explosion adding to the deafening chaos in the room. One of the glasses on the table exploded into a million glittering shards as the bullet struck it.

Mallory moved fast to seize the momentary advantage he had. Whipping out the sap he slammed it against the side of the gaunt gunman's head before the man could fire again. The man went down with a shattered skull.

Conrad dodged out of the way as the man Murtagh had grabbed upset the table and shoved it at him. Still loyal to his boss. The man tackled Conrad with an angry roar, sending them both to the floor. Landing on top of him, the man locked his fingers around Conrad's throat. The thumbs dug in, trying to crush Conrad's windpipe.

Knowing he had only seconds left to live, Conrad jabbed the muzzle of his gun into the man's body and pulled the trigger. The Lightning's explosion was muffled. The man stiffened and fell away, rolling onto his back. A worm of blood crawled from the corner of his mouth.

That left Murtagh. The gang leader grabbed one of the lamps and threw it at Conrad, who ducked out of the way. The lamp smashed against the wall, spreading flaming oil.

Serrano kicked the door open then, still wearing his apron even though he had a big revolver clutched in each fist. The weapons spouted fire and noise. He swept the room with lead, not caring who he hit.

Conrad and Mallory dived out of the way. As he hit the floor again, Conrad caught a glimpse of Murtagh ducking out through a narrow opening on the far side of the room and realized it must be a bolt-hole concealed by the wallpaper.

The fire was spreading, and Murtagh was getting away. Conrad had nothing against Serrano, but the big Italian tavernkeeper was going to be responsible for their deaths if he kept throwing lead around. Tilting the Lightning's barrel up Conrad squeezed off a shot. The bullet ripped through Serrano's meaty thigh and dumped him off his feet with a pained yell.

The Italian's men could get him to safety and chase everybody else out of the building before it burned down.

Conrad scrambled to his feet, grabbed Mallory, and hauled him toward the opening where Murtagh had escaped. "Come on!"

They ducked through the hidden door and found themselves in a dark, narrow passage. Using the flames behind them to see where they were going they raced through an open door at the far end and burst into an alley. Running feet slapped against the pavement to their left.

Conrad went after Murtagh, trusting that Mallory would follow him. The clang of a streetcar bell caught Conrad's attention. Looking in that direction, he saw Murtagh running toward the car and sprinted after him.

Seeing the gun in Conrad's hand, women screamed and men yelled, but they all got out of his way. He saw Murtagh swing up onto the street-car and lunged after him, closing the gap just in time to reach up with his free hand and grab the railing next to the car's steps. He let it pull him off his feet and clambered up.

Murtagh was waiting on the platform and launched a kick that thudded into Conrad's chest, nearly knocking him off the streetcar. Conrad dropped the revolver to grab hold of the railing and save himself. The fall from the streetcar wouldn't have been fatal, but Murtagh would have gotten away.

Conrad tackled him around the knees, and both of them sprawled on the tiny platform at the rear of the car.

It was a desperate, wordless struggle as they fought. Conrad was bigger, but Murtagh was wiry and slippery—an experienced brawler, as well as a vicious killer.

Spotting a knife coming at him Conrad grabbed Murtagh's wrist, twisting it aside. His grip didn't slacken when Murtagh's knee dug into his belly, driving the air from his lungs. He hammered his other fist against Murtagh's ear.

"Where did she go?" he grated, his face only inches from Murtagh's. His greater size and strength were beginning to give him a slight advantage. He twisted Murtagh's wrist, so the knife was pointed toward the gang leader's neck. With a heave, Conrad forced the point closer to Murtagh's throat. He was yelling as he repeated, "Where did she go?"

"K-Kansas City!" Murtagh said. "I heard her say that. Beyond that . . . I don't know!"

The point of the knife dug into Murtagh's throat enough to make a drop of crimson well out around it.

"The records she took from Futrelle's sanitarium! Where are they? Did she take them with her?"

"No! She burned them! She didn't want anything . . . linking her to the kids . . ."

"But she took them with her when she left? The children?"

"Aye. Her and . . . the nanny! I never saw any of 'em . . . again!"

The streetcar lurched to a halt. Shouts filled the night. People had seen the two men engaged in their life and death struggle and reported it. Conrad heard whistles blowing and knew the police were on their way.

Suddenly, Murtagh grinned. "She told me . . . if I ever talked to you . . . to tell you that you'll never find them, Browning. She said to tell you . . . that they're lost to you, for all time!"

Conrad suddenly went cold all over. Could Pamela have been threatening to kill the twins? Her own children? That would be a monstrous thing to do, even for her.

And yet, if anyone was capable of such evil, simply to get the revenge she desired, it was Pamela Tarleton.

Murtagh took advantage of Conrad's stunned realization and exploded into action again, jerking his head one way and shoving the knife the other. He smashed his forehead against Conrad's, and then, like one of the snakes Saint Patrick drove out of Ireland, Murtagh wriggled free. Dropping the knife, he leaped down and dashed away, pushing through the crowd that had gathered around the stalled streetcar.

Shaking his head to clear the grogginess, Conrad grabbed the knife and forced himself up. He had only taken a couple steps to go after Murtagh when strong hands grabbed him from either side.

"Look out!" a man shouted. "He's got a knife!"

Something hard smashed into the small of Conrad's back. Pain shot through him. His hand opened involuntarily and the knife clattered to the cobblestones. He tried to pull free, and as he did, he saw the blue uniforms of the men surrounding him.

"You're not going anywhere, bucko!" The officer swung a club of some sort.

Conrad tried to get out of the way, but they had him hemmed in. The club smashed against his head, and another drove into his belly. He folded up and fell to his knees. He felt his arms being jerked behind his back, then cold, hard steel closed around his wrists. He crumpled the rest of the way to the street and the angry shouting around him faded, washing away on a black tide of pain and then welcome oblivion.

Chapter 14

A balding, thick-bodied police inspector named McLaughlin glared across the desk at Conrad. "You're lucky you got out of the place alive."

Conrad rubbed his wrists where the handcuffs had chafed his skin. "I know. I guess I wasn't quite thinking straight." His voice hardened. "A man gets that way when his children are stolen from him."

"We've only your word for that," McLaughlin pointed out. "Dr. Vernon Futrelle is an important man in this town, and he claims you're delusional. He says you showed up at his sanitarium this afternoon and tried to attack him like some sort of crackbrained brute. He had to summon his orderlies because he feared for his life."

"Futrelle is lying."

McLaughlin leaned back in his chair and spread his meaty hands. "Where's the proof of that? He offered to let us go through his records. He swears we won't find anything to indicate your fiancée was ever there, let alone gave birth to any children while a patient under his care."

Conrad's jaw tightened. He would have honored the bargain he'd made with Futrelle, but after being arrested, he'd known that spilling the whole story was probably his best chance of getting out of there. He had found out everything in Boston he was going to find out.

The trail now led to Kansas City.

Unfortunately, as McLaughlin pointed out, he had no proof of anything. There were also dead men at Serrano's to be accounted for, not to mention heavy damage from a fire.

Conrad had kept his mouth shut about the dead men, but clearly there was a possible connection between him and them since he'd been seen fighting with Eddie Murtagh, their employer. Nor had he given away Jack Mallory's identity. The private detective had been able to slip away from the scene without the police nabbing him. Mallory and Arturo represented Conrad's best hope of getting out of that jam.

"I've told you . . . I had reason to believe that Murtagh knew something about the whereabouts of my children. He got away from me at Serrano's and I went after him. We argued on the streetcar—"

"Tried to kill each other is more like it, according to the testimony of the witnesses," McLaughlin put in.

Conrad shrugged. "It was a heated argument."

"Speaking of heated, you still claim you don't know anything about the fire at that dive of Serrano's?"

"Everything was fine there when I left to go

after Murtagh," Conrad lied. "Does Serrano say otherwise?"

The beefy policeman scowled. "Serrano never says anything, good or bad. He never sees anything or hears anything, either. He's all three monkeys rolled up into one."

"Then you don't have any proof that I did anything except get mixed up in an altercation on a streetcar. Charge me with disturbing the peace. I'll pay the fine."

"How about assault and attempted murder?"

It was Conrad's turn to spread his hands. "Who did I try to kill? Has Murtagh or anyone else come forward to press charges against me?"

"Eddie Murtagh talk to the coppers of his own free will?" McLaughlin gave a snort of disgust. "That's not likely to happen, and you know it."

Conrad reached up and gingerly fingered the knot on his head where he'd been clouted with a billy club and knocked out. "When my attorney gets here, there'll be more discussion about assault charges, but I'll be the one bringing the complaint."

McLaughlin slapped a palm down on the desk. "My men were trying to put a suspect in custody. A suspect who had a knife, mind you. Nobody assaulted you. I know you're a rich man and used to throwing your weight around, Browning, but that don't mean shit to me."

"Suit yourself, Inspector."

McLaughlin's scowl darkened. "Get out of here," he growled.

"You're releasing me?"

"I said get out, didn't I? What more do you need to hear?"

Conrad got to his feet. He thought about saying that an apology for the rough treatment would be nice, but he decided not to press his luck.

"You might look into some of the things that go on at Futrelle's sanitarium," he said.

"Nobody's looking into the activities of a well-respected man like Dr. Futrelle," McLaughlin snapped.

Conrad knew it was useless to pursue that angle. Anyway, he'd found out what he wanted to know from Futrelle. Trying to cause more trouble for the doctor wouldn't serve any useful purpose.

He had just turned toward the door when it opened. A well-dressed man with graying hair and a neatly clipped Vandyke beard came in. Conrad smiled in recognition. "Hello, Charles."

The newcomer gave him a curt nod. Charles Harcourt was one of Boston's leading attorneys, the senior partner of an exclusive practice. He had been one of the many lawyers representing the Browning financial interests for years.

Harcourt fixed steely eyes on McLaughlin and demanded, "Inspector, you *are* aware that Mr. Browning is one of Boston's leading citizens?"

"He hasn't lived here for several years," McLaughlin said. "Anyway, I just released him. There'll be no charges brought against him."

Harcourt glanced over at Conrad. "Is that true?"

"It is," Conrad replied with a nod. "I was just about to leave."

"Well, then . . . I suppose my presence here wasn't needed after all."

Conrad gripped the lawyer's arm. "But I'm very glad to see you anyway, Charles. I need to fill you in on everything that's been happening."

"Your personal secretary gave me some of the details. I'd like to hear more."

Good old Arturo, Conrad thought. Mallory must have gone back to the hotel with the news that Conrad had been arrested, and Arturo had sprung into action and summoned Harcourt.

As they turned toward the door, McLaughlin warned from behind the desk, "Tell your client to keep his nose clean the rest of the time he's here in Boston, counselor."

"Don't worry about that," Conrad said. "I'll be leaving as soon as I can. I've had enough of this town to last me for a long time."

Arturo and Mallory were waiting at the hotel when Conrad and Harcourt got there. Arturo paced anxiously back and forth on the expensive rug while Mallory sprawled in an armchair, apparently at ease but with a worried frown on his rugged face.

Mallory got to his feet and said without preamble, "I didn't want to leave you there, but I didn't see what good I could do you by getting arrested, too."

Conrad nodded. "You did the right thing, Jack. When I came to my senses, one of the first things

I hoped was that you had come back here to tell Arturo what happened."

"Did Murtagh tell you anything before he got away?"

"He did."

Harcourt held up a hand to stop Conrad from going on. "Why don't you tell the story from the beginning, so I don't get any more confused than I already am?" he suggested.

Conrad complied. He, Harcourt, and Mallory sat down, and Arturo brought snifters of brandy for them before helping himself to one as well. Conrad ran through the entire affair, holding back nothing. He paused from time to time to sip the smooth liquor. Its bracing effect was welcome after the day he'd had.

When Conrad was finished, Charles said, "What a terrible thing to find out."

"It's been difficult," Conrad acknowledged with a slight nod of his head.

"Are you certain it's true? As you said, there's no real evidence that it happened, other than the testimony of several people."

"That's enough for me. You can see how it all ties together."

"Yes, it does," Harcourt admitted. "Perhaps I can do something to help you. I might be able to bring some pressure to bear on Futrelle—"

Conrad stopped the attorney with a shake of his head. "There's a good chance some of Futrelle's patients are also clients of your firm, Charles. Stirring everything up could come back to hurt you. I don't want that."

"You know what a high opinion I had of your mother, Conrad. I don't mind—"

"No. We'll let it rest." A solemn smile touched Conrad's lips. "I wouldn't mind knowing what names Pamela gave them . . . but let's face it, she could have changed their names a dozen times before she hid them . . . wherever she hid them."

Harcourt frowned. "I might be able to learn more about the maid Pamela had with her. I don't know if that would be any help."

"It can't hurt," Conrad said.

Harcourt sighed. "To think that at one time I represented the Tarleton family. I was shocked when I found out that Clark was little more than a common criminal."

"There's nothing common about the Tarletons," Conrad said.

"Evidently not. From what you've told me about Pamela and her cousin Roger, the whole lot of them seem quite mad."

"But there's a method to their madness, and more important, a motivation. Revenge is what Pamela lived for."

"And died for," Harcourt said quietly.

Conrad nodded. "And died for."

A grim silence hung over the luxurious sitting room for a moment. Mallory broke it by clearing his throat and saying, "I can try to find Murtagh if you want, Mr. Browning. He's probably gone to ground somewhere in South Boston. It's a cinch he won't be going back to Serrano's any time soon. That big-nosed Eyetie would put a slug in him on sight."

"No, that's all right, Jack. I'm confident Murtagh told me everything he knows. He seemed to have a little bit of a grudge against Pamela himself."

Probably because she had promised to share her bed with him if he did what she wanted and then gone back on her word, Conrad mused. That struck him as something Pamela would do.

"You seem to be a competent investigator, Mr. Mallory," Harcourt said. "My firm might be able to throw some work your way."

Mallory nodded. "I'd like that. I'll do a good job for you."

The lawyer turned back to Conrad. "What do you plan to do now?"

"There's a westbound train leaving for Chicago at ten o'clock in the morning," Conrad said. "From there I can make a connection to Kansas City."

"It's become quite a populous city in recent years," Harcourt pointed out. "How do you intend to pick up Pamela's trail once you get there?"

Before Conrad could answer, Arturo said, "Knowing Mr. Browning, I suspect he'll barge in, wave some guns around, and demand answers of everyone he meets."

Harcourt frowned at what he undoubtedly considered a show of disrespect from a servant, but Conrad laughed.

"It seems to have worked so far, hasn't it?"

Chapter 15

Conrad and Arturo checked out of the hotel and headed for the train station early the next morning. Now that he was ready to take up the trail again, Conrad didn't want to risk being delayed in any way.

Harcourt met them at the station. "I've engaged Mallory to see what he can find out about Pamela Tarleton's maid or nanny or whatever you want to call her. How can I get in touch with you if I have any information, Conrad?"

"I'm afraid I don't know where I'll be, other than in Kansas City a couple of days from now." Conrad shook his head. "I'll wire you when we get there, Charles, and I'll stay in touch by telegraph whenever it looks like we're going to be in one place long enough to make that practical."

"All right." Harcourt held out his hand. "Good luck in your search. Don't hesitate to let me know if there's anything I can do to help."

Conrad had engaged a Pullman compartment

for himself and Arturo, rather than taking his private car. He might need to make a connection in a hurry somewhere, and having the private car hooked up to a train always took quite a bit of time.

They boarded the train and settled in for the trip to Chicago and then Kansas City. Conrad knew it would be difficult to find out where Pamela had gone from Kansas City, but he carried considerable influence with the railroad. Any records that might still exist would be three years old, but he intended to have a look at all of them.

If Pamela had paid cash for her and the maid's tickets, there would be no record of her name. On the other hand, Pamela's beauty and her imperious attitude made her easy to remember. Conrad held on to the hope that someone connected to the railroad might recall her and even remember where she had been going.

He wore the shoulder harness for the two Colt Lightnings again and didn't intend to be without them during the journey. The civilized East had proven to be just about as dangerous as the so-called uncivilized West.

Arturo brought him a light lunch from the dining car, but by the time evening rolled around, Conrad wanted an actual meal. He announced his intention to walk up to the dining car for supper. "Join me, Arturo."

"That would hardly be appropriate, sir," Arturo said with a frown and a shake of his head. "You're my employer."

"I know that, but I consider you a friend as well."

"But I don't consider *you* a friend," Arturo said

stubbornly. "You're my employer," he repeated, as if that explained everything.

Maybe it did for some people, but Conrad had spent too much time around Frank, Rebel, and other Westerners to worry about false distinctions like that. "Come on. I'll make it an order if I have to."

Arturo sighed. "Very well. Are you going to order me to enjoy myself as well?"

"I just might," Conrad said with a grin.

"Well, in that case I shall do my best to comply." Arturo pasted an artificial-looking smile on his face.

Two regular passenger cars were between the dining car and the Pullman where Conrad's compartment was. He and Arturo walked through the passenger cars and were soon seated at a table in the dining car where a white-jacketed waiter brought them a bottle of wine and a couple of steaks with numerous trimmings.

The railroads weren't noted for their cuisine, but Conrad thought the food was all right. It beat prairie hen roasted over an open fire . . . but not by much, he decided. Of course, on the trail he'd be washing down his meal with water from a creek or his canteen, not a decent bottle of Chateau Fargeaux.

The train was traveling through western New York on its way to Pennsylvania. Outside the windows all was dark except for occasional lights from a farmhouse or a small town. As always, the combination of food, wine, and the regular rhythm of the rails began to make Conrad sleepy. It was early yet, but he'd had a busy few days in Boston.

He patted his lips with his napkin and said, "I think I'm going to turn in."

"A splendid idea, sir," Arturo said. He had relaxed some during the meal and seemed to enjoy it. "I'll prepare your berth as soon as we get back to the compartment. In fact, if you'd care to wait here for a few minutes, I'll go ahead and have it ready for you when you get there."

Conrad picked up the bottle, which had a little wine left in it. "All right. That's a good idea. I'll just finish this off, and then stroll back to the Pullman."

"Excellent." Arturo got to his feet and hesitated. "Thank you, sir."

"What for?" Conrad asked with a smile.

"For the fine meal. And for saying . . . you know . . ."

"That we're friends?" Conrad chuckled. "Don't worry about it. Once you've spent more time west of the Mississippi, you'll understand."

"I suspect that I won't, but I appreciate the sentiment anyway."

Looking vaguely embarrassed by the show of any emotion, Arturo quickly left the dining car and headed back to the Pullman. Conrad took his time, lingering over the last of the wine. When he finally finished it off, he scrawled his name on the bill the waiter had left and stood up.

As he walked through the passenger cars, he was aware of the looks people were giving him. Some of the men appeared to be openly resentful of his youth, his good looks, his obvious wealth. The women, on the other hand, were more circumspect in their glances, which were frankly approving. Some of the younger women even had bold invitation in their eyes as Conrad passed. Any time anyone, male or female, caught his eye, he smiled, nodded, and moved on.

He had finally moved far enough past Rebel's death that he could be attracted to a woman again without feeling too guilty about it. The striking, redheaded bounty hunter Lace McCall had made him realize that.

But the matter of his missing children had come up, and he had shoved everything else to the back of his mind. He didn't have time for anything except the quest to find his stolen son and daughter.

He would see Lace again one of these days, he promised himself as he stepped through the vestibule of the second passenger and onto its platform. One of these days . . .

The shape came out of the darkness and slammed into him with terrific force, knocking him sideways. The impact rammed his hip against the railing around the platform and his momentum nearly carried him over it. He caught a bare glimpse of the ground rushing past beneath him as the train rocked along at a mile-a-minute clip. His hand shot out and grabbed the railing.

He felt himself flip completely over in the air, heels over head, as he fell. Maintaining his grip on the rail he hung by one hand with his feet dangling mere inches above the roadbed. Grunting with the effort, he reached up with his other hand and managed to clamp it onto the rail.

The shape of a man on the platform loomed over him, then laughed. "Did you think you could get away with what you did to me, Browning? Did you really?"

As Conrad gritted his teeth in the effort to hang on, he recognized Eddie Murtagh's voice. He didn't know where Murtagh had come from. He would have sworn the platform was empty when he'd stepped out of the passenger car's vestibule.

"I don't care about that Tarleton bitch or those little bastards of hers," Murtagh went on. "It's personal now. You came into Serrano's and killed my friends. You tried to kill me. You will pay for that."

Murtagh must have been on top of the car, Conrad thought. He had waited for his intended victim to come along and then swung down from the roof, kicking Conrad and nearly knocking him all the way off the train.

Through clenched teeth, Conrad said, "I made you . . . beg for your life . . . too. That's what you . . . can't swallow."

"Go to hell," Murtagh snapped. Light from somewhere glinted briefly on the blade of a big knife he held in his hand. "We'll see how long you can hang on once I start sawing your fingers off."

Conrad knew he couldn't hang on. He was about to let go with one hand and reach under his coat for one of the revolvers in the shoulder harness, an awkward, risky move he probably couldn't complete before that blade came chopping down into his fingers, when more light suddenly spilled over the platform and a furious voice shouted, "Get away from him!"

Arturo lunged across the gap between cars from the platform of the Pullman. Murtagh whirled toward him and thrust out the heavy-bladed knife. Arturo grabbed the gang leader's wrist with both hands and twisted, keeping Murtagh from sinking that cold steel into his belly. Murtagh cursed and crashed his left fist into Arturo's face.

Conrad knew Arturo didn't stand a chance against Murtagh and wouldn't be able to hold him off for more than a few seconds.

Those few seconds were precious, giving Conrad time to pour all his strength into his arms and shoulders and heave himself up far enough that he could hook a leg over the railing. With a grunt of effort, he swung over the rail and sprawled onto the platform, putting him in a good position to grab Murtagh's knees and pull the man's legs out from under him just as he tore free of Arturo's grip and slashed the knife at the servant's face.

With a yell of surprise, Murtagh toppled over backward and the knife stroke missed. Conrad clambered up the man's body, grabbed Murtagh's wrist, and slammed his knife hand against the edge of the platform. Murtagh yelled again as his fingers opened involuntarily and the knife went flying away into the dark.

Murtagh brought a knee up sharply, aiming to bury it in Conrad's groin. Conrad twisted aside and took the blow on his thigh. His left hand caught hold of Murtagh's throat. His right balled into a fist that he brought down with stunning force into Murtagh's face.

The blow wasn't strong enough to knock all the fight out of the man. He brought the heel of his hand up under Conrad's chin, forcing his head back and making him loosen his grip on Murtagh's throat.

Proving as hard to hang on to as he had in their previous battle, Murtagh writhed away and aimed a kick at Conrad's head. The kick landed on his left shoulder making Conrad's arm go numb. He struggled to get up while Murtagh scrambled nimbly to his feet.

Before Murtagh could do anything else, Arturo went after him, swinging wild punches.

"Arturo, no!" Conrad yelled. The servant was no match for a brawler like Murtagh, who proved that by easily blocking the valet's blows and throwing a punch of his own that rocked Arturo's head back. Stumbling backward, he cried out in horror and toppled off the platform, falling into the gap between the cars.

"No!" Conrad bellowed again as he surged up. Curling his right hand in a fist, he hammered a punch into Murtagh's face, then another and another, driving Murtagh toward the railing at the side of the platform. Conrad bulled into him, using his superior size and strength to pin Murtagh against the railing. The numbness in his left arm was wearing off so he locked both hands around Murtagh's throat, forcing the man farther and farther back, bending him over the railing in a way the human spine wasn't meant to bend. Murtagh punched and kicked and gouged, but Conrad shrugged it all off and never loosened his grip. Murtagh's wide, terrified eyes stared up at him out of a sweat-slick face.

Even over the loud rumble of the train's wheels on the rails, he heard the sharp crack of Eddie Murtagh's back breaking.

Conrad let go of his neck. Murtagh screamed once, a hoarse scream that died away in a whimpering moan. Conrad bent, took hold of Murtagh's useless legs, and lifted. Murtagh screamed again as he realized he was going over the railing.

Conrad flipped him up, over, and away. Murtagh was gone in the blink of an eye.

It was only when Conrad swayed forward and gripped the rail that he saw the train was passing over a trestle, high above a river. Conrad began to laugh hollowly. The fall would have killed Murtagh, even without the broken back.

Three sharp, unexpected slaps caught Conrad's attention. As he swung toward the sound, he heard Arturo's weak voice calling, "Mr. Browning?" A hand reached over the back of the platform and slapped the boards three more times. "Mr. Browning?"

Unable to believe what he was seeing and hearing, Conrad leaped forward and leaned down to grab the wrist just as Arturo was about to knock on the platform again. Arturo's other hand had hold of the coupling between the cars, and both of the servant's legs were wrapped around an iron rod projecting from the apparatus.

Conrad hauled up on Arturo's wrist and then grabbed his coat. He lifted Arturo onto the platform and threw his arms around him in a hug. "I thought that bastard Murtagh had killed you!"

"Yes, well, it wasn't for lack of trying." Arturo was trembling all over from the strain of having to hang on for dear life as the roadbed rushed past right below him.

"Come on, let's get you back to the compartment."

Behind Conrad, the door into the passenger car opened and the conductor strolled out, too late for all the excitement he was blissfully unaware of. "Mr. Browning!" he said when he recognized Conrad. "Something wrong?"

"Yes, my friend here isn't feeling well," Conrad explained as he put an arm around Arturo's shoulders. "I was helping him get some fresh air."

"Oh, I'm sorry to hear that. Is there anything I can to do help?"

Arturo said, "No, thank you, I'll be fine. Perhaps if I lie down for a short time . . ."

"Lemme give you a hand there, Mr. Browning," the conductor offered.

Between them, they got Arturo into the Pullman compartment, where he stretched out on one of the short divans that pulled out into a berth. The conductor said, "Let me know if there's anything else I can do help."

Conrad nodded. "I certainly will."

When the man was gone, Conrad sat down on the opposite berth and asked, "How did you happen to come out there just in time to save my life?"

"I thought you would be back here sooner," Arturo explained. "I just stepped out to see if you were coming."

"Another few seconds and I would have been a dead man. Thanks, Arturo. I'm obliged to you."

"Nonsense, sir. It's my job to assist you in any way possible."

Conrad laughed. "It's not your job to take on cold-blooded killers, but you jumped right in anyway."

"Was that Mr. Murtagh?"

"It was," Conrad said with a nod.

"What . . . what happened to him?"

"He won't bother us anymore," Conrad said, thinking about Murtagh's broken back and the long fall from that trestle.

The train rolled on, heading west into the night.

Chapter 16

The bustling city of Kansas City, Missouri sat on the border between the states of Missouri and Kansas, but it was a border town in other ways, too. For years Westport Landing, one of the frontier communities that had developed into Kansas City, had been a major jumping-off place for the wagon trains carrying immigrants to the West. Later, as civilization extended itself past the Missouri River, Kansas City had become the primary market for grain grown in the vast, flat farmland surrounding the city. But it was also a cowtown, as the railroads brought shipments of cattle from the empire-sized ranches of Texas and elsewhere. Huge stockyards covered much of the area known as West Bottoms, just west of downtown, and you were just as likely to see cowboys walking down the street, spurs jingling, as you were to bump into sober-suited businessmen. Kansas City was the true boundary between east and west, Conrad thought as he stepped down from the train in Union Station, followed by Arturo.

The servant hurried off to supervise the unloading of their luggage. Conrad set off across the crowded platform toward the stationmaster's office. He had sent a telegram to the stationmaster from back up the line, advising the man when to expect him.

The woman who sat at the desk in the outer office recognized his name. She stood up and smiled at him. "Please sit down, Mr. Browning. I'll let Mr. Crowley know you're here."

Conrad noticed she was quite attractive, with upswept brown hair and a fine figure that the high-necked, long-sleeved dress she wore failed to conceal. Evidently, more and more women were working in business offices.

The secretary came back a moment later and motioned for him to go through the door to the inner office. "Mr. Crowley will see you now," she murmured.

Conrad went in and shook hands with a tough-looking, gray-haired man. "It's good to see you again, Mr. Browning," Crowley said.

"We've met before?" Conrad asked with a faint frown.

"Not exactly. I used to be a conductor, and your mother rode on my trains several times. You were with her, but you were only a boy so I don't expect you to remember."

Conrad smiled. "My mother traveled a lot. She had so many different business interests, and she liked to keep up with all of them, as personally as she could."

"I imagine you're the same way." Crowley gestured toward a leather armchair in front of the desk. "Have a seat. Would you like a cigar or a drink?"

"No, thanks."

When both men were settled in their chairs, Crowley went on. "What can I do for you, Mr. Browning? Your wire said something about the records from three years ago . . ."

"I'm looking for two women who would have been traveling with a pair of infants. Twins. I'd like to find out where they went when they left Kansas City."

The stationmaster's forehead creased. "Two women and two children. That's all you know? And this was three years ago?" With a vaguely uncomfortable look, Crowley moved some papers on his desk. "You realize, of course, Mr. Browning, that thousands and thousands of passengers have come through this station since then?"

Conrad suppressed the surge of irritation he felt. "Of course. But I can narrow it down to a fairly short period of time, and surely there are records of how many tickets were sold and what the destinations were."

Crowley sighed. "Mr. Browning, what you ask is impossible. Yes, there are records of how many tickets were sold, but there's no way to tell which passengers bought which tickets. All we have are totals."

Conrad's heart sank. He leaned his elbows on

his knees and hung his head. The news was bitterly disappointing. As he mulled over the stationmaster's words, it occurred to him perhaps there was another way—a longer shot even, than checking the railroad's records—but it might provide at least *some* information.

He straightened in the chair. "Do you have someone who's worked here for several years? Someone who would have been here three years ago during the period I'm interested in?"

"Yes, of course. A number of our employees have been here for a long time."

"If I could talk to them, ask them some questions . . ."

"Do you really think that would do any good?" Crowley asked. "Mr. Browning, with all due respect, so many people go through here I doubt if any of the employees would remember someone from last week, let alone three years ago."

"They might remember one of the women I'm looking for." With Pamela's beauty and the way she carried herself like some sort of royalty, with all the attendant arrogance and abrasiveness, she was hard to forget. Or so Conrad hoped.

"Certainly you can talk to them," Crowley said. "I have no objection to that at all. I just think you should be prepared for the possibility that you won't find out anything."

"Can you give me a list of the people who were working here three years ago?"

The stationmaster nodded. "Give me a couple of hours."

Conrad got to his feet. "Fine. I appreciate this, Mr. Crowley."

The man smiled. "I'm glad to do it. You're a major stockholder in this railroad, Mr. Browning, as your mother was before you. Should I send the list to your hotel?"

"That's fine. I'll be at the Cattleman's Hotel."

"All right." Crowley extended his hand across the desk. "I'm not sure exactly what you're looking for, Mr. Browning, but I wish you the best of luck in your search."

The best of luck was exactly what he was going to need, Conrad thought.

Arturo had engaged a buggy for the two of them and a wagon for their luggage while Conrad was talking to the stationmaster. It didn't take long to reach the Cattleman's Hotel in downtown. With ranchers and cattle buyers making up most of its guests, Conrad thought he would feel more comfortable there than in some stuffier place. His time in the West had changed him, made him less tolerant of the artificiality that pervaded much of the East.

Which was not to say that the Cattleman's wasn't a nice place. The lobby was luxuriously furnished, and the dining room was famous for its steaks. The desk clerk greeted Conrad warmly and summoned bellboys to take the luggage up to the suite he'd reserved.

As promised, a messenger delivered the list of long-time employees that Crowley sent over, but it was too late in the day to return to Union Station and start interviewing them.

The next morning Conrad used the stationmaster's office to talk to them, but it didn't take long to realize that Crowley had been right. Even though the ticket clerks, porters, and other employees wanted to be helpful, again and again Conrad got nothing but blank looks as he described Pamela Tarleton and explained that she would have been traveling with another woman and two babies. He added that she would have been hard to please and likely would have bossed around anyone she encountered, but that didn't help.

As one ticket clerk put it, "We see hundreds of people a day, Mr. Browning. There's just no way to remember anything that far back."

Conrad was polite, but he felt his frustration growing. When he had talked to everyone on Crowley's list, the stationmaster came back into the office and asked, "Any luck?"

Conrad slumped in the chair behind the desk and shook his head. "Not a bit. No one remembers her."

"I was afraid of that. I did some checking through our records, just in case I might turn up something, but no luck."

"It's a dead end," Conrad said glumly. "The trail's too cold. There's no way to find out where she went." He looked at the list he had tossed onto the desk, and a thought occurred to him. Tapping the list, he asked, "What about people who were working here three years ago, but aren't now?"

Crowley rubbed his jaw and frowned in thought. "Yes, there are some folks who fit that description, beginning with Ralph Potter."

"Who's that?"

"He ran this station before I did."

Conrad sat up straighter. "Where can I find him? He's still alive, isn't he?"

"Oh, yes, he's still alive. I can give you directions to his place. I don't know if he'll help you, though. Ralph can be a little . . . difficult."

"I'll take that chance," Conrad said. Now that he thought about it, the odds of Pamela having much to do with a ticket clerk or a porter were small. Given her personality, if she'd encountered any sort of trouble with the railroad in Kansas City, she would have gone directly to the stationmaster to complain.

Crowley explained that Ralph Potter had bought a small farm south of town when he retired from the railroad. He told Conrad how to find it and then warned him again that Potter didn't like strangers.

Conrad smiled. "I'm sure I can handle him."

Still clinging to a shred of hope that the trail wasn't completely lost, Conrad left the depot and went back to the hotel. When he told Arturo what he was going to do, the servant asked, "Would you like me to come with you, sir?"

Conrad shook his head. "No, I'll be fine. I'm going to rent a horse and take a ride down to Potter's farm this afternoon."

The buckskin he had ridden while he was drifting across the Southwest was being well cared for

at a livery stable in Santa Fe. Conrad had paid the
man for several months' care in advance, and if it
was longer than that before he got back to pick up
the buckskin, the man knew how to contact the
law firm of Turnbuckle & Stafford in San Francisco to get more money. The dangers Conrad
had shared with the buckskin while he was known
as Kid Morgan had made the two of them friends,
at least as much as man and horse could be. But
since he hadn't known where his quest would lead
him, he'd had to leave the buckskin behind and
would have to rely on other mounts.

After lunch in the hotel's dining room, Conrad
found a nearby livery stable and picked out a
rangy gray gelding, renting the horse for the rest
of the day along with a saddle and tack. He
mounted up and made his way out of Kansas City.
It took awhile because the town was so big and
sprawling.

Eventually, Conrad found himself following a
road that ran through mostly flat farmland. Here
and there, a small hill rose, and there were
stretches of uncultivated land as well.

He wasn't quite sure if he was still in Missouri
or had crossed into Kansas. The border ran right
through the area, and a swing of a hundred yards
as the road curved could easily mean he was crossing from one state to the other. Not that it really
mattered to him which state Ralph Potter lived in.
He just wanted to talk to the man.

Following Crowley's directions brought Conrad
to a small farmhouse with a sod roof that looked

like it had been there almost as long as the region had been settled. Corn grew in the fields on both sides of the narrow lane that ran from the road for a quarter of a mile to the house. A couple of cottonwoods shaded the house itself. A barn stood behind it, along with two smaller outbuildings. Conrad saw a covered well at the side of the house.

It was a nice-looking place, especially for a man who had retired from being the stationmaster of a busy depot at one of the country's busiest railroad hubs, or for someone who wanted to live out the rest of his days in peace.

Conrad reined to a halt in front of the house and was about to swing out of the saddle when a pack of four or five huge, shaggy dogs exploded around the corner of the building and charged at him in a yapping frenzy. The rented horse panicked and started to buck and rear. Conrad was a fine rider and normally would have been able to stay in the saddle, but he'd been in the act of dismounting and was thrown off balance. He grabbed for the saddle horn but missed.

With a breath-robbing impact, he crashed to the ground.

Instantly, the growling, snarling curs were all around him. His impulse was to reach for his guns and shoot them, but they held back, not attacking him, just surrounding and threatening him.

He was glad he hadn't started any gunplay when he heard a shotgun being cocked. He glanced around to see the menacing twin barrels of a greener approaching him. What really shocked him was the person pointing the scattergun at him.

She was a beautiful girl, no more than seventeen or eighteen years old, with long, straight blond hair hanging around her face and down her back. She had a sweet, innocent, heart-shaped face, but there was nothing sweet or innocent about her voice as she said, "Keep your hands away from them guns, mister, or I'll blow your damn head off."

Chapter 17

Conrad swallowed hard and kept his hands well away from the guns under his coat. His hat had fallen off when he tumbled from the horse, and a hot prairie wind stirred his hair. The same wind moved several strands of the girl's long, fair hair in front of her face, but she didn't move to brush them away. All her attention was focused on the stranger who lay there surrounded by the dogs.

From where he lay, Conrad couldn't help noticing the thrust of her breasts against the thin cotton dress she wore, or the way the wind molded the fabric to the curves of her hips and thighs. She was young, but a full-grown woman or next thing to it, no doubt about that.

He licked dust off his lips. "Listen, take it easy. I mean no harm—"

"Shut up! Come out here from town to take our land away from us. I know your type of skunk when I see it."

The scornful lash of the girl's voice bothered

Conrad almost as much as the shotgun she was pointing at him or the slavering muzzles of the dogs all around him. She had taken him for some sort of town scoundrel with his tweed suit and rented horse.

"Sara Beth!" a man's voice called. "What you got there, Sara Beth?"

"I think it's another fella from the bank!" the girl replied without taking her eyes off Conrad.

An elderly man limped into view. He wore gray-striped trousers with suspenders over a faded pair of red longjohns. A black cap with a stiff bill perched on his head. Conrad looked at it for a second before he realized it was the same sort of cap worn by many men who worked for the rail-road. The man was short and thin, with a leathery face and a spiky white beard.

"Mr. Potter?" Conrad guessed.

The man's pale blue eyes were deep set under shaggy brows. Those brows rose as his eyes widened in surprise. "You know me?"

"Of course he knows you," the girl, Sara Beth, snapped. "The bank sent him out here to cause more trouble for us, didn't it?"

"I'm not from any bank," Conrad said, "and I'm certainly not here to cause trouble for you. My name is Conrad Browning. If you'll call these dogs off, I'll tell you why I came to see you."

The old man tugged thoughtfully at his beard. "Maybe we ought to listen to him, Sara Beth—"

"No! You can't trust anybody from the city. You told me that."

"Yeah, but there's somethin' about this young

fella . . ." The old man's voice trailed off as he looked surprised again. "Browning, did you say your name is? Any relation to Mrs. Vivian Browning?"

"She was my mother," Conrad said.

That made up the old-timer's mind. He reached over, took hold of the shotgun's barrels, and pushed them aside. "Get away from him, you blasted varmints!" he told the dogs as he advanced, kicking at them. "Let the man alone!"

"But you told me—" Sara Beth began angrily.

"I know what I told you, girl. But this fella is the son of one of the most decent ladies to ever walk the face o' the earth. Ever' time a train she was on stopped in Kansas City, she made a point of it to come to my office and say hello to me."

"Then you *are* Ralph Potter, the former station-master?" Conrad asked.

"That's right, young fella." Potter held a hand down to Conrad. "Lemme help you up."

Conrad started to say he didn't need any help, but changed his mind and grasped the gnarled old hand. He climbed to his feet and brushed his clothes off. Potter picked up the hat and handed it to him.

Sara Beth stood off to the side, scowling darkly at Conrad in suspicion.

"I reckon Crowley told you where to find me," Potter said.

Conrad nodded. "That's right."

"I heard about your mother passin' away, God rest her soul. Was sure sorry to hear about it, too."

"Thank you."

"I reckon you must own her share of the railroad now."

Conrad nodded again, not wanting to take the time to explain that he shared the Browning interests with Frank Morgan. "I've come to talk to you about the railroad, in fact."

"But I've been retired for a couple years now," Potter said. "I don't have anything to do with it anymore."

"What I want to talk to you about happened three years ago, while you were still the stationmaster."

The old-timer looked confused, but he nodded. "All right. Why don't we go inside and get out of this hot sun?"

Conrad smiled. "That'll be fine. Thanks."

"Sara Beth, you fix us some lemonade," Potter said as he ushered Conrad toward the farmhouse.

The girl snorted as if she didn't like being ordered around, but she didn't say anything.

The furnishings in the house were old and shabby, but the place was clean, almost spotlessly so. Potter and his granddaughter—she was too young to be his daughter—might be a little down on their luck, judging by Sara Beth's talk about the bank, but they weren't allowing that to make them give up. Potter motioned Conrad into an armchair next to a small, round table with a lace doily and a lamp sitting on it. The old-timer pulled up a ladderback chair and sat on it while Sara Beth disappeared into the kitchen.

"Now, Mr. Browning, what can I do for you?"

"Like I said, I want to ask you about something

that would have happened about three years ago. A young woman came through Kansas City on the train, probably heading west. She was traveling with another woman—I don't really know how old she was—and a couple of small children. Infants. Twins. A boy and a girl."

Potter took off the black cap and gave him a dubious frown. "Lots of folks come through Kansas City, Mr. Browning."

"Yes, that's what people keep telling me," Conrad said, trying not to sigh in frustration.

"I can't hardly remember—"

"It's possible this woman would have come to see you. She probably would have been upset about something and might have demanded some sort of special treatment."

"Oh, you're talkin' about Miss Tarleton."

Conrad sat there, thunderstruck with surprise.

"I remember her, all right," Potter went on. "Be hard to forget a lady like Miss Tarleton, if you ever had to deal with her."

Conrad managed to nod. "That's putting it mildly. Go on, Mr. Potter."

"Well, like you said, she was upset because the train she was on was a mite late, and she'd missed her connection to Denver. I don't know what she thought I could do about it. It's not like I could reach out and catch that westbound and make it back up all the way to Kansas City just so's she could get on it."

"She was going to Denver, you say?" Conrad's heart slugged heavily in his chest, but he managed to keep his face and voice calm.

"Well, that's where she was bound next. I seem to recall her sayin' she was gonna stop there for a while. But the tickets she had would take her and the lady with her all the way to San Francisco. No charge for the two little ones, of course. Wee babes like that ride for free."

Conrad felt a little dizzy. This was exactly the sort of information he'd been looking for. He had Pamela's intinerary laid out before him.

Sara Beth came back from the kitchen carrying a tray with a couple of glasses of lemonade on it. She handed one to Potter and one to Conrad, not being very gracious about it. Conrad smiled and said, "Thank you," anyway.

Potter took a drink of the lemonade and licked his lips. "Talkin' is thirsty work."

"You're being very helpful, Mr. Potter," Conrad assured him. "I had a feeling someone, some-where along the way, must have remembered Pamela. You called her Miss Tarleton. Did you know her before she introduced herself?"

"Well, not really, but when she said she was Clark Tarleton's daughter, I knew *him*, all right. He had an interest in the railroad at one time, too, but whenever he came through the station, he wasn't near as nice as your mother always was. He seemed to think the world pretty much re-volved around him, and I reckon Miss Tarleton in-herited that same feeling from him."

Conrad nodded. That was Pamela, all right.

"Did she tell you the two children were hers?"

Potter shook his head. "Nope. Didn't offer any explanation for them." He pursed his lips in disapproval. "I figured as much, though. I saw she didn't have no wedding ring on her finger, but it's not my place to judge." The old-timer squinted shrewdly at Conrad. "Mr. Browning, you can tell me to go to hell if you want . . . but were those your kids?"

Grimly, Conrad nodded. "That's right. Now you understand why I'm trying to find out where she went."

"She stole your kids away?" Potter shook his head. "That's a mighty bad thing to do to a man."

"I didn't even know about them until recently."

"And now you want to find her and them?"

"Not Pamela," Conrad said. "She's dead."

Potter looked shocked, and so did Sara Beth, who had set the tray on a side table and withdrawn to a divan across the room. "What happened to the young'uns?" Potter asked.

"That's what I'm trying to find out. Pamela left them somewhere, probably in the care of the servant who was traveling with her, and then"—the whole story was too complicated and sordid, and at that moment Conrad didn't have any stomach for telling it again—"she was killed in an accident. But my son and daughter are still out there somewhere, and I'm going to find them."

"Good Lord," Potter muttered. "What a terrible thing."

"I'd followed her trail to Kansas City, but I didn't know where she went from there. Now I do." Conrad paused. "I assume she took the next train heading for Denver?"

Potter nodded. "That's right. Since she missed

her connection because the train she came in on was late, I made arrangements for her to stay at the best hotel in town, and the railroad paid for it. I didn't have to do that, it's not what we usually do, but I figured for somebody like Miss Tarleton . . ." He shrugged his narrow shoulders.

"And it got her off your back," Conrad said with a faint smile.

"Yeah. That, too. The next mornin' I sent a buggy and a wagon for them, and I saw to it personal-like that her bags got loaded on the train and she and the other lady were settled in a nice compartment with the children. She was only delayed about twenty-four hours."

"But you don't know what happened after that?"

"After the train pulled out?" The old man shook his head. "No, sir, I don't have any idea. Miss Tarleton and those kids rolled right on outta my life, and I ain't seen any of them since."

Conrad expected as much. Still, he had learned a great deal. The twins had to be somewhere between Kansas City and San Francisco. That was a vast stretch of territory . . . but it was better than having to search for them across the entire country.

To cover the emotions coursing through him, he took a sip of the lemonade. It was pretty sour—Potter probably couldn't afford much sugar. The corn crop Conrad had seen on his way there had looked like a good one, but Potter might be cash-poor at the moment. A lot of farmers wound up that way, with a crop in the fields that might save them but circumstances that closed in and didn't give them any time.

"I can't thank you enough for your help," Conrad said as he set the glass on the table beside him. "I'd like to give you something for your trouble."

"Shucks, that isn't necessary—" Potter began.

"Yes, it is," Sara Beth snapped. "If the man wants to pay you for your help, it wouldn't be polite to turn him down. Besides, we have a payment due on that note."

Potter nodded wearily. "Yeah, I know, Sara Beth."

"Don't worry, Mr. Potter," Conrad said with a smile as he withdrew his wallet from an inner pocket of his coat. "The help you've given me is well worth it."

Not to mention the hope, Conrad thought.

He took two hundred dollars from the wallet and held it out toward Potter.

Before the old-timer could take it, Sara Beth was on her feet and had come across the room to pluck the bills from Conrad's fingers. "I handle the money around here."

Potter didn't challenge her. He nodded and said, "She's got a better head for it than I do."

It didn't matter to Conrad who got the money. He'd gotten the information he needed. He stood up. "Thank you for your hospitality, and for your help."

"You're mighty welcome, Mr. Browning. Like I said, your mother was always as nice as she could be to me."

The two men left Sara Beth counting the money and walked out of the farmhouse. As they paused on the front porch, Potter asked, "Where are you stayin' in town, Mr. Browning? Just in case I think of anything else that might help you."

"I'm at the Cattleman's Hotel," Conrad replied. "I'm not sure how long I'll be there. Until tomorrow, anyway."

He was going to have to do some thinking about how to proceed now that he knew what Pamela's destination had been three years earlier. It wouldn't do to take the train straight to San Francisco. Her letter had indicated she'd hidden the children somewhere in the West.

They could be anywhere, Conrad thought. Anywhere.

"Thanks again." He shook the old-timer's hand. "I'm glad your granddaughter took the money. I hope it helps you out as much as you've helped me."

"Granddaughter?" Potter repeated with a puzzled frown. "Sara Beth isn't my granddaughter. She's my wife!"

Chapter 18

During Conrad's ride back to Kansas City, he thought about the old man's surprising revelation. On the frontier, it wasn't uncommon to see young women married to much older men. It made sense. An older man usually had more to offer a wife, financially. However, that didn't appear to be the case with Potter and Sara Beth, and the age gap wasn't usually quite as wide as it was between them. Conrad hadn't known whether to congratulate the old goat or condemn him.

He hadn't done either. He had something more important on his mind: how to carry out his search from there.

One thing was certain. He couldn't continue traveling west on the train. The thought of rolling right past the place where his children were hidden made his stomach turn.

No, Conrad decided, he was going to have to follow the steel rails, but on horseback so he could stop at every town and ask questions.

His heart sank a little as he realized it was going to take months, unless he was incredibly lucky and found the twins right away. He considered that unlikely. Pamela wouldn't have made it that easy.

But if it took months . . . if it took a year or more . . . he wouldn't give up the search until it was successful. He reined in for a moment before he reached the city and turned in the saddle to gaze off toward the west. His son and daughter were somewhere out there. "I'm coming to find you," he promised them, speaking the words softly. "Count on it."

Arturo was waiting anxiously when he reached the hotel. "How was your visit with the old station-master, sir? Any results?"

"For a change, yes. That man Potter remembered Pamela. Even better than that, he knew where she was going. San Francisco."

"I'll begin packing," Arturo murmured. "I assume we're taking the next train west?"

Conrad shook his head. "Not the train."

"Then how *are* we traveling?" Arturo asked with a puzzled frown.

"*We're* not traveling. Sorry, Arturo, but from here on out I'll be going it alone."

Arturo's frown deepened. "What are you talking about? I thought you said Conrad Browning wouldn't travel without a valet."

"Maybe Conrad wouldn't. But Kid Morgan would."

"Really? You're actually going to resurrect that . . . that dime-novel masquerade?"

Conrad didn't take offense at the question. "I

told Claudius Turnbuckle and John Stafford that The Kid would ride again. I wasn't sure how or when, but I had a feeling I wasn't done with Kid Morgan just yet."

"You realize, of course, that you sound a bit mentally disturbed, talking about this mythical Kid in the third person, as if he actually exists."

Conrad laughed. "Who's to say he doesn't, Arturo? Just because you're born with one name doesn't mean that's who you really are. Many of the Indians believe that when a young warrior goes on a vision quest, he becomes another person when the truth is revealed to him, and because of that he takes another name. Maybe what I was doing all that time when I was drifting around as Kid Morgan was going on my own vision quest, finding out who I really am."

Arturo looked at Conrad like he had gone completely mad. "And what am I supposed to do? I gave up my previous employment to come east with you, you know."

"I'm well aware of that. You'll continue to draw your full salary until you find another job that suits you, no matter how long it takes. I'll wire Claudius and make sure he understands that. You can take the train to San Francisco and he can help you, like he did before. You'll be fine, Arturo."

"Begging your pardon, sir, but *this* job suits me."

Conrad shook his head. "Sorry. I'll be traveling by horseback. I'm going to have to stop at every little town on the railroad between here and California. Maybe the twins are in San Francisco, but

Pamela could have stopped anywhere along the way and made arrangements to leave them."

"Abandoned her own children, you mean?"

"A she-wolf has a lot more motherly instinct than Pamela Tarleton ever did," Conrad said, letting some of the bitterness he felt toward her creep into his voice. "I suspect she found some family to take them in and paid the people well. Finding them isn't going to be easy."

"You never thought it would be. But I can help—"

"That's all, Arturo." Conrad's tone was a bit sharper than he intended. He reached for his hat. "I'm going out to look for a better horse to buy. The one I rented won't do for a long trip. I'm going to need at least one pack animal, too. I'll eat in the hotel dining room tonight."

"Very well, sir," Arturo said stiffly. "Would you like me to lay out the garb you wear as Kid Morgan?"

"No, there'll be time for that later."

Conrad left the suite. He felt bad about Arturo's hurt feelings, but he couldn't see Arturo riding a horse all the way to California.

The quest might not even stop there, Conrad thought. But it didn't matter. He would ride all the way to hell and back to find his kids if he had to.

He returned the rented horse to the livery stable and had a look at the other stock the liveryman had to offer. None of them impressed him enough to buy one. There were other stables in

Kansas City, and he would check all of them if he had to.

By late afternoon, he found what he was looking for. He purchased a big, blaze-faced black gelding, along with a saddle and everything else he would need. Some men considered a blaze on a horse's face to be a flaw, a sign that the animal was lacking somehow, but Conrad had never felt that way.

At the same barn, he purchased a large, sturdy mule to use as a pack animal. The mule would be able to carry the supplies he needed. He told the livery owner he would pick up both animals early the next morning.

He was on his way back to the hotel when several cowboys stepped up onto the sidewalk in front of him. At least, he took them for cowboys because of their well-worn range clothes, but as they came closer he saw the hard eyes, the beard-stubbled jaws, the guns worn in thonged-down holsters. Conrad glanced at their hands and knew the truth.

Their hands were callused, but different from a puncher's hands would be. The calluses were signs of long hours spent practicing with a gun.

Seeing the arrogant expressions on their faces as they strode along, Conrad moved to the edge of the sidewalk. It went against the grain for him to step aside for any man, but he was prepared to do so to avoid trouble. His mind was full of thoughts of his missing children. He was ready to step down into the gutter for a moment and let the hardcases have the sidewalk.

It wasn't that simple. The nearest of the men reached out suddenly, grabbed Conrad's coat, and hauled him back so he blocked their way.

"Where you goin', dude?" the man demanded. "You ain't good enough to share the sidewalk with the likes of us?"

Instantly, alarm bells rang in the back of Conrad's mind. He knew without being told that if he *hadn't* tried to step aside, the hardcase would have challenged him about that, too. The man was looking to start a fight. His left eye rolled a little to the side, seemingly independent of the right eye, which had a loco anger burning in it.

Though the men seemed to be on the prod, Conrad thought he might be able to avoid trouble. "I was just trying to get out of your way, friend."

The man sneered at him and closed his left hand tighter on Conrad's coat, balling up the fabric. "What the hell makes you think I'd be friends with a fancy-pants varmint like you?"

"Just let me go," Conrad said. "I don't want any trouble."

A couple men laughed. One of them said, "Hear that, Rankin? Sounded like a threat to me. Ain't you scared?"

"Scared of this sissy varmint? Hell, I'll bet he's about to piss his pants right now!"

Conrad looked into the man's good eye and said coldly, "Not even close. You may be if you don't back off." He didn't have much patience to start with, and it had just run out.

The man who had spoken to Rankin hooted derisively. "Dude's got a mouth on him!"

"Yeah," Rankin growled, "and I intend on shuttin' it."

A Kansas City police officer was probably within hearing distance of a shout for help, but Conrad didn't call out.

Kid Morgan stomped his own snakes.

The clothes were different, but suddenly it was The Kid who glared defiantly at the man confronting him.

For a second, the hardcase's good eye widened slightly, as if he recognized the change that had come over his intended victim. But it wasn't enough to make him change his mind about what was going to happen next. He grated a curse and swung a fist at The Kid's head.

Jerking his head aside The Kid hooked a punch into the hardcase's midsection, burying a fist deep in his belly, and knocking the man's grip loose from his coat. As the man doubled over, The Kid grabbed his shoulders and shoved him into the other troublemakers, who had started toward him with clenched fists and angry faces.

A couple got their legs tangled up and fell on the sidewalk, but the other two closed in on The Kid. Pedestrians nearby scattered, not wanting to get in the middle of a brawl, leaving a clear space on the sidewalk around The Kid and the men attacking him.

He ducked under a roundhouse punch, reached up and took hold of the man's arm, and pivoted sharply at the waist in a wrestling move that sent the off-balance hardcase flying into the street with a startled yell. He came crashing down on the pavement on his back, leaving The Kid open to the other man's attack.

A fist grazed The Kid's ear painfully, and another thudded into his chest. He sent a jab of his own into his opponent's face that rocked the man's head back. A looping blow from The Kid landed cleanly on the man's jaw and sent him spinning to the sidewalk.

Rankin and the other two had climbed back to their feet, and they closed in around The Kid. A fist drove into the small of his back and sent pain shooting through him. A booted foot was thrust between his ankles to trip him. He knew if he went down to the sidewalk, they could kick and stomp him to death if they wanted to.

It appeared that was exactly what they *did* want. The man with the crazy eye said, "Kill the son of a bitch! You don't get the money unless he winds up dead!"

Chapter 19

That changed everything.

The Kid knew instantly—it wasn't a random encounter with some toughs eager to push somebody around. It was an ambush by hired killers who had been waiting for him to return to the hotel.

It also told The Kid several other things, but he didn't have time to ponder them. He devoted all his attention to not winding up dead.

His hands shot out and grabbed the shirtfronts of two men to keep himself from falling. Braced that way, he lifted a leg and slammed a savage kick into the groin of the third man. The man screamed and doubled over, clutching at himself. That cut down the odds by one.

The Kid lowered his head and hunkered his shoulders so he could more easily shrug off the blows that rained down on him. He bulled forward, forcing the two men he had hold of to stumble back toward the building behind them. He ran them into the wall hard enough to make the back of their heads bounce off the bricks. The impact was enough to stun them and put them out of the fight for a few moments.

When The Kid whipped around toward the two men in the street who were back on their feet, he saw them clawing at the guns on their hips. The pretense of making it look like a casual encounter and a simple fight turned deadly was over. It was outright attempted murder now.

The two Colt Lightnings were in the shoulder holsters under his arms. He couldn't draw them from there as quickly as he could if they had been in the cross-draw rig belted around his waist. Because of that, both of the would-be killers cleared leather first. Shots blasted from them as The Kid shucked his irons. A slug whined past his ear and splattered against the brick wall behind him. The Lightnings flashed .38 caliber death in return.

One of the men dropped his revolver and clutched at his bullet-torn throat as crimson welled from it. The other man staggered as The Kid's bullet drove into his chest, but he stayed on his feet and kept shooting. The Kid went to a knee and triggered both guns again, aiming at the remaining hardcase's belly. The man bent forward as the slugs punched into his gut. His gun exploded one more time as his hand clenched on it spasmodically, but the bullet smacked into the sidewalk between him and The Kid.

People down the street were yelling in alarm over the shots. The Kid heard someone moan behind him, sending him surging to his feet. He whirled around with the Lightnings leveled and saw that one of the men he had run into the wall was down on the sidewalk, writhing in pain. The Kid guessed instantly that one of the bullets aimed at him had missed, and struck that man instead.

The wounded man suddenly stiffened, and his breath came out of him in a long sigh that turned into an ugly rattle. The hardcases had succeeded in killing someone, but the dead man was one of their own.

With whistles shrilling and guns drawn, a couple of Kansas City police officers charged toward the scene. The Kid knew they would be there in mere moments, so he moved quickly, stepping over to the only one of the hardcases who was relatively unhurt. The man stood against the wall of the building, eyes wide with fear.

They widened more when The Kid put the barrel of a Lightning under his chin and asked in a low, hard voice, "Who hired you?"

"R-Rankin!" the man answered without hesitation.

The one with the loco wandering eye, The Kid recalled. He glanced around. Rankin was the man he'd shot in the throat. He wouldn't be answering any questions even if he weren't dead . . . which he damn sure was.

"Why?" The Kid demanded. "Why did he want me dead?"

The man swallowed as best he could with the barrel of The Kid's gun digging painfully into his neck. "I-I dunno." He tried to shake his head. "I swear I don't, mister. He just rounded up a few boys he knew and said he had a-a job for us. Said there was a man who . . . who needed to wind up dead."

"You don't know who I am, or why Rankin wanted to kill me?"

"I got no idea, I swear."

Before The Kid could say anything else, a loud, harsh voice ordered, "Get away from that man and drop those guns! Do it or we'll shoot!"

The Kid didn't have to look around to know the police had arrived. He knew they would make good on their threat. He stepped back, bent over, and carefully placed the Lightnings on the sidewalk. He didn't want to take a chance on damaging the guns by dropping them.

He knew he wouldn't be able to ask any more questions of the two survivors from the gang that had tried to kill him, but that didn't really matter.

He knew somebody else he could ask, just as soon as he got the chance.

The soft yellow glow of lamplight through a window guided The Kid through the dark night. He rode the big black gelding he had bought that afternoon. The horse's hoofbeats were enough to alert the dogs. They came charging out from under the farmhouse's porch. The black shied a little, spooking as the curs clustered around and barked furiously. The Kid brought the horse under control with a firm hand on the reins and waited.

Not for long. He saw the light in the window go out abruptly, then a second later the door swung back just enough to allow the barrel of a rifle to be thrust out. "Who . . . who's there?" a quavery old voice asked.

"I think you know the answer to that, Mr. Potter," The Kid called.

He was ready for the reaction he got. Muzzle flame lanced through the darkness as the rifle cracked. The Kid didn't know where the bullet went, but it didn't come anywhere close to him. He had figured that accurate shooting in the darkness would be more than the old, terrified retired stationmaster could manage.

Drawing his gun—not one of the .38 caliber Lightnings but rather the Colt .45 he wore in a holster on his hip—The Kid sent the black surging forward, scattering the dogs. When he was close enough he left the saddle in a leap that carried him to the porch as the horse veered away.

By the time The Kid's boots hit the boards of the porch, Potter had managed to work the rifle's lever. The Kid crouched low and drove a shoulder against the door. It banged inward, crashing into Potter and knocking the old man backward. He fired again, but the shot went wild.

Normally The Kid wouldn't be too rough with an old-timer like Potter, but the retired stationmaster had tried to have him killed. The Kid dropped to a knee beside Potter and grabbed the Winchester with his free hand, wrenching it out of the old man's grip. Then he said, "You'd better be careful with that shotgun, Sara Beth. You shoot me and you'll blow the hell out of your husband with it, too."

He saw the pale blur of her dress on the other side of the shabby living room. He couldn't see the greener but thought there was a good chance she was pointing it at him.

His hunch was confirmed by the way she asked, "Why shouldn't I? The old buzzard ain't much use to me. Most of the time he can't even—"

A groan came from Potter, cutting across her words.

"Anyway," Sara Beth went on, "if he's dead, this place would belong to me."

"Yeah, that's what you want," The Kid said mockingly. "A hardscrabble farm that the bank's going to take away from you sooner or later anyway."

"You shut up!" she snapped. "You don't know anything about it."

"I know more than you think I do. I know he took Pamela Tarleton's money so he could buy this farm and ask you to marry him. I know you're the granddaughter of an old friend of his and he's been lusting after you ever since you started sprouting. I found out a lot about both of you this evening after the men he sent to kill me didn't do their job."

From the floor, Potter rasped, "I didn't . . . didn't send them to kill you. I didn't know what Rankin was gonna do. I just went to see him and . . . and told him you were the man Miss Tarleton said might come after her. That's what she paid me to do, three years ago. I reckon she . . . she must've paid him, too."

"Spill it all," The Kid ordered. "Did she tell you to be so cooperative with me if I showed up and started asking questions? Did she pay you to lie to me about where she went?"

"No! No, it was the truth, the God's honest truth!"

The Kid took hold of the nightshirt Potter was wearing and hauled the old man into a sitting position. "Keep talking."

"Sara Beth, put that shotgun away and strike a light," Potter said.

With obvious reluctance, she did so, scratching a lucifer to life a moment later. She lit the lamp that one of them had blown out a few minutes earlier. As its glow filled the room, The Kid saw that she was dressed for bed, too, in a long nightgown that repeated washings has faded from blue to almost white.

Potter rubbed a lump on his forehead where the door had hit him. "I'm sorry, Mr. Browning. I never meant for you to get hurt."

"What did you think Rankin and his hired guns were going to do?"

The old-timer grimaced. "I . . . Well, I just tried not to think too much about that. I surely did." He looked at The Kid and his bushy eyebrows rose in surprise, as if he had just noticed what the visitor was wearing.

The tweed suit of Conrad Morgan had been replaced by high-topped black boots, black whipcord trousers, a soft buckskin shirt that was open at the throat, and a flat-crowned black Stetson with a concho-studded band. It was the gunfighter Kid Morgan who hunkered next to Potter, a heavy .45 revolver held with deceptively lethal casualness in his hand. "Tell me the whole thing."

Potter rasped his tongue over dry lips. "Everything I told you was true. Miss Tarleton and the other lady and the babies showed up in Kansas City. I helped 'em out because they missed their connection. It was Miss Tarleton who told me where they were going, just like I told you. And she said . . . she said you might come looking for them someday."

"What did she want you to do if I showed up?" The Kid asked.

"Just what I did. Tell you the truth. But . . . there was something else."

"Go find Rankin and tell him I was in town and on Pamela's trail?"

Potter swallowed and nodded. "Yeah. She paid me, paid me well, to do both those things. So I did. And she said, once I had done it, if I sent a wire to a man in Boston and told him what I'd done, he'd see to it that I got some more money for my trouble." A whining note entered the old-timer's voice. "I really need that money, Mr. Browning. This farm ain't been near as successful as I thought it would be, and it's hard work."

Sara Beth snorted. "He wouldn't know how hard it is. He makes me do most of the work."

"Well, you're young and strong," Potter muttered without looking at his wife.

The Kid didn't care about the problems between them. "What's the name of the man you were supposed to get in touch with in Boston?"

"D-Davenport. Willard Davenport." Potter hesitated. "I already sent the wire to him."

"To collect your blood money," The Kid snapped.

Potter winced as if he thought The Kid was going to hit him . . . or shoot him. "I didn't know," he insisted. "I didn't know what was gonna happen."

Maybe in the strictest sense, the old man was telling the truth. He had to have guessed, though, that whatever Pamela had planned for Conrad Browning wouldn't be anything good.

Despite that, Potter had given him a lot to think about, and The Kid was grateful for that. The pieces of Pamela's plan were falling into place.

"I-I'd like to make it up to you," Potter went on. He nodded toward the blond girl on the other side of the room. "Why don't you and Sara Beth go into the bedroom for a while? She . . . she won't mind, and I'm sure you could do her a hell of a lot more good than I ever could."

The sour taste of disgust rose in The Kid's mouth, and it grew stronger when he glanced at the girl and saw the look of interest, even avarice, that sprang up in Sara Beth's eyes.

"Forget it," he said. "That's not going to happen."

Sara Beth made a little sound of disappointment.

"What are you gonna do to me?" Potter asked in obvious fear.

The Kid straightened to his feet and slipped the

Colt back into leather. "If you've told me the truth, nothing. But if I find out you've lied to me, I'll be back to see you one of these days. Until then, you can live with your own greed and misery. I've heard Davenport's name. He's a lawyer in Boston. He'll probably send you the money Pamela promised you." The Kid shook his head. "I don't think it's going to make any real difference."

Potter swallowed again. "That's because you got plenty of money, Mr. Browning, and always have. You don't know what it's like. You just don't."

The Kid thought about everything *he* had lost, everything he had struggled, and was still struggling, to get back. "Nobody does, Potter. Nobody does."

Chapter 20

During the ride back to Kansas City, The Kid thought hard about everything he had learned.

After the shootout on the street near the Cattleman's Hotel, the police had taken him into custody and questioned him about the attempt on his life. Enough witnesses to the incident had spoken up that there was no question about his actions being self-defense.

The Kid hadn't told the police the ruckus was deliberate on the part of Rankin and the other men. He let them think it was an ugly fight that had spiraled out of control into deadly violence. The fact that all five men had bad reputations had helped convince the authorities. Rankin was well-known as a troublemaker, and he was suspected of being involved in bank robberies and train holdups in Missouri, Kansas, and Nebraska.

Just the sort of man Pamela Tarleton would hire to carry out a killing, The Kid mused. He had no doubt she had promised Rankin more money once Conrad Browning was dead. Rankin had probably had instructions to get in touch with Willard Davenport, too.

Maybe Pamela had told Eddie Murtagh the same thing, as well as Dr. Vernon Futrelle. The lure of an extra payoff would have been necessary to insure the men did exactly what Pamela wanted them to do.

The Kid couldn't help but wonder how many other men between there and San Francisco had received similar instructions from Pamela Tarleton.

He was convinced Potter had told him the truth that afternoon. Pamela really had been headed for San Francisco when she came through Kansas City with her maid and the two children. She had *wanted* Conrad to know that. She was deliberately leaving a trail he could follow, luring him farther and farther west.

At the same time, she had set up traps along the way, like the one with Rankin. The point of the whole thing was to torment Conrad. If he fell victim to one of the ambushes, then Pamela would have her revenge that way. But if he survived, as he had so far, he would continue to be tormented by the knowledge that she had stolen his children away from him. The whole thing was a two-edged sword, and it was one of the most diabolical schemes he had ever encountered.

What made it even more impressive, in its own macabre way, was that it was actually a contingency plan on Pamela's part. The main thrust of her vengeance had been Rebel's kidnapping and murder, along with the attempts to kill The Kid after that.

There were no limits to her evil, he thought. She had come up with ways to torture him from beyond the grave.

When he got back to the hotel, he would send wires to Charles Harcourt and Jack Mallory, asking them to investigate Willard Davenport and his dealings. It would be a long shot, but maybe they could find out something about other traps that might be waiting for him somewhere up ahead on Pamela's trail.

With that decision made, he reconsidered another one. When he reached Kansas City, he took the horse back to the stable where he had bought it. As the hostler put the animal in a stall for the night, The Kid said, "I'll be back for him in the morning."

The clerk in the hotel lobby looked puzzled by The Kid's clothes, but he recognized the tall, sandy-haired man as Conrad Browning. The Kid got a couple of telegraph forms from the clerk, printed his messages, and shoved them back across the desk. "See that these are sent right away."

"Of course, sir. Is there anything else I can do for you?"

The Kid smiled faintly. "Where's the closest wagon yard? I need to buy a buggy in the morning."

Armed with that information, he went upstairs. Arturo was still awake and fully dressed, of course. He would have been no matter what time it was when The Kid got back.

"Did you find out what you wanted to know,

sir?" Arturo asked as The Kid took off his wide-brimmed Stetson and dropped it on a table.

"I did," he replied. "Pamela was behind the whole thing. She paid off Potter and the leader of the men who jumped me later in the afternoon. She promised them more money, through a Boston lawyer, if they were successful in carrying out her orders."

"To have you killed, you mean," Arturo murmured.

The Kid inclined his head in agreement.

"No offense, sir, considering that you were once engaged to the lady in question . . . but was there no end to the woman's deviousness?"

"Evidently not," The Kid said. "That's the reason I've made up my mind about something."

"And what might that be, sir?"

"You're coming with me after all."

Surprise leaped into Arturo's eyes, but he concealed it quickly and kept his usual unflappable expression on his face. "An excellent decision, I must say. But what prompted you to reconsider the one you made earlier, if you don't mind my asking."

"I'm liable to run into one trap after another, all the way to San Francisco," The Kid explained. "I'm going to need somebody watching my back. And you *did* save my life on the train coming out here. I know I can count on you, Arturo."

"Indeed you can, sir. You won't regret this."

"You know, of course, it's going to be dangerous."

"Of course," Arturo said. "But after all, I'm going

to be in the company of a notorious gunfighter, aren't I?"

First thing in the morning, they went to the wagon yard. The Kid couldn't imagine Arturo riding horseback all the way to California, if that was what it took, but the valet *could* drive a buggy that far, as long as they didn't have to travel through territory that was too rough for such a vehicle. If they did . . . well, The Kid would deal with that when the time came.

They settled for a buckboard with a single seat and enough room behind it to carry quite a bit of their gear. The Kid wouldn't have to leave behind as much as he had expected to. Between the buckboard and the pack mule, they would be able to take plenty of supplies with them. The Kid made arrangements to have a cover added to the buckboard so Arturo would have at least a little protection from the sun and the rain.

"Really, sir, that's not necessary," Arturo protested. "I can travel without that luxury."

"It's not a luxury," The Kid said. "The cover will protect our gear, too."

The owner of the wagon yard promised to have the buckboard ready to roll by that afternoon. The Kid and Arturo went back to the hotel to pack.

When they entered the lobby, the clerk saw them and called, "Mr. Browning."

The Kid went over to the desk. "What is it?"

"I have a response to the telegrams you sent out

last night." The man handed over a Western Union envelope.

The Kid tore it open and slid out the yellow flimsy inside. His eyes quickly scanned the words printed on it.

The wire was from Charles Harcourt and explained that the lawyer hired by Pamela, Willard Davenport, was refusing to cooperate and wouldn't admit he knew who Pamela Tarleton was. Harcourt could sue in an attempt to force him to open his records, but that would take a long time and might not be successful in the end.

In the meantime, Jack Mallory was conducting a more discreet investigation of his own. Reading between the lines, The Kid knew Harcourt and Mallory were trying to come up with something they could use to blackmail Davenport into talking.

Mallory was enough of a big Irish bulldog that he stood a good chance of finding something they could use against the attorney. It was a dirty way to play the game, but not nearly as dirty as the tricks Pamela had pulled.

Anyway, it wasn't a game, The Kid thought. It was business, deadly serious business.

That afternoon, Arturo returned to the wagon yard and picked up the buckboard while The Kid got the black gelding and the pack mule from the livery stable. It was late enough in the day that they wouldn't get very far before having to stop and make camp for the night.

"Are you sure you wouldn't rather wait and

get a fresh start in the morning?" The Kid asked Arturo.

"Really, sir, I think I know you better than that by now," Arturo replied. "I can tell you're anxious to be on your way, and this will give me a chance to become accustomed to driving the buckboard before I have to handle it for an entire day."

"Well, that's a good point," The Kid said with a smile. "We'll load up and light a shuck out of here."

"Light a shuck . . . what an odd expression."

The Kid chuckled. Crossing the country by train was vastly different from doing it on horse-back and in a buckboard. It was going to be a real education in frontier life for Arturo. He had experienced some of that while he was working for Count Fortunato, but not like he was about to.

They carried their belongings downstairs, The Kid refusing the help of a porter. Now that he had slipped back into the personality of Kid Morgan, his impulse was to do things for himself, rather than waiting for somebody else to take care of a chore for him. It was different where Arturo was concerned. The Italian undoubtedly still saw himself as a servant, but to The Kid's mind, they were rapidly becoming partners.

That was what happened when you fought side by side with a fellow and shared danger together. Those bonds went deeper than boss and employee.

The sun was still fairly high in the sky when they crossed the bridge that paralleled the railroad trestle over the Missouri. The Kid rode slightly ahead, leading the pack mule, and Arturo guided the buckboard after him. The shrill whistle of a train made The Kid look to his left, where he saw a locomotive crossing the trestle with a long string of cars behind it. Smoke puffed from the big engine's diamond-shaped stack.

Westbound. Headed for California and all the bright promises that lay between here and there, The Kid thought. Headed into the unknown, because no man truly knew what the next day would bring.

He and Arturo were headed in the same direction, and The Kid was ready for whatever the journey might bring.

Chapter 21

They covered several miles the first day and camped on the bank of a creek that flowed into the Kansas River from the north. They planned to follow the railroad tracks, which ran along with the river past Abilene, to the point where the Saline and Smoky Hill Rivers flowed together to form the Kansas. From there the railroad continued running almost due west, The Kid knew, though the rivers twisted and turned away from the steel rails and then came back again.

Over the campfire that night, as trains rumbled past on the tracks several hundred yards away, The Kid mused as he sipped from a cup of the good coffee Arturo had brewed. "If Pamela hid the twins somewhere along the way, she likely would have done it someplace the train was already scheduled to stop. If she'd gone too far away from the railroad, she'd have had to hire a wagon and a driver, and I don't see her doing that. We'll have to stop in every settlement where the train stops."

"But I was under the impression Miss Tarleton was capable of almost anything, sir," Arturo said. "You can't be sure she didn't leave the train and strike out on her own with the children and her servant."

"No, that's true, I can't be sure," The Kid said with a shrug. "But that's what my gut tells me, and I've learned to play my hunches."

"If you're wrong, it's possible we may travel all the way to San Francisco without finding the children."

"I know. Believe me, I know."

"What will you do then?"

The Kid took a sip of the hot, strong coffee. "Reckon we'll turn around and start back this way. Do it all over again."

"That could take years."

"Yeah. It could."

The Kid's tone made it clear that if the search took years, he was fully prepared to spend that much time on it.

Arturo didn't say anything for a long moment. Off in the distance, a wailing sound arose, joined by another and another until they formed a discordant melody. Arturo lifted his head to listen. "Are those . . . wolves?"

"No. Coyotes."

"Are they dangerous?"

"Not to a man who can stand on his own two feet. If you were wounded and there was a whole pack of them, they might come after you, but otherwise you don't have anything to worry about."

"I see." Arturo hesitated. "Mr. Browning?"

"Just call me Kid."

Arturo sighed as if that was going to be difficult. "Are there savages out here?"

"You mean Indians?"

"Yes, sir. Kid."

"There may be some still roaming around. Most of them are on reservations now, though."

"Are *they* dangerous?"

The Kid smiled. "There haven't been any Indian fights in these parts for a long, long time, Arturo."

"Well, that's good to know. I wouldn't want to be scalped."

"Neither would I," The Kid said, looking off into the night for two reasons. He knew better than to stare into the fire, because it would ruin his night vision, and he didn't want Arturo to see the grin on his face.

Yeah, this trip was going to be an education for Arturo, he thought.

Lawrence was the first good-sized settlement they came to. It had been raided twice by jayhawkers, first before the Civil War and then during the war by William Quantrill's marauders, who had burned the town to the ground. Lawrence had rebuilt and was now a peaceful farming community, with few if any reminders of the bloody violence that had taken place there.

They spent two days camped outside town while The Kid and Arturo asked questions of the settlers. Nobody seemed to know anything about Pamela.

Nobody tried to kill The Kid, either, which told him she probably hadn't disembarked the train there.

It was a good break for Arturo, too, since he wasn't used to sitting on the hard, bouncing seat of a buckboard all day long. His skin was already starting to tan, and he was handling the four-horse team with more confidence.

They moved on to Topeka. For a capital city, the settlement was on the smallish size, but still large enough that The Kid and Arturo spent a week there, poking around and asking questions. The Kid wired Charles Harcourt to find out if there had been any new developments in Boston, but Harcourt reported that he and Jack Mallory had been unsuccessful in their efforts to uncover any more facets of Pamela's far-reaching plot.

After a week, The Kid thought it was time they moved on. He began to have the feeling that Pamela wouldn't have hidden the children in a large town or city where he wouldn't have any realistic chance of finding them. She hadn't wanted that. She'd *wanted* him to stay on the trail, and he wouldn't do that if the chances of finding the twins were so small as to be hopeless. She'd wanted him to keep going, so he could keep stepping right into the traps she had prepared for him.

The Kid was convinced it was much more likely the children were hidden away in some small settlement along the rail line, and that was where he and Arturo would devote their efforts.

Abilene was still famous for everything that had

happened during its days as a wild, hell-roaring cowtown. The sleepy little farming community bore little resemblance to that bloody hell on wheels where Wild Bill Hickok had ruled as city marshal. It was just the sort of place where Pamela might have stashed the twins, The Kid thought as he and Arturo rolled across the bridge over Mud Creek and down Front Street.

Dusk was settling over the town. The Kid turned in the saddle and pointed toward a two-story brick hotel. "We'll stay there tonight. Be nice to sleep in a real bed, won't it?"

"I don't know. I'm getting used to being uncomfortable. How will I know what to do if there aren't insects biting me and rocks jabbing me all night?"

"You'll figure it out," The Kid said with a smile. "Here's a livery stable." He swung down from the saddle and led the black and the pack mule through the open double doors into the barn. Arturo brought the buckboard to a halt just outside.

An elderly hostler, quite spry despite his age, greeted them. "You gents want to put them animals up for the night?"

The Kid nodded. "And I reckon we can park the buckboard out back?"

"Sure, sure, no charge for that. Two bits a night for the critters, though."

"Fair enough," The Kid said. He took a five-dollar gold piece from his pocket and handed it to the old man. "That'll cover three nights with a little left over. Give them a little extra grain. They deserve it."

"I sure will. You fellas been travelin' a far piece?"

"Far enough." The Kid paused. "Have you been around these parts for long?"

"Oh, shoot, yeah. Twenty years or more." The hostler held out a hand. "Name's Barlow."

The Kid shook with him. "Morgan. My friend's Vincent." Arturo's last name was really Vincenzo, but The Kid had given the moniker a more American sound. With his neutral accent, Arturo didn't sound Italian.

"Pleased to meet you both," Barlow said.

"We're looking for some old friends of ours. You might remember if they've been here."

A grin split the old-timer's face. "I see 'most ever'body who comes through town, except for the folks who never get off the train when it stops."

"This lady would have come in on the train," The Kid said. "A very beautiful lady with two young children, traveling with a friend of hers. She brought the children out to let them stay for a spell with either some friends or relatives of hers, I'm not sure which."

The Kid had devoted considerable thought to the matter and figured that was the story Pamela might have used. The sudden, unexplained presence of two new children in a family might draw too much attention, but people took in youngsters belonging to friends or relatives all the time, when there was some sort of hardship or other circumstance that warranted it. Pamela would have made it worth the trouble to any family where she left the twins to spread that lie.

Barlow scratched his jaw, which bristled with silvery beard stubble. "That don't sound familiar. About how long ago are we talkin' about, Mr. Morgan?"

"Three years or so. Maybe not quite that long."

"Three years, huh? That's a long spell, especially to a fella like me who's gettin' older and don't remember so good anymore."

The Kid slid a hand in his pocket. "Would a double eagle improve your memory?"

"What?" Barlow looked confused, then suddenly moved his hands back and forth in front of him as he figured out what The Kid meant. "Oh, no, no, I'm tellin' the truth, not hintin' for more money. I been right on the straight and narrow ever since me and my brothers got in some trouble with the law years back. I really don't remember so good no more, Mr. Morgan. But I'm thinkin' I never heard tell about no lady bringin' some kids here like that and leavin' 'em."

The Kid tried not to sigh. "Well, if anything comes to you, my friend and I will be staying over at the hotel for a day or two. Let us know, will you?"

"I sure will." Barlow's eyes widened as a thought occurred to him. "Say, I know who you ought to talk to. Marshal Fisher. He's been around Abilene even longer'n I have."

The Kid had been trying not to involve the law in his search, but maybe the suggestion was a good one, he thought. "I'll do that," he told

Barlow. "We'll get these horses unhitched and unsaddled—"

"Let me do that," the hostler said. "I got to earn my keep. I been an honest businessman for a long time now. You get whatever you want to take to the hotel with you, and I'll lock up your saddle and the rest of your gear in the tack room."

The Kid nodded. "Much obliged."

He slid his Winchester from the sheath strapped to the black's saddle and draped the pair of saddlebags over his shoulder. Arturo took a pair of small valises from the back of the buckboard.

"Well, he was quite a colorful character," Arturo commented as the two of them walked toward the hotel.

"I'm sure he'd think the same thing about you," The Kid said. In the fading light, he spotted a squarish, solid-looking building made of stone, up ahead on the left across the street. An oil lamp burned in front of the building, and the windows glowed yellow with lamplight. A sign attached to the wall beside the door read MARSHAL'S OFFICE.

Since the lawman appeared to be in his office, The Kid said to Arturo, "Why don't you go on to the hotel and get a couple of rooms for us? I think I'll stop and talk to the marshal, like Mr. Barlow suggested."

"Do you think he'll be willing to help you?"

"I don't know, but Barlow said that he'd been around Abilene for a long time. If he's been packing a badge all that time, he's probably kept a pretty close eye on the comings and goings in town. He might be more likely to remember seeing Pamela than anybody else."

"That strikes me as a reasonable assumption. Good luck."

"Thanks." The Kid started to step down from the boardwalk so he could angle across the street to the marshal's office, then paused. "Get us rooms in the back if you can. Quieter that way."

"Of course."

Arturo continued on his way, and The Kid stepped into the broad, dusty street. He was only partway across when he heard the sudden rataplan of hoofbeats. Stopping, he saw a group of riders coming quickly toward him. The red glow from the setting sun in the sky behind them cast them in stark silhouette. Four men on horseback, and they didn't seem inclined to slow down or go around him. With his mouth tightening in anger, The Kid took a fast step back to avoid being trampled.

He wanted to call out to them and tell them to watch where the hell they were going, but that could lead to an argument or a fight and he didn't have time to waste. Once the horsemen were past him, he started toward the marshal's office again.

He slowed as he saw the riders pull their mounts to a stop in front of the stone building. They swung down, stepped onto the boardwalk, and then paused for a second. Even in the fading light, The Kid's keen eyes saw the men reach down and check to make sure their guns were loose in their holsters.

That was a sure sign trouble was brewing, The Kid thought as one of the men jerked open the door and all four of them marched into the marshal's office.

Whatever was about to happen, it was none of his business, he told himself. He didn't know who those four men were, and he had never even heard of Abilene's Marshal Fisher until a few minutes earlier. The smart thing to do would be to turn around, follow Arturo to the hotel, and come back to see the marshal later.

But suppose there *was* trouble, and Fisher got himself shot full of holes. He might know something about Pamela and the children . . . but a dead man was no use to Kid Morgan.

The Kid drew a deep breath through his nose and started walking again. He still had the Winchester in his hands, and he worked the lever to throw a round into the rifle's chamber.

The four men had left the door partially open. As he stepped onto the boardwalk, The Kid heard a harsh voice say, "You can let him outta there, Marshal, or by God we'll *take* him out! You won't like what happens if we have to do that."

It was enough to give The Kid a pretty good idea of what was going on. Using the Winchester's barrel to push the door open the rest of the way, he stepped into the doorway and drawled, "And I don't reckon you boys will like what happens if you try."

Chapter 22

In a matter of seconds, The Kid's eyes took in the scene in the marshal's office, noting the position of each of the five men who stood there.

The four who had just entered had arranged themselves in a threatening half-circle around a man who stood with his back to the thick wooden door that separated the office from the cell block in the rear of the building. The man was in his forties, slender as a whip, with graying fair hair and a mustache. He was dressed all in black and had a holstered Colt on his hip, along with a marshal's badge pinned to his leather vest.

The oldest of the four intruders was older than the marshal, with a derby hat on thinning red hair and a grizzled beard of the same shade sprouting from his jaw. The youngest was no more than twenty. Curly brown hair fell around his shoulders. Despite his youth, the eyes he turned toward The Kid were flat and devoid of humanity, like the eyes of a snake.

The other two were in their thirties, typical hardcases in worn range clothes. One of them, who had a prominent beak of a nose over a thick, drooping black mustache, glared at The Kid and demanded, "Who the hell are you?"

The old-timer in the derby growled, "This ain't none o' your business, mister. You best skedaddle."

"My business is with the marshal," The Kid said coldly. "So you'd best conclude whatever brought you here and then leave, so I can get on with it."

Big Nose said, "You're makin' a bad mistake. Haul your freight outta here." He was the one who had been threatening the marshal as The Kid reached the doorway.

The long-haired youngster laughed. "Yeah, you don't want to get on our bad side, mister. We work for Court Elam."

"Never heard of him," The Kid snapped.

Big Nose ignored him and looked back at the marshal. "How about it, Fisher? You gonna let Barnes out?"

"Not hardly," the lawman replied. "We don't know yet if that girl's going to live or not, and even if she does, Barnes will have to answer for what he did to her."

Big Nose's face flushed with anger. "Court's not gonna like this. He wants his men treated with respect."

"I don't give a damn what Elam likes or doesn't like. As far as I'm concerned, none of you varmints have earned a lick of respect from me or anybody else in Abilene. Why don't you just ride on back to Powderhorn?"

The youngster said, "We can take 'em, Jim. There's four of us and only two of them."

"Yeah, but one of them is behind us with a Winchester." Big Nose grimaced. "We'll go, Fisher. But this ain't over."

The old-timer with the derby pointed a finger at the marshal and blustered, "Yeah, you'll be seein' us again."

"More than likely over the barrel of a gun," Fisher drawled, and The Kid's instinctive liking for him increased.

The Kid moved aside from the door to let the four hardcases file out of the office. He kept them covered the whole time. When they were gone, he toed the door shut and lowered the rifle as he turned toward the marshal.

Before The Kid could say anything, Fisher snapped, "Get down!" and leaped toward the desk where a lamp was burning. Even as he blew out the flame, both of the windows in the office exploded inward under the onslaught of a volley of shots fired from outside.

The Kid had halfway expected something like that, so he was already diving toward the floor as shards of broken glass sprayed around him. He had an arm over his face to protect his eyes. He rolled over as he landed and came up on one knee still holding the Winchester. He thrust the rifle through the busted window closest to him and aimed at the muzzle flashes in the street, cranking off three rounds as fast as he could work the lever.

Marshal Fisher had snatched a loaded rifle

from the rack on the wall behind the desk and crouched at the other window to open fire. He and The Kid raked the street with their shots, and that was enough to make the four mounted men dig in their spurs and send their horses lunging away from the marshal's office.

"Hold your fire!" Fisher called to The Kid. "They're leaving. Don't want any stray bullets hitting anybody else."

The Kid pulled the Winchester back from the window. The rifle was chambered to use the same rounds as his Colt, so he took fresh cartridges from the loops on his shell belt and thumbed them through the Winchester's loading gate, working in the dark with the ease of long familiarity.

It sounded like Fisher was reloading, too. When he was finished, the marshal asked, "You hit?"

"I picked up a scratch or two when those windows broke, but that's all. How about you?"

"Not even a scratch." Fisher stood up. "There are shutters on the windows. Let's close them before I strike a light again."

That sounded like a good idea to The Kid. He closed and latched the shutters on the window where he had been firing at the gunmen, and heard the marshal doing the same at the other window. The scratch of a lucifer came a moment later. Light flared up from the match.

Fisher lit the lamp. In its glow, The Kid studied the shutters, which had a double layer of thick boards that would stop most rifle bullets and anything smaller than that. The office door was formidable, too. With the building's stone walls, it would take a cannon to bust in there.

Fisher put his rifle back in the rack. "Stranger in Abilene, aren't you?"

The Kid nodded. "That's right. A friend and I just rode in a little while ago."

"That was good timing as far as I'm concerned." The marshal came around the desk and stuck out his hand. A faint smile relieved the naturally grim cast of his face. "I'm obliged to you for your help, Mister . . . ?"

"Morgan," The Kid said.

"Morgan." The lawman nodded. "You said you had some business with me?"

The Kid tucked his Winchester under his arm. "We stopped at the livery stable down the street, and the old-timer running it said you'd been a lawman here in Abilene for quite a while."

"About twenty years. Started out as a deputy under Marshal Travis. Took on the top job when he retired."

"Then you've probably seen most people who have come and gone during that time."

Fisher shrugged. "Most of them, I guess." He gave The Kid a shrewd look. "I take it you're looking for somebody in particular."

"A woman," The Kid began.

Fisher held up a hand to stop him. "Wait a minute. Stories that start out with a fella looking for a woman generally take some time and require a cup of coffee." He gestured toward the pot that sat on a stove in the corner.

"Don't mind if I do," The Kid said with a smile.

Fisher filled tin cups and nodded The Kid into a chair in front of the desk. The lawman took a seat behind the desk and propped a booted foot on its corner. "Go ahead."

"This woman would have come into Abilene on the train." The Kid described Pamela, not downplaying her beauty. It was a shame that such a lovely exterior had concealed such an evil soul, but that's how it was. "She would have been traveling with another woman—I don't know much about her—and a couple of kids a few months old. A boy and a girl."

Fisher shook his head. "I don't recall anybody like that moving to Abilene recently."

"It would have been about three years ago. And the woman wouldn't have stayed here. Maybe the other woman did, I don't know. But she might have left the children."

Fisher frowned and sat up straighter. "Abandoned them, you mean?"

"No, she would have found somebody to take them in. She probably would have paid them to spread the story that the kids belonged to some relative of theirs."

The marshal's face wore its bleak look again as he shook his head. "I don't know absolutely everybody in Abilene, Mr. Morgan, but I can promise you I never heard tell of anything like that happening around here, certainly not in the past three years. Anybody who's gotten any kids has had them show up the, ah, normal way."

The Kid's instincts told him Fisher wasn't lying, hadn't been paid off by Pamela to lie. For one thing, that would have required a certain degree of crookedness on the marshal's part, and The Kid had a hunch Fisher was as straight-arrow a lawman as anybody would ever find.

"Well, I can't say as I'm surprised."

"Who is this woman you're looking for, Morgan? If she's not wanted by the law, I suppose you can tell me it's none of my business, but—"

"She's not wanted," The Kid said. "She's dead. Has been for more than a year."

"Was she the mother of those kids?"

"That's right."

"And you're the father." It was a statement, not a question.

The Kid drew in a deep breath. "I didn't even know about them until a long time after she'd taken them and hidden them away somewhere."

Fisher took his foot off the desk and sat up straight in his chair. "That's a damned rough thing for a man to have happen. I wish I could help you, but I can pretty much guarantee the children aren't here in Abilene. Tell you what I'll do, though. If you're going to be around here for a day or two, I'll put out the word, just in case I've overlooked something."

"I'd appreciate that, Marshal."

"If you don't mind indulging my curiosity, how do you know she hid them somewhere?"

"I got a letter from her after she died," The Kid explained. "She had left it with a relative of hers, along with instructions that I was to get it after a certain amount of time had passed."

Fisher shook his head again. "That's a pretty damned low thing to do."

"Yeah, it sure is." Since his mission in Abilene was probably going to be a failure, The Kid went on. "Now indulge my curiosity, if you would, Marshal. Who were those men, and what did they want?"

Fisher made a face like he had just bitten into something that tasted bad. "Hired guns who work for a man named Court Elam." He jerked a thumb at the cell block door. "I've got another of Elam's men locked up back there. He was drunk and got too rough with a soiled dove. Slapped her around until she passed out, and she hasn't regained consciousness." Fisher sighed. "That was two nights ago, so it doesn't look very good for her. I figure the varmint will hang for murder before it's all over."

"And Elam doesn't like that, does he?"

"Not one damned bit. He's the big skookum he-wolf of a town called Powderhorn, about thirty miles west of here. He and his gunnies have everybody there buffaloed, and he doesn't like it when anybody challenges him. He seems to think he ought to run things in this whole part of the state and can get away with whatever he or his men want to do."

"But you don't agree with that."

Fisher shook his head. "Inside the town limits of Abilene, I sure don't."

The Kid got to his feet. "Well, Marshal, I wish you the best of luck with this problem."

The marshal regarded him through narrowed

eyes and asked, "You wouldn't be interested in pinning on a deputy's badge, would you? Just temporary-like, until I see what's going to happen."

The Kid smiled and shook his head. "Sorry. I'm not a lawman."

"Yeah, that's what I was afraid you'd say. And you've got those kids to look for, too. I can't blame you for thinking that's more important." A look of surprise came over Fisher's lean face as something occurred to him. "Say, I just thought of something that might help you. There's an orphanage not far from here. What better place to hide a couple kids than some place where there's a whole passel of them to start with?"

The Kid's heart began to beat faster as he thought about the marshal's question. "You're right. All Pamela would have had to do was claim they were orphans and leave them there!"

Fisher nodded. "Yeah, you'll want to check that out for sure."

The Kid's hands tightened on his rifle. "Where is this orphanage?"

"Well, that might be a little problem for you. You see, it's in Powderhorn . . . and after tonight, I don't think Elam's gun-wolves are going to be too happy to see you again."

Chapter 23

By the time The Kid reached the hotel, Arturo had rented two rooms for them. They were on the second floor, in the back as The Kid had requested, and were next to each other. Arturo had taken the valises upstairs and placed one in each room. He was waiting in an armchair in the lobby when The Kid came in.

"I heard a considerable amount of shooting a short time ago. I suppose it's too much to hope for that you weren't involved in that, Kid."

"I had a hand in it," The Kid admitted.

"I suspected as much." Arturo frowned as he spotted a bit of dried blood on The Kid's face where a piece of the flying glass had cut him. "Good Lord. You're wounded! Do you require medical attention?"

"I'm fine. It's just a tiny scratch. Don't worry about me, Arturo."

"It's my job to worry," Arturo pointed out. "Did you get a chance to talk to the marshal, or were you set upon by crazed gunmen before you reached his office?"

"I talked to him," The Kid replied as a grim tone came into his voice. "He doesn't remember anyone like Pamela ever stopping here, and he's convinced that no children have shown up mysteriously in Abilene in the past three years. But he's going to investigate just to be sure."

"Why would he do that?"

"Because I pitched in and gave him a hand when some hired guns tried to bust a friend of theirs out of jail."

"Ah," Arturo said. "The light dawns. Those were the shots I heard."

"That's right."

"Was anyone killed?"

"Not this time." In a low voice, The Kid quickly filled him in on what had happened at Marshal Fisher's office.

When The Kid was finished, Arturo frowned in thought. "Wait just a moment. You said that no one was killed *this* time. Do you plan to have another violent encounter with these men?"

"I'm not planning on it, but it could happen. You see, they're from a place called Powderhorn, and that's where we're going from here." The Kid gestured toward the stairs. "Come on. I'll tell you all about it."

They went up to The Kid's room, where The Kid told Arturo about the orphanage in the settlement called Powderhorn. "Marshal Fisher didn't know much about the place, only that it's been there for about five years and is run by an old widow woman named Shanley. He said he couldn't think of a better place to hide a couple kids than an orphanage, and I agree with him."

Arturo considered the idea and nodded. "It certainly seems feasible to me, sir. All Miss Tarleton would have had to do was claim that the parents of the children were dead. I doubt if this Mrs. Shanley would have demanded any proof, because after all——"

"Who would lie about such a thing." The Kid finished for him.

"Exactly." Despite Arturo's habitually calm demeanor, a hint of excitement appeared on his face and in his voice as he went on. "I believe this may be the most promising development in our search so far."

The Kid nodded. "I agree. We'll stay here tonight and start for Powderhorn tomorrow."

"Where there may well be men who are, what's the expression, gunning for you?"

"We ought to be used to that by now," The Kid said.

They didn't leave Abilene until almost noon the next day. The Kid considered it unlikely the former cowtown held anything else that would help him in his quest, but he had agreed to let Marshal Fisher ask some questions around the settlement. The Kid was confident if anyone could get answers, it was Fisher.

The lawman came to the hotel late in the morning and knocked on The Kid's door. Arturo was waiting there, too. The buckboard was ready to roll down at Barlow's livery stable, and The Kid's black gelding was saddled.

Fisher came in and gave both men a curt nod. "I didn't turn up anything about the woman and the children you're looking for, Morgan. Like I told you last night, I don't think they were ever here, except to pass through on the train."

The Kid nodded in acceptance of that opinion. "Thanks anyway, Marshal." He shook hands with Fisher. "I appreciate you looking into it."

"If you want, I could ride over to Powderhorn with you," Fisher suggested. "I'd be out of my jurisdiction over there, so I wouldn't have any legal standing, but I might be able to lend you a hand."

The Kid shook his head. "I appreciate the offer, but you have enough on your plate right here. How's that injured woman doing, by the way?"

"She died early this morning. Elam's man will be charged with murder. I don't doubt that he'll wind up dancing at the end of a hangrope."

"Sounds like the best place for him," The Kid said.

"I already wired the sheriff over in the county seat. He's on his way here with some deputies to pick up the prisoner. I'll have Barnes off my hands before the end of the day, and that's just fine with me."

"Maybe we should stay here to lend *you* a hand, in case you need it."

"You mean if all of Elam's men ride back here to bust him out?" Fisher smiled and shook his head. "It was different while the girl was still alive.

Elam was willing to risk trying to get him out then. Now that it's murder, he won't try it. He's got a thin shred of respectability left in Powderhorn, and he'd like to hang on to it. He won't risk turning outlaw all the way for scum like Barnes."

"You're sure of that?"

"Sure enough." The marshal gave a humorless chuckle. "I'll say one thing, though. Court Elam's going to be in a mighty bad mood by the time you and your friend get to Powderhorn."

"We'll have to risk it. Maybe we won't have any run-ins with his men. We're just going to Mrs. Shanley's orphanage. No reason for us to get involved in anything else."

"Hope it works out for you. Good luck," Fisher added as he left the room.

Less than ten minutes later, The Kid rode out of Abilene, leading the pack mule, with Arturo following in the buckboard. The main trail was easy to follow. Even if it hadn't been, the railroad tracks lay a couple hundred yards to the south, with the telegraph poles running along beside them.

They probably wouldn't be able to cover the whole thirty miles to Powderhorn in one day, The Kid knew, but they would put enough distance behind them that they could reach the settlement the next day without any trouble.

Arturo had packed a lunch from a place back in Abilene called the Sunrise Café. They stopped to eat and rest the horses early in the afternoon, when they were only a few miles from town, then resumed the trip. A short time later, The Kid spotted some dust ahead of them. A cloud of it boiled up and moved toward them.

"Riders coming, and they're in a hurry," he called to Arturo as he held up his hand in a signal to stop. "Must be half a dozen or more horses, to be kicking up that much dust."

"Who do you think they are, and why are they in such a hurry?"

"I'm not sure, but let's get off the trail." The Kid pointed to a clump of scrubby cottonwood trees about a hundred yards to the north. Arturo turned the team and got the buckboard rolling in that direction.

The Kid hung back and watched the dust approach. When he could see some black shapes at the base of the cloud, he turned the black and galloped over to the trees.

The cottonwoods didn't provide all that much cover. If the riders had been paying any attention, they might have spotted the two men, the horses, the mule, and the buckboard, but they were racing hellbent-for-leather toward Abilene and didn't appear to even glance toward the trees.

By the time they went past, The Kid had pulled a pair of field glasses from his saddlebags and was watching them. He recognized three of them from the previous evening in Marshal Fisher's office: the longhaired youngster, the derby-wearing old-timer, and a pale-faced gunnie with jet-black hair, the one member of the group who hadn't said anything the night before.

The only one missing was the hombre with the big nose and the drooping mustache. Fisher had told The Kid that his name was Jim Mundy, and that Mundy had a reputation of sorts as a gun-slinger and killer. The old coot was Riggs, the flat-eyed youngster Chet, and the pale gunman Stevenson.

The Kid lowered the glasses. He could think of only one reason why some of Court Elam's men would be on their way to Abilene in such a hurry. They had heard about the soiled dove dying and knew the sheriff was on his way to pick up Barnes and take him back to the lockup in the county seat. It looked like some of Elam's men weren't prepared to abandon Barnes to that fate, no matter what their boss said. Mundy hadn't come along, but his place had been taken by three more gun-wolves.

"You look troubled, Kid," Arturo said.

The Kid nodded toward the trail. "Those were some of the men who shot up the marshal's office last night. I think they're on their way to Abilene to bust their friend out of jail."

"It's not your responsibility to prevent that."

The Kid rubbed his jaw. "I know. And my kids could be less than thirty miles away, right this very minute." He grimaced. "But Fisher's a good man, and he tried to help us."

"Only after you helped him," Arturo pointed out.

"That wouldn't have made any difference." The Kid said with certainty.

He reached a decision. "I'm going back. It's not that far to town. You can wait for me here. There's some shade, and I shouldn't be gone long."

"Unless you're fatally injured, of course."

"In that case, don't wait."

"Kid, perhaps I should come along—"

"You're good at a lot of things, Arturo," The Kid said with a smile, "but this is my kind of work."

With that, he heeled the black into a run and took off after the hardcases who were pounding toward Abilene.

Chapter 24

By the time The Kid came in sight of the town, he heard the faint popping of gunfire. Elam's men hadn't wasted any time, he thought grimly. They had just ridden in and started shooting.

He figured Marshal Fisher had to be alive since the battle was still going on. If the lawman had been able to fort up in the sturdy stone building that housed his office and the jail, he would be able to hold off Elam's hired killers for a while.

As long as the shooting went on, the innocent citizens of Abilene would also be in danger.

The Kid knew better than to go charging in without scouting out the situation first. Being careless was a quick way of getting killed. He pulled his Winchester from the saddle boot and reined the black to a stop on the edge of town. Dropping to the ground, he ran around one of the buildings and started up the alley that ran behind the businesses. He could tell from the steady blasting of guns when he was getting close to the ruckus.

He moved up the side of a hardware store until he reached the front corner of the building. Venturing a glance into the street, he saw that he was diagonally across from the marshal's office. Guns roared to his right. The Kid looked that way and saw four men firing at the office. One of them was stretched out behind a water trough, Stevenson crouched behind a barrel on the porch of the general store, and the old-timer Riggs and another man had taken cover behind a wagon parked in front of the store. The Kid didn't see the longhaired youngster Chet or the other man who had been in the group riding toward Abilene.

The whereabouts of Chet and the other man worried The Kid. He had a hunch they were up to no good somewhere close by.

Return fire came from one of the windows in the marshal's office. The shutters were closed except for a narrow gap that allowed Fisher to thrust the barrel of his rifle through it. Eventually Riggs and the others might do enough damage to the shutters with their heavy, continuous fire that the shutters wouldn't stop their bullets anymore. Likewise, Fisher might be able to pick off attackers even though they were behind cover, if he had long enough to work at it.

For the moment, it was a standoff. The Kid was glad to see the boardwalks along both sides of the street were deserted. The citizens had scrambled to get out of sight as soon as the shooting started. Maybe no innocent bystanders would be hurt.

None of the gunmen had spotted The Kid. He was going to take them by surprise, he thought as he lifted his Winchester. He could down a couple before they realized what was going on, and then he would take his chances with the other two.

But before he could fire, he spotted movement on top of the jail. The building had a flat roof with a low stone wall around it. The Kid saw the heads of two men moving around behind that wall.

Chet and the other man, The Kid realized as the men rose up on their knees. He recognized the longhaired killer without any trouble. They were fumbling with something between them, and as sparks suddenly flew, The Kid figured out Chet had lit the fuse attached to a small bundle of dynamite being held by the other man. The hard-case put a hand on top of the wall and leaned out. He was going to drop the dynamite right in front of the window where Fisher was shooting at the men across the street.

Without thinking, The Kid snapped the rifle to his shoulder and fired. The slug smashed through the shoulder of the man with the dynamite and threw him backward. The red, paper-wrapped cylinders of explosive flew high in the air as they slipped from his fingers, then dropped back toward the roof.

Chet let out a terrified yell and leaped off the top of the building. He might break a leg in the fall, but at least he wouldn't get blown to smithereens.

It wasn't working out exactly like The Kid had hoped. He yelled to the marshal, "Fisher, get out of there!" as he swung the rifle toward the other killers and worked the lever. It was no longer a matter of surprise since his first shot had warned them that he was there.

Riggs and the other man behind the wagon swung about and opened fire on him. The Kid ducked around the corner as flame spurted from their gun muzzles and bullets began to whip past his head.

Across the street, Chet scrambled to his feet and ran away from the marshal's office, limping heavily. Obviously he hadn't broken his leg when he landed. He hadn't made it very far when the dynamite exploded on top of the building.

The blast was powerful enough to shake the ground under The Kid's boots. The force of it sprayed chunks of rock through the air and picked Chet up, tossing him forward like a rag doll. Debris carried far enough to pelt the buildings across the street, forcing Riggs and his pals to stop shooting for the moment and duck for cover. A cloud of dust and smoke billowed up, obscuring The Kid's view of the marshal's office.

He was sure he hadn't seen Fisher come out of there before the blast.

The Kid recovered his wits and stepped out of the alley with the rifle ready in his hands. Stevenson, who still knelt behind the barrel on the porch, jerked his rifle toward him. The Kid's Winchester cracked first, the slug drilling into Stevenson's chest and knocking him on his ass.

The Kid shifted his aim toward the wagon. Riggs had fallen down, but the other man was still on his feet. He got a shot off, the bullet chewing splinters from the wall near The Kid's head. The

Kid's rifle blasted again. The man doubled over as the bullet slammed into his belly and tore through his gut.

The next instant, The Kid's Winchester was ripped out of his hands as a bullet from the man on the ground behind the water trough smashed into the breech. Pain shot up The Kid's arms as his hands went numb. He dived to the ground at the mouth of the alley. Another bullet went over his head, then another. Riggs had climbed to his knees and was back in the fight with a revolver he had yanked from the holster on his hip.

The Kid tried to force his stunned nerves and muscles to work, but he couldn't draw his Colt. It would only be a matter of seconds before Riggs and the other man filled him full of lead.

Marshal Fisher came out of the cloud of smoke and dust that still clogged the street. He was hatless and blood streaked his face, but he was alive and had a revolver in his hand. "Hey!" he shouted, causing Riggs and the other killer to turn toward him. Flame geysered from the muzzles of all the guns as the three men opened fire.

Riggs stumbled and clutched at his chest. Crimson welled between his fingers. He fell to his knees, then pitched forward onto his face. The other man's head jerked as one of Fisher's slugs exploded through it. He dropped his gun and rolled onto his side as he died.

Fisher didn't seem to be hurt any worse than he already was when he emerged from the smoke. Slowly, he lowered his gun.

Enough feeling had returned to The Kid's right

arm and hand that he was able to reach down and draw his Colt. He pointed it in Fisher's direction and pulled the trigger. Fisher jumped in surprise as the bullet sang past his head.

The slug thudded into flesh behind him, and he turned his head in time to see Chet collapse with a bright flower of blood blooming on the chest of his shirt. He smacked face-first into the dirt as his gun fell out of his hand.

Fisher looked at The Kid, nodded, and said into the sudden, echoing silence, "Obliged."

"Same here," The Kid said with a nod toward Riggs and the other man Fisher had shot.

That was all either man needed to say.

The Kid climbed wearily to his feet. He grimaced as he looked down at his Winchester lying in the dirt and saw that the rifle was ruined. He'd buy another one, of course, before he rejoined Arturo and proceeded on to Powderhorn. But the battle with Elam's men might have complicated the whole thing, he thought.

He walked over to Fisher. "How bad are you hurt?"

"Not enough to worry about," the lawman replied with a shake of his head. "A few nicks and bruises, that's all. I was damned lucky. I got blown out on top of the front wall."

The Kid looked at the marshal's office. The smoke had cleared enough for him to see some of the damage the explosion had done to the building. Most of the front wall had collapsed, and so had some of the roof. The other walls were still standing.

"What about your prisoner?"

"I don't know," Fisher said. "Reckon I'd better go see, as soon as we make sure all the rest of these varmints are dead."

That didn't take long. None of the men had survived. The Kid figured there wouldn't be enough left of the man who'd been on the roof when the dynamite went off to bury.

Guns in hand, the two men approached the ruined jail. They picked their way through the rubble of rocks and splintered roof beams until they reached the cell block. The roof had come down on top of the cell where the prisoner was being held. The Kid could see an arm and a leg sticking out from under the rubble, along with a rapidly spreading pool of blood around the remains.

"Well, his friends saved him from the hangrope, anyway," The Kid said.

Now that the shooting was over, the people of Abilene began to emerge from their hiding places. A large group of them gathered in the street to gape at the destruction the dynamite had wreaked on the marshal's office and jail.

A wagon pulled up, and a black-suited man—the undertaker—climbed down. "Some of you fellas help me load these bodies." He and some volunteers began lifting the dead gunmen into the back of the wagon.

The Kid and Marshal Fisher climbed out of the rubble. Nodding toward the gash on the lawman's forehead, The Kid suggested, "You'd better have a doctor stitch that up."

Fisher dabbed at the sticky blood with his fingertips. "I suppose you're right. Come along with me?"

"Sure," The Kid replied with a shrug. The two of them walked along the street. The air still smelled of dust and gunsmoke.

"What made you come back?" Fisher asked. "I thought you were on your way to Powderhorn with your friend."

"I was. But we spotted those riders coming and my gut told me to get off the trail. When they rode past I recognized some of the men who were here last night. Figured they were bound for trouble and thought you might be able to use a little help."

"That's for damned sure. I didn't see Jim Mundy among them."

"He didn't come along. I thought you figured Elam wouldn't try to get his man free, now that the charge was murder."

"Mundy not being here proves that," Fisher replied. "Riggs and Chet were a pair of hotheads, a lot alike even though there were probably forty years between them. Elam likely said to let it alone, but they couldn't swallow that. Barnes was their friend. So they decided to bust Barnes out anyway and talked some more of Elam's men into coming with them."

"That was a mistake on their part."

Fisher grunted. "The last one they'll make."

They had reached the trim little house where the local doctor's practice was located. The medico was young but seemed quite competent. He cleaned and sewed up the gash on the marshal's forehead, then wrapped a bandage around Fisher's head.

As they left the doctor's office, The Kid asked, "What'll you do for a jail now?"

"Don't worry, I'll find some place to lock up prisoners if I need to. There are some pretty sturdy smokehouses around here. I'll salvage what I can from the office and move into the town hall until we can fix the place."

"Rebuild it, you mean. I think Chet and the other man on the roof underestimated the amount of damage that dynamite was going to do. They were going to drop it right down in front of the window where you were returning the fire of the others and blow a hole in the front wall."

"Yeah, that would've blown me up, too," Fisher said. "How come it went off on top of the building instead?"

"I shot the man holding it and knocked him backward." The Kid didn't see any point in lying about it. "The dynamite flew up in the air and came back down on the roof, and since the fuse was already burning . . ."

He didn't have to finish the sentence. Anybody with eyes could see the devastation that had happened next.

"Well, I'm even more obliged to you than I knew," Fisher said. "You sure you don't want me to go to Powderhorn with you?"

"I'm sure. You'll have your hands full here, cleaning all this up and getting a new marshal's office and jail built. And you'll have to explain to the sheriff when he gets here that he rode all the way from the county seat for nothing. Justice has already been done."

Fisher chuckled wryly. "He won't be happy about that." He gripped The Kid's hand. "If you ever come through these parts again, stop and say hello. Maybe all hell won't break loose again."

"Maybe not."

But somehow The Kid doubted it.

Chapter 25

Arturo was still waiting in the clump of cotton-woods where The Kid had left him. When he rode up a short time later, Arturo put the rifle he'd been holding across his lap in the back of the buckboard. "I noticed what looked like quite a bit of smoke rising in the direction of Abilene a while ago. I suppose you were responsible for that, Kid?"

"Well, sort of," The Kid said with a smile. "But mainly it was the fault of the fella with the dynamite."

"Dynamite," Arturo repeated.

The Kid nodded. "Yeah. The one who blew up the jail."

"I see." Arturo paused. "Is Marshal Fisher all right?"

"Yeah, I got there in time to give him a hand. Those men of Elam's won't bother him anymore. Unfortunately, he no longer has a prisoner to turn over to the sheriff. The explosion sort of took care of that problem, too."

"Well, that simplifies matters for the marshal, I suppose. I take it we'll be continuing on to Powderhorn as planned?"

The Kid nodded. "That's right. Are you ready to go?"

Arturo lifted the reins. "Of course." But he didn't put the team into motion right away. "I was quite glad to see you ride up, sir. I would have gone on without you, but I was hoping that wouldn't be necessary."

"You'd have tried to find my kids on your own?"

"Certainly," Arturo answered without hesitation. "They're the children of Conrad Browning. They need to know that. They need to receive the legacy that would be coming to them."

A warm feeling filled The Kid's chest. He smiled, nodded. "I'm obliged to you for that, amigo."

"That's Spanish for friend, isn't it?"

"Yeah. It is."

When evening came, The Kid led the way about half a mile off the road before he found a good place to camp. He wasn't expecting trouble, but it never hurt to be careful about picking a place to spend the night.

In the morning they pushed on toward Powderhorn. They encountered several cowboys on horseback and a farming family in a run-down wagon. None of those pilgrims had represented any threat.

Around mid-morning, The Kid spotted travelers up ahead on the road, heading east toward Abilene.

He reined in and motioned for Arturo to stop as well. Something about the riders coming toward them struck The Kid as different. For one thing, there were half a dozen men on horses accompanying a black buggy. As the distance narrowed, The Kid saw that only one man sat in the buggy, handling the reins.

"Let's get out of their way, Arturo. Is that rifle of yours still handy?"

"I'll get it out of the back and put it on the floorboard," Arturo said as he lifted the reins and drove the wagon off the trail.

"Put it on the seat beside you where it's handy," The Kid advised. "Go ahead and lever a round into the chamber."

Arturo looked worried, but readied his rifle. The Kid moved his black saddle horse and the pack mule aside from the trail as well, tying the mule's reins to the back of the buckboard. Then he slid his Winchester from its sheath and laid it across the saddle in front of him.

By that time, the travelers were close enough The Kid recognized the hawklike nose and drooping mustache of Jim Mundy, the gunman who, according to Marshal Fisher, was Court Elam's *segundo.*

More than likely that made Elam the man in the buggy, The Kid thought.

The rest of the riders were typical hardcases—like the other members of Elam's gun crew The Kid had seen. He could make a guess why Elam and some of his men were on their way to Abilene.

As the group neared the spot where The Kid

and Arturo waited, Mundy scowled in recognition. He moved his horse closer to the buggy and said something to the driver. It came as no surprise to The Kid when the man hauled back on the reins and brought the vehicle to a halt. The riders reined in and arranged their horses three on each side of the buggy, with Mundy closest on the right.

The man in the buggy regarded The Kid with a cool stare. He was in his forties, The Kid judged, but already had iron-gray hair under his expensive brown Stetson. His brown tweed suit had cost plenty, as had the diamond stickpin in his cravat. He was lean in face and body, with watchful, deep-set eyes.

"You're the man called Morgan," he said as he looked at The Kid. It wasn't a question.

"That's right," The Kid said with a nod. "And you'd be Court Elam."

The man smiled thinly. "You've heard of me, I see."

"Heard plenty. None of it good."

Mundy's scowl darkened as he leaned forward slightly in his saddle. His hand moved an inch or so toward the butt of his gun.

Elam lifted a hand and motioned for Mundy to take it easy. It was a casual gesture, as if Elam knew it would be obeyed instantly and without hesitation.

"We're not looking for any trouble, Mr. Morgan," Elam said. "We're on a sad errand this morning. Some of my employees met an untimely end yesterday, as you well know. I'm on my way to Abilene to make the final arrangements for them."

The Kid grunted. "Fitting, since you sent them there to die."

Elam's narrow face hardened slightly. With a faint, solemn smile he said, "Just because a man's employees do something doesn't mean that he ordered them to do it. Sometimes they do exactly the opposite of what he might wish."

"Are you saying they came to Abilene on their own?" That was what Fisher believed had happened, The Kid reminded himself.

"That's right," Elam said. "Sometimes men will get carried away when a friend of theirs is in trouble and do something unwise."

"How'd you find out what happened?"

Still wearing that same shadow of a smile, Elam said, "Well, I'm not sure that it's any of your business . . . but Marshal Fisher notified me of the tragedy."

Fisher might do that, The Kid thought. Fisher might send a telegram to Elam in Powderhorn telling him to come get the bodies of his hired guns.

But Fisher probably wouldn't have gone into detail about The Kid's part in the events of the previous day. He suspected Elam had spies in Abilene, or at least friends who could have given him the whole story.

Tension was thick in the air. Mundy and the gunmen looked coldly at The Kid, and he knew they wanted to slap leather and blow him out of the saddle. Elam's presence was the only thing keeping them from doing exactly that.

Like all businessmen, honest and crooked alike,

he knew the secret of success was waiting for just the right moment to make his move. He also had sense enough to realize if lead started flying, he would be in the way of The Kid's first shots. "You and your friend appear to be bound for Powderhorn, Mr. Morgan. Is that the case?"

"It might be," The Kid allowed.

"If you're there for any amount of time, we'll probably run into each other again. I own a number of businesses in the settlement."

"Maybe so."

"Right now, though, we have to get on to Abilene. We have an unpleasant chore awaiting us." Elam inclined his head in a lazy nod. "So long." He flicked the reins against the back of the buggy horse.

The Kid didn't say anything as Elam got the vehicle moving again. He sat there stoically as the gunmen rode past, sending hostile looks his way. The Winchester stayed where it was on the saddle in front of him as the group from Powderhorn moved on.

"I was convinced they were going to kill us," Arturo said from the buckboard behind The Kid.

"They thought about trying. But Elam knew he'd be the first one to die if they did."

Arturo brought the buckboard up even with The Kid. "I'll never become accustomed to this, you know."

"You'd be surprised what a man can get used to when he doesn't have any other choice."

Arturo didn't argue the point as they continued on their way to Powderhorn. They didn't stop for lunch since The Kid thought they were getting pretty close to the settlement.

It was only a little after one o'clock in the afternoon when he spotted a church steeple up ahead, along with the roofs of several buildings and a smudge of green indicating the presence of trees—planted, watered, and cared for by humans, since the Kansas prairie was largely treeless.

As they drew closer, The Kid looked for a building big enough to be used as an orphanage, figuring such an institution would be located on the outskirts of town. He didn't see one.

The railroad tracks curved toward the settlement. A red brick depot building stood at the southern end of the main street, which ran due north for half a dozen blocks to a wooden bridge that spanned a creek. The stream's meandering path formed Powderhorn's northern boundary. The Kid had no idea how the town had gotten its name. He didn't see any physical features that reminded him of a powderhorn.

The trail turned into a road that ran along the front of the depot. Main Street dead-ended into it on The Kid's right as he and Arturo approached the station.

Even before they turned onto Main Street, The Kid saw a warehouse on the far corner. A sign with ELAM FREIGHT COMPANY painted on it hung on the front of the building. On the other side of the warehouse was a large barn and corral. The sign on it read ELAM FREIGHT LINES.

The Kid supposed Elam had merchandise shipped in by train, stored it in the warehouse belonging to Elam Freight Company, and delivered it in wagons belonging to the Elam Freight Lines to settlements that weren't on the railroad line. That was a handy arrangement.

It didn't end there, however. The Kid and Arturo also passed Elam's Livery Stable, Elam's General Mercantile Store, and Elam's Prairie Belle Saloon. Across the street stood the Elam Hotel.

The Kid was getting good and sick of that name.

"Mr. Elam certainly wasn't exaggerating, was he?" Arturo said. "How do you Americans put it? He appears to own half the town."

"At least," The Kid said.

He saw a building on the left with the words MARSHAL'S OFFICE on a sign that hung from the wooden awning over the boardwalk, and couldn't help but wonder if the man who occupied that office was Elam's Marshal. He would be surprised if it didn't turn out to be the case.

Deciding to start his search there, he angled toward the hitch rail in front of the lawman's office, and Arturo followed.

The Kid swung down from the saddle and looped the black's reins around the rail. "You might as well stay here until I find out something," he told Arturo. "No need for you to climb up and down if you don't have to."

"Very well." Arturo took off his hat and pulled a handkerchief from his pocket to pat beads of sweat off his forehead while The Kid went to the door of the marshal's office. The door was locked, he discovered when he tried the knob, and no one responded to his knocks on it.

A stocky man ambling along the boardwalk stopped to watch him for a moment before asking, "You lookin' for the marshal, mister?"

The Kid suppressed a surge of irritation. It was obvious what he was doing, he thought. "That's right. Do you know where he is?"

"Sure do."

The man didn't volunteer any more information, so once again The Kid had to hold his temper. "Can you tell me where to find him?"

"Yep." For a second, The Kid thought the local was going to force him to ask again, but then the man went on. "You see the church up at the end of town, on the other side of the street?"

"I see it," The Kid said.

"Go on around back and you'll find the cemetery. That's where the marshal is. Just look for the tombstone that has HERE LIES A DAMN FOOL carved on it."

Chapter 26

The townsman appeared to be completely serious. He was short and thick and had a close-cropped gray beard. His clothes were stained and had a definite odor of manure about them, which told The Kid the man probably worked in the livery stable.

"You mean the marshal is dead?"

"That's right."

"What happened to him? And I don't mean the business about him being a damn fool."

The man shrugged. "He took his job too serious-like. Tried to keep the peace one night when he should've just let it go. He knew good and well the law only gets enforced a certain way around here, or at least he should have."

"And Court Elam decides what way that is," The Kid guessed. "Who killed the marshal, Jim Mundy or another of Elam's gun-wolves?"

"Mister, I don't know you, and I've said all I'm gonna say. Probably more than I should have."

The Kid noticed that Powderhorn didn't appear to be a very busy place. Only a few people were on the boardwalks, and just a handful of horses were tied up at the hitch rails. "Is everybody taking a siesta? Or do Elam and his men have folks so scared they won't come out of their homes and businesses unless they have to?"

The man shook his head. "Like I told you, I ain't sayin' anything else. I got to get back to work."

"At the Elam Livery Stable?"

The man had started to brush past The Kid but he stopped and frowned. "A man's got to eat, and so does the rest of his family. You can work for somebody without agreein' with everything he does. If it wasn't you holdin' down that job, it'd be somebody else."

"That's a convenient way to think," The Kid said, not bothering to keep the scorn out of his voice.

The man's already florid face flushed a deeper shade of red. Instead of angry words, though, he said quietly, "You ain't from around here, mister. You don't know how it is."

"You can answer one more question for me."

"I told you—"

"Where can I find Mrs. Shanley's orphanage?" The Kid's words cut through the local's protest.

The man looked surprised by the question. His eyes widened for a second, then narrowed in suspicion. "Why do you want to know? You and your friend in the buggy there don't look like orphans to me."

"As a matter of fact, both of my parents *are*

deceased," Arturo said. "But it happened a long time ago, so I don't really think of myself as an orphan."

"And my father's still alive," The Kid said. *As far as I know*, he added to himself. As perilous a life as Frank Morgan led, he supposed he couldn't make that assumption.

The liveryman said, "I don't really care. I don't mix in things that don't concern me, and that Shanley woman and her blamed orphans are one of 'em."

With a hostile glare, he walked off down the street toward the stable.

"Well, he was certainly an unhelpful fellow," Arturo said.

"Not completely. He told us more about how things are around here. Not very good, from the sound of it. Elam and his men have this town treed."

"By that you mean everyone is afraid of them?"

"Yeah." The Kid looked up the street and rubbed his chin. "I'm curious why he didn't want to say anything about the orphanage. That doesn't seem like something that would get anybody in trouble."

He untied the black's reins but didn't mount up, leading the gelding up the street.

Arturo brought the buckboard alongside him. "Where are we going, Kid?"

"To see somebody who maybe won't mind telling us about the orphanage."

The Kid angled across the street toward the church. It was a whitewashed frame building with a square bell tower that had a tall wooden steeple on top. As he looked along the side of the building he saw the fenced graveyard behind it. A few small cottonwood trees provided shade where the citizens of Powderhorn who had passed on had been laid to rest.

It put him in mind of another cemetery, located in a small town in New Mexico. As The Kid's mouth tightened into a grim line, he put those thoughts out of his mind. It wouldn't do to think too much about the woman who was buried there, even though he would never forget her, or the happiness she had brought him.

Or the scars her murder had seared into his soul.

As The Kid tied the black's reins to the buckboard Arturo asked, "Shall I come with you, sir?"

"That'll be fine."

They stepped into the church and walked through a small foyer into the sanctuary. It was cooler inside, out of the sun. "Hello?" The Kid called. The word echoed back from the stained-glass windows and the high ceiling.

"Up here," a voice said from behind and above them.

The Kid turned and looked into the foyer where a narrow door stood open a few inches. He opened it more and saw a ladder propped inside the tiny room. Light spilled through an open trapdoor at the top of the ladder. It led up into the bell tower, The Kid thought.

"Wait there and I'll be right down," the same voice said. A moment later, a man's shape blocked off the light coming through the trapdoor. He started climbing down the ladder.

When he reached the bottom he stepped off and brushed his hands together. "I was working on the bell," he explained with a smile. "On the rope, actually. It was getting rather frayed. Wouldn't do to have it snap some Sunday morning while I'm ringing the bell to summon the faithful to services."

"No, I suppose not," The Kid said. "Are you the pastor here?"

The man nodded. "That's right." He was young, no more than twenty-five, with a friendly, slightly rounded face and brown hair. He wore a pair of corduroy trousers and a work shirt with the sleeves rolled up over his forearms. "Thomas Kellogg."

"Pleased to meet you, Reverend."

The minister shook his head. "Please, no reverend. Just Tom is fine, or Brother Tom if you insist. I saw you gentlemen ride into town." With a grin he pointed a thumb up at the steeple. "There's a good view from up there, you know. In a land as flat as this, you can see a long way from any sort of elevation."

"I'm sure you can," The Kid said. "We were hoping you could tell us where to find a lady named Shanley."

"Mrs. Shanley who runs the orphanage?" Instantly, the amiable expression disappeared from Kellogg's face and his eyes and tone became guarded. "Why do you want to know?"

"I need to ask her about something."

"And who are you, exactly?"

The Kid kept a tight rein on his impatience. "They call me Kid Morgan." That was the literal truth. He didn't want to lie to a man of God.

Kellogg surprised him by asking, "Not *the* Kid Morgan? The one in the dime novels?"

The Kid had heard the old saying about life imitating art. In his case, it was more complicated than that. When he had decided to let everyone believe for a while that Conrad Browning was dead, he had hidden his true identity behind a new name. In choosing that name, he had considered the fact that authors working for publishing companies back east had written dime novels about his father, Frank Morgan. From there it had been a natural leap to calling himself Kid Morgan. Very few people actually knew that Frank was his father, so he didn't think the name would give him away.

However, he had never expected that he would become well-known enough, quickly enough, to inspire dime novels about *him*. Evidently those lurid, yellow-backed novels had an avid readership that was always hungry for more heroes, more adventure. The Kid had seen a few of the Kid Morgan books and been baffled and amused by them.

Seeing his reaction, Kellogg hurried on, "Oh, I know, a preacher's not really supposed to read such things. But they're so exciting, and from time to time they teach good moral lessons. I mean, good always triumphs over evil in the end, doesn't it?"

"In dime novels, maybe," The Kid said, again trying not to think about Rebel.

"Well, it's really an honor to meet you," Kellogg said as he shook hands with The Kid. Then he grew more serious. "But I'd still like to know what your business is with Theresa. I mean, Mrs. Shanley."

If he was going to trust anybody, The Kid told himself, it ought to be a preacher. "I'm looking for some children."

"She has quite a few." Kellogg frowned. "Although I'm not sure that a man such as yourself . . . I mean, a man with no permanent place of residence . . . I mean . . ." The minister was starting to look really flustered.

"You mean a drifting gunfighter is not really the sort of man you'd think would want to adopt an orphan?"

Kellogg nodded. "No offense intended, but yes, that thought did cross my mind."

"I'm not planning to adopt. I'm looking for two children, a boy and a girl. Twins. Between three and four years old."

"Again, in all good conscience, I have to pry into something that may not be any of my business—"

"It's not," The Kid cut in. "But I'll tell you anyway. I don't have to adopt those children. They're already mine. I'm their father."

For a long moment, Kellogg didn't say anything. Finally, he asked, "Where is the mother?"

"Dead," The Kid said. "Do you know if Mrs. Shanley has them?"

Kellogg waved a hand. "I've only been the pastor here for a year and a half, Mr. Morgan. Before that I was in Springfield, Missouri. There are several children of that age in Mrs. Shanley's care, but I don't know how they came to be with her or if any of them are brother and sister. I can tell you that I never noticed any twins among them."

"Fraternal twins don't always look that much alike," The Kid pointed out.

"Oh, so they're fraternal twins?"

The Kid took a deep breath. "I don't know." It bothered him to admit that.

It bothered Kellogg, too. "You expect me to believe these children belong to you, and you don't even know if they're identical twins?"

"It's a long story," The Kid snapped. "Are you going to tell me where to find the orphanage or not?"

Kellogg didn't answer the question directly. "You know, when I first saw the two of you come into town, I thought maybe you were some more of Mr. Elam's men."

Arturo said, "Do I look like a hired gunman to you, sir?"

Kellogg shrugged. "I'll admit, you don't. Who are you?"

"I work for The Kid here. I'm his batman, as the British call it." When Kellogg looked baffled by that answer, Arturo added, "His valet, assistant. Call it what you will."

That just confused the minister more. "A gunfighter's got a valet?"

The Kid tried not to get too exasperated. "Another long story. Please, Reverend . . . I mean, Brother Tom. The children I'm looking for may not be with Mrs. Shanley, but I have to be sure. Just tell me where to find her place, if you will."

"I'll do better than that," Kellogg said with an abrupt nod, as if he had made up his mind about something. "I'll take you there."

"I'd be obliged for your help."

"If I can help reunite a father with some lost children, well, that's just one more way of doing the Lord's work, as I see it."

"Nobody's going to argue with you there," The Kid said.

"It's an easy walk," Kellogg said as he led them out of the church. "Up here and around the corner on Fifth Street."

The houses of Powderhorn's citizens were on the cross streets. Kellogg took them to one that rose three stories, with a gabled roof and trees growing around it. It would have been a stern, forbidding-looking place without the flower beds in front of it and the bright curtains in the windows. On his way into town, The Kid had been looking for some ugly, institutional-appearing building, probably of stone or brick. He wouldn't have picked out that place as an orphanage. It looked more like the private home of a well-to-do businessman.

"Mrs. Shanley and her husband were some of the original settlers in Powderhorn," Tom Kellogg explained as he, The Kid, and Arturo went through a gate in the whitewashed picket fence around the front yard. "He had something to do with the railroad, and he also established a very successful store here. But then a fever came through the area, he caught it, and passed away. So did the Shanleys' children. Since Mrs. Shanley was left alone, she took in the children of the families where both parents had died of the fever. That's how the orphanage got started. At least, that's the way I've heard the story. I didn't live here then, you know. But I have no reason to doubt that it's true."

Neither did The Kid. He felt his heart pounding harder as the three of them went up the walk to the front porch. His son and daughter could be in there, only a few yards away from him.

"I'm surprised the kids aren't out playing," he commented, more to have something to say than anything else.

"The younger ones are napping, the older ones are studying. Theresa insists on a good education."

Kellogg knocked on the door frame. A moment passed, and then the door swung open.

The fact that Kellogg had a habit of referring to Mrs. Shanley by her given name should have warned him, The Kid thought, and so should have the preacher's comment about her own children dying of the fever.

But in his anxiousness to find out if his kids were there, he hadn't considered those things, and so he was surprised to see that the woman standing in the doorway with a smile on her face was a beautiful blonde who couldn't be any more than thirty years old.

Chapter 27

"Hello, Tom," the woman said to Kellogg. "What brings you here?" She looked past him at The Kid and Arturo. "And who are your friends?"

"This is Mr. Morgan and his . . . helper," Kellogg introduced them. He added to Arturo, "I'm afraid I didn't catch your name."

Arturo swept his hat off and stepped forward to take hold of Theresa Shanley's hand. "Arturo Vincenzo, madame," he told her as he bowed. He pressed his lips to the back of her hand. "At your service."

Theresa looked a little surprised, as anybody would have under the circumstances. "I'm pleased to meet you, Mister . . . ah, Vincenzo, was it?"

The Kid took his hat off and suppressed the impulse to toss Arturo aside. Fortunately, Arturo didn't linger over his hand kissing. As he stepped back, The Kid moved forward and said, "Ma'am, we're looking for a couple of children who may have been left here in your care a few years ago."

Theresa's voice was a little cool and wary as she asked, "What's your relation to these children, Mr. Morgan?"

"They're my—the Kid's voice caught a little—"they're my son and daughter."

"I only have children here who have been or-phaned."

"That's just it. The woman who brought them here would have told you some sort of story to ex-plain why she had to leave them with you. She probably told you that their parents were dead."

"Why would she have done a thing like that?" Theresa wanted to know.

Tom Kellogg said, "It's probably a long story."

The Kid nodded. "It is."

"So why don't we go inside?" Kellogg suggested.

"Of course," Theresa said. "Where are my man-ners? Come in, please."

She stepped back and ushered them into the house. They went into a comfortably furnished parlor.

"Would you like some coffee or lemonade?"

Kellogg smiled. "Lemonade would be nice. I've been replacing that worn-out bell rope in the steeple this afternoon. It was thirsty work."

"Sit down, gentlemen. I'll be right back."

Though he was trying hard not to show it, The Kid's emotions were running wild inside him. After all the danger and worry, he might be on the verge of reclaiming his children. Or rather, claiming them for the first time, he told himself, because he had never seen them before. It was a thrilling moment and a frightening one, all at the same time.

He and Arturo sat down in armchairs while Kellogg took a seat on a sofa. While Theresa was gone, the minister said, "Something just occurred to me, Mr. Morgan. If the children *are* here . . . how are you going to prove that they're yours?"

The Kid drew in a sharp breath. "What do you mean?"

"Well . . . do you have any sort of records, any documents that prove you're the children's father?"

The Kid's heart slugged in his chest. He had never thought about that. He had been so consumed with finding the twins, with the search itself, the idea of proof hadn't entered his mind. He couldn't come up with any words to say.

"We have a letter from the mother of the children," Arturo spoke up. "It explains why she set out to conceal from Mr. Morgan not just the location of the children, but also their very existence."

Kellogg held up a hand to stop him. "You might as well wait until Theresa gets back. Then you'll only have to go through the story once."

"That's a good idea." The brief delay would give The Kid a chance to get his thoughts in order.

Theresa returned a few minutes later with a tray and glasses of lemonade. The drink was considerably better than what he had had at the house of Ralph and Sara Beth Potter, The Kid discovered as he sipped the cool, sweet yet tart liquid.

"Mr. Morgan is going to explain the situation,"

Kellogg told Theresa as she sat down at the other end of the sofa from him.

She nodded. "I'm eager to hear that explanation." Caution, even outright suspicion, was still plain to see on her face.

The Kid took a deep breath. "Several years ago, I was engaged to a woman named Pamela Tarleton. Our engagement ended before we were married. What I didn't know at the time was that she was already . . . with child." He glanced at Kellogg. "Sorry, Reverend. I mean Brother Tom."

Kellogg waved a hand. "I'm not here to judge, Mr. Morgan, just to listen."

"Well, I found out recently that Pamela—Miss Tarleton—gave birth to a son and daughter. Twins."

"You never knew about this?" Theresa asked.

The Kid shook his head. "Not until a few weeks ago. I got a letter that she had left behind with a relative. She was upset with me, blamed me not only for ending our engagement but for the death of her father as well."

"Did you have anything to do with that?"

"No, ma'am, I did not. But that didn't stop Pamela from being angry with me. She deliberately withheld the news of the twins' birth from me, and she informed me in the letter that she had hidden them away where I would never find them."

"That's terrible," Kellogg murmured.

"I thought so," The Kid agreed.

Theresa asked, "What did you do when you found out about this, Mr. Morgan?"

"Naturally, I set out to find the children. I tracked

Pamela, the children, and a servant to a train bound for San Francisco. It seems like she might have stopped somewhere along the way and left the children in a place she thought they wouldn't be found. So Arturo and I are having a look around in every likely settlement we come to."

"So when you heard there was an orphanage in Powderhorn . . . ?"

"What better place to hide a couple of kids," The Kid finished for Theresa.

"I take it that Miss Tarleton has dropped out of sight, too, so you can't just ask her? I would think a court might compel her to talk."

The Kid shook his head. "She's dead," he said flatly. He didn't offer any explanations for that.

"I see." Theresa regarded him solemnly. "Mr. Morgan, you have my sympathy. I'm sure it was quite a shock for you to find out that you're a father, and I can understand why you want to locate your children. But I'm afraid I can't help you."

"Are you sure you don't remember?" The Kid said. "It would have been about three years ago—"

"There are no twins here. I'm certain," Theresa said in a firm voice. "You see, I keep good records. I know where each of the children living here came from, and I assure you, no woman got off the train and dropped off a couple of infants."

The Kid felt a surge of anger and frustration. He had convinced himself that he might be close to the end of his quest. "No offense, Mrs. Shanley, but would you mind if I took a look at the children? I'd like to see for myself—"

"What would you like to see, Mr. Morgan? That none of them the right age bear a resemblance to you or your late fiancée?" Theresa's voice was sharp with some anger of her own. "Why would I lie to you about such a thing?"

"Pamela Tarleton had a lot of money." The Kid's words were hard and blunt. "In tracking her movements, we've run into several people that she paid off to do what she wanted."

"I'm not one of them, and I resent the implication that I am," Theresa snapped.

The Kid shrugged. "Like I said, I meant no offense. But I don't know you, ma'am. Taking care of a bunch of kids can't be easy, and it probably costs quite a bit, too."

Tom Kellogg leaned forward. "I *do* know Mrs. Shanley, Mr. Morgan, and I can promise you she's a truthful woman."

"Thanks, Tom, but I can defend myself." Theresa gave The Kid a cool, level stare. "My husband left me fairly comfortable as far as money is concerned, and the members of Tom's church have been very generous with both time and money to help me out. There haven't been any problems until—" She stopped short and didn't finish.

The Kid took note of that. "Until when? Until Pamela showed up?"

"I told you, I never met the woman. And any problems I may have are none of your business." She added with scathing scorn, "No offense meant."

"I'd still like to—"

She didn't let him finish. She stood up and said,

"This visit is over. Good day, sir. Tom, would you please show Mr. Morgan and Mr. Vincenzo out?"

Kellogg looked uncomfortable. In his profession, he was used to being a peacemaker, and he unwittingly had brought conflict into that house. But clearly, he was on Theresa's side in the dispute. He stood up. "Gentlemen, please."

The Kid and Arturo got to their feet as well. The Kid gave Theresa a nod. "I'm sorry, ma'am. It wasn't my intention to cause trouble. I just want to find my children."

"I understand that, but they're not here." She crossed her arms over her chest. Her face was firm and inflexible.

Kellogg ushered them out of the parlor to the front door. As they reached it, a sudden clatter of footsteps on the stairs made The Kid pause. He looked back and saw several youngsters coming downstairs. His heart took a leap as spotted a young boy and girl, each with dark hair like Pamela's. As they reached the bottom of the stairs they paused to look curiously at the strangers. The Kid didn't see any sign of either himself or Pamela in their features. He also could tell they were a little older than his twins would be. "Come on, Arturo," he muttered, trying not to let his disappointment get the better of him.

They went through the gate in the fence and onto the street. Tom Kellogg lingered behind them, talking to Theresa Shanley through the open front door.

Quietly, Arturo asked, "Do you believe the lady, Kid?"

"She certainly sounded and acted like she was telling the truth," he replied with a shrug. "I knew Futrelle was lying as soon as he opened his mouth. The question is, how much do I want to trust my instincts?"

"I agree. Mrs. Shanley doesn't strike me as the sort to be involved in anything nefarious. But it's difficult to be sure what money can persuade a person to do, isn't it?"

"That's the truth," The Kid said.

Behind them, Kellogg came through the gate and hurried after them. "Wait up, gentlemen," he called.

The Kid and Arturo stopped and let the minister catch up to them.

"I'm sorry things didn't work out as you'd hoped they would, Mr. Morgan. I promise you, though, Theresa—I mean Mrs. Shanley—wouldn't lie. She's the most honest woman I know." Kellogg paused. "Do you believe me?"

The Kid smiled thinly. "I'd be sort of risking my immortal soul to doubt the word of a preacher, wouldn't I?"

"Not at all. Preachers are as human as anybody else."

The yearning look he cast back toward Theresa Shanley's house was proof of that, The Kid thought. Kellogg was seriously smitten with the young widow. The Kid didn't know if she returned the minister's interest and frankly didn't care.

But he was curious about something. "What sort of trouble has she been having lately?"

Kellogg hesitated. "I don't know that it's my place to say anything . . ."

The Kid made a guess. "Something to do with Court Elam?"

Kellogg's eyes widened in surprise. "How in the world did you know that?"

"Arturo and I have had our own run-in with Elam and his men. I was involved in that dustup over in Abilene yesterday."

"You killed those men who went over there to break Barnes out of jail?" Kellogg sounded impressed and a little scared at the same time, as if it might be dangerous walking down the street with Kid Morgan.

Which was certainly true from time to time, The Kid reflected wryly.

"I gave Marshal Fisher a hand defending himself. Then this morning we ran into Elam, Jim Mundy, and some more of his men on the trail between here and Abilene. Nothing happened, but the conversation was a mite tense. When we got here to Powderhorn we saw Elam's name plastered on what looks like half the businesses in town. A man like that thinks he runs everything, and he doesn't like it when anybody stands up to him."

"That's certainly true of Courtland Elam," Kellogg said with a nod. "I try to think the best of everyone, but sometimes it's difficult. Very difficult."

The Kid hooked his thumbs in his belt as they walked toward the church. "Tell me about Elam."

"Well, I don't really know all that much. Like Mrs. Shanley, he was here when I came to Powderhorn. From what people tell me, he came here several years ago and bought out the freight company. Nobody knew that Ben Jeffords had any interest in selling out, and the rumor was that Elam forced him into it. Elam had Jim Mundy and several other men like that with him. More gunmen drifted into town . . . I don't think it was an accident . . . and Elam began buying up other businesses."

"Forcing the owners out in the process?"

"I'm told he paid fair prices. It was more a matter of taking over businesses the original owners didn't really want to get rid of. Then there was what happened to Jephtha Dickinson . . ."

They had reached the shade under the trees in front of the church. "Go on," The Kid said.

"It's not very Christian to repeat a lot of gossip."

"What happened to Dickinson?" The Kid asked.

Kellogg sighed. "He owned the livery stable and wouldn't sell out to Elam. Early one morning, when he was in the stable alone, a horse kicked him in the head and killed him."

"A horse kicked him . . . or one of Elam's men stove in his skull and made it look like a horse had done it?"

"I don't know." Kellogg shook his head. "People talked about that possibility, of course, but there was no way to prove it."

"Did anybody look into it? Do you have any law here?"

"Not really. Not since the marshal was killed."

"And what happened to him?"

"Shot from behind, from the mouth of an alley one night. No one saw who did it . . . but he'd ar-rested one of Elam's men for disturbing the peace that day. The man resisted, and the marshal had to knock him around pretty good."

"Jim Mundy strikes me as the back-shooting type," The Kid mused.

"Like I said, no one knows. There's been some talk about having the town council hire another marshal, but nothing has ever been done about it. By the way, Court Elam is the mayor and the head of the town council."

The Kid grunted in surprise. "Why would folks vote a man like that into office?"

Kellogg looked at him like that was a stupid question.

"Yeah, I suppose they were scared not to. So nothing was done about Dickinson's death?"

"No. His wife sold the stable to Elam not long after that."

"What about the store that Elam owns? Is it the same one that Mrs. Shanley's husband had before he died?"

"That's right," Kellogg said. "And before you jump to any conclusions, Mr. Morgan, there was nothing suspicious about his death. He and their children passed away because of a fever. So did a number of other people in town. For a while it looked like Powderhorn might dry up and blow away, as the old saying goes." The minister's mouth tightened. "I suppose if there's one good thing you can say about Elam, it's that he didn't allow that to happen. He kept the town in business, and eventually everyone got over the tragedy. As much as they could, anyway."

The Kid nodded slowly. "Probably that's one

more reason why Elam thinks Powderhorn is his and nobody can defy him. Sounds like a lot of businessmen. Maybe a little more heavy-handed than most. There's still the matter of Dickinson's death."

"Yes, but it hasn't stopped there," Kellogg said. "His men have gotten bolder, more brazen. They take what they want and run roughshod over anybody who gets in their way. Also, other men have started riding into town and then riding back out again as the lawlessness in these parts has increased. Trains have been held up, the bank down in Hutchinson was robbed, ranches have been raided and stock run off."

"Sounds to me like Elam's recruited a bunch of outlaws and is using this as the gang's headquarters," The Kid said.

"That's what people think, but again, there's no proof."

"It's a pretty sorry situation. But what does it have to do with Mrs. Shanley? Did he pressure her into selling the store she inherited from her husband?"

Kellogg shook his head. "No, she was more than willing to sell. She didn't want to run the place once her husband was gone, and I don't blame her. She was more interested in caring for the children she had taken in. The money Elam paid her allowed her to do that. Her problem with Elam is more . . . personal."

Kellogg fell silent, and after a moment The Kid prodded him, "Go on."

The minister drew in a deep breath and let it

out in a sigh. "Elam didn't want to just buy the store from Theresa. He wanted a merger."

"What do you mean?" The Kid asked, although he suddenly had a hunch that he knew.

"Elam wanted her to marry him . . . and he's never been a man who's willing to take no for an answer."

Chapter 28

The Kid's mouth tightened as he looked at Tom Kellogg. "Go on."

"There's not much else to tell," the minister said with a shrug. "Theresa refused his proposal, of course. Her husband and children had only been dead for about a month."

"And he asked her to *marry* him?" Arturo said. "How uncivilized."

"It's more like arrogance on Elam's part, I think. He's just so used to getting what he wants, he can't accept it when somebody says no to him. But I guess he saw that he'd overplayed his hand with Theresa, because he backed off for a while. Nearly a year, in fact. But then he started pressing her again to marry him. Of course, it wouldn't have mattered how long he waited. She was never going to marry a man like him."

"But he hasn't given up," The Kid guessed.

Kellogg shook his head. "No. He's asked her several more times. She always says no. But lately . . .

things have started to happen. Some of the older girls who live with her, the ones who are fifteen and sixteen, have been approached in town by Elam's men. Crudely approached," Kellogg added with a note of angry disapproval in his voice. "And one of the young men was beaten up. He says he didn't see who grabbed him, but I'm sure it was some of Elam's hired toughs. Then Elam cut off Theresa's credit at the store. As you can imagine, with more than a dozen children in the house, she needs plenty of food and other supplies. Money is tight at the moment. The members of the church help out as much as they can, but having Elam and his hired guns around here is starting to strangle the town."

It was a long speech, and Kellogg looked and sounded weary when he finished it.

The Kid nodded slowly as he took in what the minister had told him. "I suppose all these problems would go away if Mrs. Shanley agreed to marry Elam."

"He's never come right out and said so, as far as I know, but that's certainly the feeling Theresa got."

"That's a real shame, all right. Is there only the one hotel in town?"

The abrupt change of subject seemed to take Kellogg by surprise. "That's right. Just the Elam Hotel."

"I don't feel like putting any more money in the varmint's pockets. Are you up to camping out again tonight, Arturo?"

"Of course. I wouldn't feel comfortable in any hostelry owned by that man, either."

"You're moving on, then?" Kellogg asked.

"I've still got those children to find," The Kid said. "If they're not here, that means Pamela left them somewhere else."

"It's just that I thought . . . I mean, I hoped . . ." Kellogg stopped and shook his head. "Never mind. It doesn't matter what I thought. Of course you want to keep looking for your children. I understand."

The Kid put out his hand. "I appreciate all your help."

"Of course." Kellogg shook hands with The Kid in front of the church. "God bless you, Mr. Morgan."

The Kid untied his horse from behind the buckboard as Arturo climbed aboard. "The people who live here have themselves quite a predicament," Arturo commented.

"Yes, they do," The Kid agreed, as he swung up into the saddle.

"It's a shame there's no one around here who might be able to help them." Arturo turned the wagon down the street.

"Who do you think could do that?" The Kid asked as he rode next to the wagon. "Elam's got probably a dozen hired guns at his disposal, maybe even more if the preacher's right about those outlaws who have been plaguing these parts. One or two men wouldn't stand much of a chance against a gang like that, would they?"

"Perhaps not. But if the townspeople could be rallied to take action themselves, it might be different. What they need is someone to lead them."

The Kid looked narrowly at Arturo. "What are you trying to get us into?"

"Nothing. I was indulging in pure speculation, nothing more. After all, we have a task of our own to complete."

"That's right. A very important task." They had reached the edge of town. The Kid paused and looked back down the street. His eyes lingered on all the business that bore Court Elam's name. He studied the mostly empty boardwalks. He sensed the air of fear that gripped the town.

"Maybe somebody ought to do something," he said slowly. "And I've got an idea what it could be. First, though, let's go find a place to camp for the night."

He pretended not to see the look of satisfaction in Arturo's eyes.

They followed the creek that ran past the north end of the settlement for about a mile west of Powderhorn, then made camp in a grove of cottonwoods on the bank. The Kid didn't expect any trouble, but slept lightly anyway. It was a habit with him, the sort of habit that helped him stay alive.

The next morning, he and Arturo returned to town and went straight to the general store. As they walked in, The Kid saw the few customers casting suspicious glances in his direction. Maybe they took him for a new member of Elam's gun-crew, as Tom Kellogg had at first the day before.

A balding, middle-aged man in a white apron was behind the counter at the rear of the store.

"Something I can do for you, mister?" he asked as The Kid came up to him.

"I understand that Mrs. Theresa Shanley owes a bill here."

The clerk frowned. "Maybe she does, but I reckon that's between her and Mr. Elam."

"Not anymore. Tell me how much she owes."

"I don't know if I can do that." The clerk's frown had turned into a look of nervousness. Clearly, he didn't want to do anything that might get him on Elam's bad side.

"Then maybe you can tell me if the amount is more than a hundred dollars."

The clerk didn't want to admit even that much, but after a moment of enduring The Kid's flinty stare, he shrugged. "Yeah, she owes more than that."

"More than two hundred?"

Now that he had answered one question, he couldn't very well refuse to answer another. "No, it ain't that high yet."

The Kid nodded and said, "All right. Thank you." He took ten double eagles from his pocket and placed them on the counter in two stacks of five. "There's two hundred dollars. I want you to apply that to Mrs. Shanley's account. Any that's left over, you can carry on the books as credit."

He spoke loudly and clearly enough that the other customers in the store couldn't help but overhear him. He didn't want there to be any questions later on about what was happening.

"But . . . but, mister," the clerk said. "You can't pay off somebody else's account."

"Why not? There's no law against it. In fact"—
The Kid dug into his pocket again and added another stack of five double eagles to the gold pieces
already on the counter—"put another hundred
dollars of credit on the books for her as well. And
I want a receipt for all of it."

The clerk looked a little like he wanted to cry.
The Kid was sorry to be putting the man in a bad
position, but the sooner the word started getting
around town that things were about to change in
Powderhorn, the better.

"Go ahead," The Kid prodded. "I'll take that receipt now."

The clerk sighed and pulled a pad of paper to
him—one he probably used to jot down orders
that people gave him. Picking up a stub of pen-
cil he scrawled a receipt for the three hundred
dollars.

The Kid watched what the man was writing. "Be
sure to write on there that it goes on the account
of Mrs. Theresa Shanley," he reminded the clerk.

The man nodded as he added that information. He tore off the paper, slid it across the
counter to The Kid, and raked the gold pieces
into a drawer. "Are you satisfied now, mister?"

The Kid smiled as he tucked the receipt in his
shirt pocket. "Not really, but I'm getting started in
that direction."

He left the store with Arturo, who asked once
they were outside, "Where are we going now?"

The Kid tapped his pocket. "I want to give this
receipt to Mrs. Shanley."

"May I ask why you didn't just give her sufficient

funds to settle her account at the store? It seems like that would have been simpler."

"You saw her. She's a woman with a lot of pride. She'd have turned it down. She probably would have wanted to spit in my face while she was doing it . . . but I figure she's too much of a lady for that."

"Court Elam won't be happy when he finds out he no longer has that particular lever to use against Mrs. Shanley."

"Court Elam's happiness is just about the last thing in the world I'm worried about."

As The Kid and Arturo turned onto Fifth Street and started toward the big house that served as the orphanage, The Kid spotted a buggy and a couple of saddle horses tied up in front of the house. He frowned slightly as his pace picked up. He thought he recognized that buggy.

Arturo saw the vehicle, too. "Mrs. Shanley appears to have visitors. That looks like—"

"Yeah," The Kid snapped. "Elam's buggy."

They reached the gate in the picket fence. The Kid opened it and strode up the walk. He saw three men standing on the porch. The well dressed one was Court Elam, who was talking through the screen door to Theresa Shanley. The other two were Jim Mundy and another of Elam's gunwolves. They saw The Kid coming toward them and tensed. Their hands moved slightly closer to the revolvers holstered on their hips.

"Boss," Mundy said in a low, urgent voice.

Elam swung around with an irritated look on his narrow face. "What is it?" Then he stiffened, too, as he caught sight of The Kid and Arturo. "You two again." He didn't sound pleased.

"That's right." The Kid came to a stop at the bottom of the porch steps.

"What are you doing here?"

The Kid nodded toward the woman who stood behind the screen door with a worried look on her face. "We have business with Mrs. Shanley."

"I don't think so," Elam said. "I don't know what you're doing in Powderhorn, but I'm certain you don't have any business here, period."

"I don't see how you can be so sure about that."

Elam smiled coldly. "It's my town. If you don't have business with me, you might as well move along."

"I've already done all the business with you that I'm going to." The Kid slipped the piece of paper from his pocket and spoke past Elam. "Mrs. Shanley, your account at the general store is paid up, and you have a line of credit there again. Here's the receipt to prove it."

Theresa looked surprised. So did Elam, but his face darkened with fury. "What in blazes are you talking about?" he demanded.

The Kid started up the steps. "See for yourself."

Before he could reach Elam, Jim Mundy got in his way. "Back off, mister," the gunman warned. "I buried some friends yesterday, and you're to blame for some of 'em being dead."

"No, they're to blame for trying to break a murderer out of jail," The Kid shot back. "Get out of my way, Mundy."

"You know who I am?"

"That's right."

Mundy bared his teeth in a savage grin. "Then you must know I'm a dangerous man with a gun."

"Gentlemen!" Theresa's voice was sharp as she spoke through the screen. "Please. I can't have any gunplay on my front porch. For God's sake, there are children in this house!"

"Mrs. Shanley is right," Elam said. "Your gun stays in its holster, Jim, you understand that?"

Mundy understood it, but he didn't like it. Lifting his lip in a snarl, he said, "Sure, boss."

"But that doesn't mean you can't teach these two a lesson," Elam added.

"That's more like it," Mundy said.

Instantly, he shot a big fist straight at The Kid's head.

Chapter 29

Expecting something like that, The Kid was ready when Mundy struck. He pulled his head aside so the gunman's fist whipped past his ear. Reaching up to grab Mundy's arm it was easy to twist around, pull hard on the man's arm, and send him sailing off the porch. Arturo leaped out of the way as Mundy crashed on the ground, hard enough to knock the air out of his lungs and make him gasp for breath.

"Stop that!" Theresa cried. "Stop that brawling!"

It was too late. The second gunman tackled The Kid, and the two of them tumbled down the steps, landing in a heap at the bottom.

Elam's man was on top. He hooked a vicious punch into The Kid's side, then tried to dig his knee into The Kid's groin. Writhing out of the way The Kid hammered a fist against the side of the man's head, knocking the gunman away from him. The Kid rolled and came up on one knee.

Mundy had gotten to his feet and swung a kick

at The Kid's head. At that same moment Arturo leaped on Mundy's back and threw him off balance. With a startled yell, Mundy went down again.

Elam stood at the edge of the porch watching the battle. His face was pinched and had gone white with anger, but he didn't make any effort to get in the middle of the ruckus.

The Kid made it to his feet as the second gunman scrambled upright and waded in, swinging wild punches. The Kid blocked a couple, but one of the flailing haymakers got through and landed cleanly on his jaw. It was a lucky punch, but it was enough to knock The Kid to the ground again. The gunman rushed in, clearly intending to stomp him half to death.

The Kid caught hold of the booted foot that descended toward his face and gave it a twist and a heave. The gunman toppled with an angry curse. The Kid rolled over, pushed himself to his hands and knees, and looked around.

A few feet away, Jim Mundy had climbed back to his feet. His left hand was bunched in Arturo's shirtfront, holding him up. His other hand was clenched in a fist and drawn back, poised to smash into Arturo's face.

The Kid dived at Mundy from behind before he could hit Arturo, catching him around the knees and knocking his legs out from under him. The man lost his grip on Arturo's shirt, and Arturo scrambled backward, out of the way.

Mundy kicked out at The Kid, catching the younger man in the chest. For a second, The Kid felt paralyzed and unable to breathe. He wasn't even sure if his heart was still beating.

Rubbing his chest he took a deep breath. Relieved that he wasn't seriously hurt he blocked a looping punch that Mundy threw and landed a sharp jab of his own to Mundy's nose, rocking his head back.

The Kid wrapped his hands around Mundy's neck and locked them in place. Jerking Mundy up a little he slammed the back of the man's head into one of the paving stones that formed the walk. As angry as he was, he might have smashed Mundy's head against the rock several more times and crushed his skull, but a foot crashed into The Kid's side and knocked him sprawling.

As he pushed himself up yet again, the second man rushed him, swinging wildly and letting out a harsh, furious yell.

The Kid stepped inside that blow and lifted an uppercut that smashed home under the man's chin. His teeth clicked together, biting right through the tip of his tongue. He screamed in pain as blood spurted between his lips. The Kid finished him off with a left hook that stretched the gunman on the grass in front of the porch.

Swinging around, ready to continue the battle, The Kid saw that Mundy had pushed himself up on an elbow and was shaking his head groggily. That was as far as Elam's segundo had gotten, and it didn't look like he was going to be continuing the fight any time soon.

The Kid backed off, bending down for a second to pick up the black Stetson with the concho band that had gotten knocked off when the fight started. He kept one eye on Elam and one eye on Mundy. Elam was still just looking on. Obviously he had no interest in joining the battle himself. Paying somebody to do his fighting for him was more Court Elam's style.

The Kid heard excited voices and glanced toward the house. He saw young faces peering from every window. Several of the smaller children had crowded up behind Theresa and ignored her efforts to shoo them back away from the door. They had been watching the fight from around her.

"Is that quite enough violence?" she asked as her eyes locked with those of The Kid.

He brushed the hat off and settled it on his head. Coolly, he said, "They started it."

"No, you started it by sticking your nose in where it doesn't belong," Elam said. "What business is it of yours whether Mrs. Shanley's bill at the store is paid?"

"I'm making it my business, just like I'm making it my business to put a stop to all the hell you and your hired guns have been raising around here, Elam."

"If you have proof of anything, produce it." Elam sneered.

The Kid shook his head. "I don't intend to take you to court . . . Court. I'm going to settle this myself."

Mundy was starting to come around and struggled to his feet. The Kid rested a hand on the butt of his gun, but Mundy had had enough trouble for one day. He said thickly, "We better tend to Fred, Mr. Elam. He's bleedin' all over the place."

The man who had bitten through his tongue was lying on the grass whimpering. Elam gave Mundy a curt nod. The gunman helped Fred to his feet and led him shakily toward the horses.

Elam looked back at Theresa. "You have me all wrong, Mrs. Shanley. I don't want trouble between us. Far from it, in fact. I think we'd do much better working together."

"That will never happen, Mr. Elam. Good day."

He continued to look at her for a long moment before he finally shrugged. "If that's the way you want it," he murmured.

There was a note of dangerous finality in his voice that The Kid didn't like.

Elam came down from the porch. As he passed The Kid, he said under his breath, "This isn't over, Morgan."

"Never thought it was," The Kid said.

Mundy had gotten the injured man on one of the horses. He mounted up on the other and the two of them headed for Main Street. Elam followed in the buggy.

"Mr. Morgan," Theresa said from the porch, having stepped out of the house.

The Kid turned toward her. Glancing around, he spotted the receipt for the money he had paid at the store, and picked it up from the ground. "I imagine you'll be wanting this." He held it out to her.

"What I want is for everyone to leave me alone so I can raise these poor children to the best of my ability." After a second, she took the receipt from him. "Thank you. It was a generous gesture." Her eyes widened slightly as she noticed the amount. "Very generous. Are you sure you can afford this?"

"I'm sure," he said.

"Well, I appreciate it, but you really should have ridden on." She lowered her voice so the children in the house couldn't hear. "You realize you've put a big target on your back, just like the marshal and Jephtha Dickinson did by defying Court Elam?"

"I know that. That was sort of my intention."

"To get yourself murdered?"

"To get Elam worked up enough to make a mistake. When he left here, he looked like he was just about there."

Theresa frowned. "I don't understand. He'll send his hired killers after you. You and your friend can't fight a dozen men, Mr. Morgan."

"Not just the two of us. There have to be some men in this town who can handle a gun." The Kid's voice hardened. "Men who should have gotten together and stood up to Elam a long time before now."

"You're talking about average citizens fighting professional gunmen," Theresa argued. "Elam's men might wipe out the whole town."

The Kid shook his head. "They can't do that. Elam needs folks to run all those businesses he finagled his way into. Without the people, Powderhorn isn't worth anything to him."

Theresa drew a deep breath. "Powderhorn's

not worth anything anyway. If Elam has his way, a year from now the town won't even be here."

The Kid's forehead creased in confusion. "What are you talking about? Of course the town will be here."

"No, Mr. Morgan, you're wrong. There's a very good chance that Powderhorn is going to vanish from the face of the earth."

Chapter 30

A long moment passed before The Kid said quietly, "You're going to have to explain that one."

"I don't have to explain anything." Theresa tilted her chin defiantly.

"You are if you want me to help you."

"Who said that I did? And why would you want to help me, anyway?"

He gestured toward the piece of paper she still clutched in her hand. "That receipt proves I'm on your side. I think the folks in this town deserve better than to be buffaloed by Elam and his men. And I'm mighty curious to know why you think something's going to happen to wipe out the whole town."

Theresa regarded him stubbornly for a moment longer before she sighed. "Not the people. Just the buildings. Everyone's going to have to pack up and move." She motioned for The Kid and Arturo to follow her. "Come around back. I'll tell you about it. For some reason . . . I think you're telling the truth when you say you want to help."

The three of them sat down at a picnic table under a shade tree in the backyard. Theresa tucked the receipt into a skirt pocket and went on. "My late husband worked for the railroad for a number of years before we moved here to Powderhorn. He was a surveyor and helped lay out the route to start with. He had a number of friends among the men who actually run the line, and some of them have stayed in touch with me. Several months ago, I got a letter from one of them. He told me about some rumors he'd heard. The railroad is making a deal with one of the big meat packing companies in Chicago to establish a stockyard here."

The Kid frowned. "When you say here . . ."

She pointed at the ground. "I mean right here. The town will be demolished and hundreds of cattle pens will take its place."

The Kid leaned back on the bench he was sitting on. "That's crazy. With all the open land around here, why would they put their stockyards right here?"

"Because of the creek. It's closer to the tracks here than anywhere else for miles in either direction. This is where it makes a big loop to the south. They'll need plenty of water, and the creek can supply it. It's already being piped over to the water tower at the depot, which is the only thing they're planning to leave standing."

The Kid thought it over and nodded slowly. "I

suppose that makes sense. But what about all the people who live here?"

"The meat packing company will pay them for their property—the ones who actually own the land. Quite a bit of the acreage in town is owned by the railroad and is leased to the people who live on it or have businesses on it. Everyone will have to get out."

"Does Elam know about this?" The Kid asked, his eyes narrowing with suspicion.

"I'm certain he does. When he first came here, I'm convinced he tried to take over as much of the town as possible simply because he's a greedy, arrogant man. But he knows he stands to make even more from the railroad and the meat packing company. He wants to marry me so he can get his hands on this house and the other property I own in town."

"But he couldn't have known about the stockyards when he first proposed to you," The Kid pointed out.

Arturo spoke up, saying, "Any man would be interested in marrying Mrs. Shanley, no matter what the financial considerations might be."

She smiled. "Thank you, Mr. Vincenzo. You're very gallant."

"Simply an honest observer, madam."

"Anyway, that's the situation," Theresa went on. "Elam plans to make a fortune with his land grab before the stockyard plans become public knowledge. I don't think he'll stop at much of anything to force people out. So you see, Mr. Morgan, that's why it doesn't matter whether he has people to run the store and the livery stable and the freight line. Soon those businesses won't exist anymore."

The Kid mulled over everything she had told him. It rubbed him the wrong way that folks could lose their homes and their livelihoods because the railroad and some meat packing company wanted to make more money than they were already making. It wasn't right. It bothered him more knowing it was entirely possible some of the companies in the vast Browning financial empire could have been involved in such shenanigans in the past.

Fortunately, he was one of the few people who could actually do something about that. "Listen to me. Nobody's going to lose their home or their business if I have anything to say about it."

She gave a hollow laugh. "No offense, Mr. Morgan, but Tom Kellogg told me about you. He says you're some sort of drifting gunfighter. You might be able to shoot it out with Jim Mundy and the rest of Elam's men, although they'd probably kill you in the process, but you can't stop a couple of big companies from doing whatever they want to do."

"You'd be surprised," The Kid said with a faint smile. "There's a telegraph office in the train station, I suppose?"

"That's right."

The Kid got to his feet.

"What are you going to do?" Theresa asked.

"Burn up some wires," he said.

* * *

He didn't go straight to the depot when he left the orphanage, however. First he and Arturo stopped at the church to talk to Tom Kellogg. "You know most of the honest men in town, don't you, Tom?"

"I suppose so," the minister replied. "I heard the talk about how you paid off Theresa's account at the store, Mr. Morgan. You have folks in Powderhorn buzzing this morning."

The Kid smiled. "I have a hunch they'll have more to buzz about before this is over. Can you round up as many men as you can get, men who will fight for what's right, and bring them to the orphanage this afternoon?"

Kellogg stared at him in surprise. "You think there's going to be a fight?"

"I think Elam will come after me when he finds out what I've done," The Kid replied with a nod. "I plan to fort up at Theresa's place, and it would be nice to have a few men on my side. It's your chance to rid Powderhorn of Elam and his killers."

"But the children!" Kellogg protested. "That would be putting them in great danger."

The Kid shook his head. "They'll be split up through the town, put with families who can take care of them and keep them safe until after the showdown is over." He smiled. "Who knows, some of those folks might decide they want to give the kids a permanent home."

"I really don't understand any of this," Kellogg muttered. "How do you know Elam will come after you?"

"He's already got a grudge against me," The

Kid explained. "When he finds out how I've
pulled the rug right out from under him, all he'll
be able to think about is getting even with me."

"Pulled the rug out . . . What are you going
to do?"

"Leave that to me," The Kid said. "I'll explain it
all later."

"If you're still alive!"

"I plan to be. I've got another job to finish."

"Your children," the minister said. "That's right.
I'd forgotten about them. You're not just risking
your life, you're risking being able to find them,
too. Why would you do that for people you didn't
even know until yesterday?"

"I don't know." The Kid thought about how
Rebel would never let him turn his back on people
who were in need . . . and about how she would
never run away from a fight. His mother had been
the same way. "I guess I've listened to too many
ghosts in my time."

As he had promised Theresa, he had the telegraph wires smoking between Powderhorn and an
assortment of places both east and west of there,
all the way from Chicago to San Francisco. The
first set of replies warned him that what he wanted
to do wasn't possible, at least not as quickly as he
wanted to do it.

The Kid sent more wires, instructing his lawyers
to make it possible. At the same time, he dis-
patched messages directly to the board of directors of the railroad. At one time, Vivian Browning

had been one of those directors, and her son Conrad could have a seat at that table any time he wanted one.

By mid-afternoon, the messages he wanted to read began trickling in. Deals had been struck. Papers hadn't been signed yet—that would take time, of course—but agreements in principle had been made. The Kid had no doubt everything would go through just as he wanted. He had the best lawyers in the country making sure of that.

The telegrapher, an old man with a green eye-shade and sleeve garters, looked increasingly confused as the messages flowed back and forth. When the negotiations were concluded, The Kid smiled at him. "You want to go tell Court Elam about all of this, don't you?"

"You got me all wrong, Mr. Morgan," the old-timer protested. "Court Elam can go to hell as far as I'm concerned." He hesitated. "That ain't necessarily true for some of the other fellas who work here at the depot, though. Elam spreads some money around to keep informed of everything that goes on."

"Then you might as well collect some of it while you can. Tell Elam whatever you want. And tell him that if he wants to find me, he'll know where I am if he thinks about it."

The telegrapher sighed. "Whatever you say. You sure do know how to stir up a hornet's nest, don't you?"

"It's one of the things I'm good at."

Now it was just a matter of waiting. Maybe he had misjudged Elam, he mused as he walked back toward the orphanage. Maybe when Elam found out what was going to happen, he would abandon his scheme to seize the parts of Powderhorn that he didn't already control. Maybe he would just go on like he had been, content to own half the businesses in town, like before that stockyard deal had come up.

Maybe . . . but considering the pride, arrogance, and anger he had seen in Elam's eyes, The Kid didn't think so.

Actually, he was counting on it.

Chapter 31

Arturo had gone back to the orphanage with instructions for Theresa Shanley. The Kid wasn't sure she would go along with the plan, but now that events had been set in motion, she wouldn't have much choice in the matter if she wanted to keep the children safe. He figured that was more important to her than anything else.

When he reached the big house with its tree-shaded yard, everything looked quiet and peaceful. But as he opened the gate and started up the walk to the porch, Tom Kellogg stepped out of the house with a rifle in his hands.

The Kid stopped at the bottom of the steps and smiled. "I know I told you to gather up some men who were willing to fight, Brother Tom, but I didn't expect you to take up arms yourself."

"A man of God can fight, as long as it's in a righteous cause. I can't think of a cause more righteous than battling murderers."

"Nothing's been proven against Elam and his men in a court of law," The Kid reminded him.

"No one else had any reason to kill Jephtha Dickinson or Marshal Reed. Anyway, we're not taking the fight to them, are we, Mr. Morgan? If Elam doesn't want trouble, he doesn't have to come here."

The Kid nodded. "True enough. How many men are inside?"

"Counting me, eight."

The Kid frowned. He and Arturo would make ten. They would be facing odds of at least two to one. True, they would be defending the house, which would give them a slight advantage, but it might not be enough to balance out the superior numbers Elam would have.

"Theresa insists that she's going to stay and fight, too," Kellogg added. "She says she can handle a rifle just fine."

"Blast it," The Kid muttered. "I was hoping she'd be well out of harm's way." He glanced toward Main Street. "We may not have much more time."

"I tried to talk some sense into her head. She can be a very proud, stubborn woman when she wants to be."

"Yeah, I got that impression. When this is all over, Tom, you'd better tell her how you feel about her."

The preacher's face turned pink. "Is it that obvious?"

"Yeah . . . except maybe to the lady who ought to know it the most."

"Then I have one more reason to ask God to help us prevail. I'll take your advice, Mr. Morgan . . . provided we live through this."

The Kid looked again at the street. He saw a couple of men carrying rifles come around a corner and start up Fifth Street. Neither of them was Court Elam or Tom Mundy, but he had no doubt they were Elam's men.

"Are all the kids gone?" he asked quickly.

"Yes, they're all safe. Members of the church took them in and are caring for them for the time being."

"That's one thing we can be thankful for, anyway." The Kid went up the steps. "I thought there might be more volunteers to help us, but it's too late now. Elam's men are on their way."

As he withdrew into the house with Kellogg, he spotted two more men darting from the concealment of a shed to a spot behind a parked wagon. The Kid suspected a dozen or more men were working their way toward the orphanage, getting into position for the attack.

The question was whether or not Elam would order them to start shooting, or if he would give the house's defenders a chance to surrender first.

The answer came when a buggy rounded the corner and rolled slowly toward the house. From inside the doorway The Kid watched it coming.

A footstep behind him made him glance over his shoulder. Theresa Shanley stood there, a rifle clutched in her hands. "Is Elam coming?"

The Kid nodded. "Yeah. You might still have time to get out the back before he gets here."

"I'm not going anywhere." Her hands tightened on the Winchester. "This is my home, Mr. Morgan. My children may not have been born here, but they . . . they died here, and so did my husband. It's home to all the children I've taken in, too. I won't abandon it."

"Your choice," he said curtly. Anyway, it was probably too late. Elam might have men behind the house, and if he did, they would grab Theresa if she tried to leave. That would be the same as handing over a valuable hostage to Elam.

Kellogg stood behind Theresa. The Kid looked at him and said, "Get the men spread out so they cover as many windows as they can. Make sure each man has plenty of ammunition. Where's Arturo?"

"Upstairs at one of the gable windows," the minister replied. "He says he's a good shot and can pick off some of Elam's men from up there when the shooting starts. I've got a man in one of the attic windows in the back of the house, too."

"Good idea." The Kid commended him with a nod.

The buggy came to a stop in the street in front of the house. The Kid recognized Court Elam's well-dressed figure at the reins. Elam stared at the house for a moment, then called, "Morgan! Morgan, I know you're in there!"

The Kid called through the open door, "I'm here, Elam!"

In a voice that shook with anger, Elam demanded, "What the hell have you done?"

"You know what I've done. That stockyard is

going to be built west of here, on land I sold to the meat packing company for half of what they'd have to pay for this site."

"That's impossible!" Elam shouted back. "Who in blazes *are* you? How does some damn gunfighter pull off a deal like that?"

The Kid glanced at Theresa and Kellogg and saw that they were equally confused. He grinned reassuringly at them and told Elam, "That doesn't matter now. What's important is that you don't have any reason to run people out of their homes and businesses anymore. Why don't you take your hired guns and get out of Powderhorn?"

"Blast it, this is *my* town, Morgan. I'm going to kill you for interfering with my plans!"

That was exactly the reaction The Kid expected from Elam. The man was too arrogant and power-hungry to listen to reason.

"Nobody else has to die, though," Elam went on. "Come on out of there and I give you my word that'll be the end of it."

"What about Mrs. Shanley?"

"Theresa is going to be my wife!" Elam insisted.

She stepped up beside The Kid and shouted, "Never! Go to hell, Elam!" Before either The Kid or Tom Kellogg could stop her, she lifted the rifle to her shoulder and fired.

The whipcrack of the shot filled the street. The rifle's recoil was strong enough to knock Theresa back a step. The Kid wasn't sure where the bullet went, but it didn't hit Elam. He hauled on the reins and jerked his buggy team around, then sent the horses racing back toward Main Street. The

Kid heard him shouting something but couldn't make out the words.

It must have been an order to open fire, because shots suddenly blasted from the hiding places Elam's gunmen had worked themselves into. Slugs thudded into the walls of the big house, but the thick planks stopped them.

The Kid pulled Theresa away from the door and kicked it shut. "Well, that's one way of opening the ball," he said dryly.

"I shouldn't have shot at him like that." She rubbed her shoulder where the rifle's recoil had pounded. "I could have killed him in cold blood."

"But you didn't," The Kid pointed out, "and even if you had, he likely ordered the murders of two men. And that's just the ones we know of. There's no telling what else Elam has done."

"Mr. Morgan's right, Theresa," Kellogg said. "When there's no law, good people have to deal out justice themselves."

The shots from outside continued, and the defenders inside the house returned the fire. Glass shattered under the onslaught, and bullets made curtains flutter as if the wind were blowing through them. The attack seemed to be centered on the front of the house, so The Kid, Theresa, and Kellogg took up the defense there. The Kid and Kellogg crouched by the big window in the parlor that had already been broken out by flying lead. Theresa went to a smaller window at the side of the room, raised the pane, and poked the barrel of her rifle out as she searched for a target.

"Stay down as much as you can, Theresa," Kellogg

warned her between shots. "I don't want anything happening to you before I . . . before I get a chance to tell you something important."

She glanced at him but didn't say anything.

The Kid's Winchester spat fire as one of Elam's men tried to dash from one tree to another. The steel-jacketed slug punched into his chest and flipped him backward like he'd been swatted with a giant hand. He crumpled in a lifeless heap on the grass.

The Kid heard Arturo's rifle crack from upstairs and saw a man topple out from behind a parked wagon. He figured Arturo had had an angle on the gunman from the gable window. Facing the odds they were, it was just the sort of shooting they needed. They had to make nearly every shot count.

Feet clattered on the stairs. The Kid glanced around to see a stranger descending from the second floor. "Brother Tom!" the man called to Kellogg, which identified him as one of the church members.

"What is it, Will?" Kellogg asked.

The man stopped at the bottom of the stairs. "From that attic window I saw a big dust cloud headin' for town. Has to be a bunch of riders to be kickin' up that much dust."

"What direction is it coming from?" The Kid asked.

"From the north," the townie answered.

The Kid's mouth tightened grimly. In all likelihood, the arrival of a large group of riders from that direction meant Elam had summoned the outlaws he'd been working with to help him clean out the opposition in Powderhorn. All the cards were on the table, and neither side could back down.

"What does this mean, Mr. Morgan?" Kellogg asked.

"It means the odds against us are about to get a lot worse," The Kid said bluntly. "If you know any more prayers besides the ones you've already said, Tom, now's the time for 'em."

Chapter 32

Another of Elam's men tried to shift his position. The Kid drilled him cleanly and knocked him down. Shots continued pouring into the house from the attackers, but the sturdy walls gave the defenders good cover.

The Kid glanced over at Theresa and caught her eye. "You're going to have plenty of damage to clean up when this is over."

"I don't mind. It'll be worth it to rid the town of Elam."

The gunfire from outside suddenly increased. The Kid and his two companions in the parlor ducked as a storm of lead smashed into the house. Bullets zinged through the broken windows and thudded into the interior walls. A framed picture fell from its nail, shaken loose by the slugs striking it.

The Kid knew there had to be a reason why Elam's men had stepped up their attack. When he risked a glance over the windowsill, he saw why. A dozen men on horseback were charging the house with guns blazing in their hands. The horses smashed into the picket fence and crashed right through it.

An instant later, a couple men leaped their horses onto the porch. The Kid and Tom Kellogg had to throw themselves aside as one of the animals came right through the empty space where the big window had been.

The Kid rolled across the rug on the parlor floor and brought his Winchester up as he levered a fresh round into the chamber. The man on the horse had stayed in the saddle. He swung his revolver toward The Kid and fired. The bullet smacked into a floorboard only inches from The Kid's head.

The Winchester cracked as The Kid fired it one-handed. The bullet caught the outlaw under the chin and bored on up into his brain, flipping him backward out of the saddle. The Kid scrambled to avoid the slashing hooves of the panic-stricken horse. The other gunman who had reached the porch burst through the front door and tracked his gun toward The Kid.

A rifle blasted and knocked the outlaw back out through the open doorway. The Kid glanced over and saw smoke curling from the barrel of Tom Kellogg's Winchester. Another man started to clamber through the window behind Kellogg. The Kid snapped his rifle to his shoulder and sent a slug boring into the center of the would-be killer's forehead. The man flopped back onto the porch.

Another gunman replaced him an instant later. Several of them had reached the house, getting close enough the defenders at the windows no longer had a shot at them. The Kid knew if more of them managed to pour into the house, they could go through the place and clean it out, killing all the defenders.

It would have helped, he thought bitterly, if more than eight men had stepped forward to help in the battle. But sometimes you had to fight for folks anyway, whether they seemed to deserve it or not.

More determined than ever The Kid wheeled toward the window and fired as the man charged through, shooting blindly. He doubled over and fell when The Kid's bullet punched into his belly. His momentum carried him forward and he crashed into The Kid's legs, knocking him down.

Another man loomed close behind. His gun was chopping down toward The Kid when a blast from the stairs sent him spinning off his feet. Arturo stood there, halfway down the staircase, with a smoking Winchester in his fists.

As The Kid shoved the gut-shot man aside and leaped to his feet, he heard shouts and renewed gunfire outside. Not sure what was going on, he moved cautiously to the door and peered out.

Once the outlaws on horseback had breached the house, it appeared the rest of Elam's men had left their hiding places and joined the charge, eager to get in on the carnage. They were caught in a crossfire as a number of men from town, armed with rifles and shotguns, attacked them from the rear. A grim smile tugged at The Kid's mouth. The citizens of Powderhorn had come through after all. It had just taken most of them a little longer to realize it was time to stand up and fight.

"Come on!" he called over his shoulder to Kellogg and Arturo. "Let's give them a hand!" He jumped off the porch and advanced toward the knot of hired killers in the street. Bracing the Winchester against his hip, he emptied it as fast as he could work the lever and crank off the rounds. Arturo, Kellogg, and several other defenders from the house joined in. Elam's men didn't stand a chance, trapped between the two forces the way they were. Clouds of powdersmoke rolled, and the stench of burned powder and the cries of dying men filled the air.

When the shooting stopped, it was eerie in its abruptness. A few of Elam's men were still alive but wounded. They threw their guns down and begged for mercy.

The Kid looked over the bodies but didn't see Court Elam or Jim Mundy among them. Since his rifle was empty, he tossed it aside and drew the Colt on his hip. Leveling it at one of the wounded men, he asked in a voice as cold as the grave, "Where are Elam and Mundy?"

The man was pale from terror and loss of blood. "Don't shoot!" he wailed.

"Tell me where they are," The Kid ordered.

"They . . . they took off when the fight started goin' against us. Looked like they were headed for . . . the railroad station."

The Kid looked over at Tom Kellogg, whose face was grimy from gunsmoke. Blood dripped down Kellogg's face from a scratch on his head. He didn't look much like a preacher.

"When's the next train due through here, do you know?"

"Sometime this afternoon," Kellogg replied. "Could be any minute."

The Kid nodded. He wasn't surprised. Despite his arrogance, Elam was cunning. He had timed the attack so he'd have a way of escaping if things went bad.

Turning back to the man he'd questioned, The Kid said, "Elam ordered the marshal and Dickinson killed, didn't he?"

The man swallowed hard and nodded. "Mundy did the actual killin', but Elam gave the orders."

"You'll testify to that?"

"Sure."

"All right." The Kid holstered his gun. "Arturo, you and Tom stay here and start getting things cleaned up. Make sure Mrs. Shanley is all right."

"Where are you going, Kid?" Arturo asked.

"To make sure Elam and Mundy get what's coming to them."

"I'll come with you—"

"No, stay here. You know what you have to do if I don't come back."

With that, The Kid strode quickly toward Main Street. On the way, he thumbed a cartridge into the Colt's chamber he usually left empty. He wanted a full wheel for the last act in the drama.

He broke into a run when he heard the shrill blast of a train whistle.

Swinging into Main Street, he saw the plume of

smoke from the locomotive's stack as it approached the town from the east. The whistle blew again. Main Street was empty—as if Powderhorn was a ghost town. Everybody was lying low until the battle was over.

It would be soon, one way or the other.

The Kid circled the depot at a run and came up the stairs at the west end of the platform. The train was about five hundred yards away, slowing to pull into the station.

In the middle of the platform, Court Elam and Jim Mundy stood waiting. Elam nervously clutched a carpetbag. Mundy had a gun in his hand. He was watching the door from the depot lobby, not the end of the platform.

"Elam!" The Kid called. "Mundy!"

Both men jerked toward him. The train whistle screeched again as Mundy's gun came up. The killer's mouth worked, no doubt spewing curses, but The Kid couldn't hear them over the rumble of the engine, the hiss of steam, and the clatter of the train's brakes.

Flame spouted from the muzzle of Mundy's gun. The Kid fired at the same time. He felt the wind-rip of Mundy's slug as it sizzled through the air next to his ear. Mundy staggered. His gun hand drooped. When he tried to bring it back up, The Kid shot him again.

Mundy folded up. His face hit the platform, but he was past feeling it.

That left Elam. The Kid expected him to surrender, but was surprised when the man pulled a pistol from under his coat and started firing as he broke into a run toward the far end of the platform. The Kid squeezed off a shot that clipped Elam's thigh. Dropping the carpetbag and the gun, he flung his arms in the air, and cried out in pain as he fell. He clutched at his wounded leg and rolled over.

The Kid leaped forward, calling, "Elam, look out—"

Elam rolled right off the edge of the platform and landed across the tracks as the train rumbled into the station. The Kid heard him scream, even over all the racket, but the scream didn't last long before it was cut short.

Arturo and Tom Kellogg burst through the doors from the depot lobby, followed by several more townsmen. Kellogg said, "Mr. Morgan! I know you told us to wait, but we had to find out what happened."

"You got your town back, that's what happened," The Kid said as he started to reload the Colt.

Since the orphanage was shot full of holes, Theresa moved into a suite at the Elam Hotel . . . or as it would soon be known, the Powderhorn Hotel, which was its original name. She would stay there until the damage done to her house could be repaired. The children would stay with the various families that had taken them in. The Kid figured there was a good chance some of them wouldn't want to give up the kids when the time came and would welcome them permanently into their homes. He hoped that was the way it turned out.

The next morning, Theresa and Tom Kellogg had breakfast with The Kid and Arturo in Theresa's suite. She said, "I'm not sure how I'm going to pay for all this."

"It's taken care of," The Kid assured her. "Just like the repairs to your house will be."

"What about all the property Elam owned?" Kellogg asked. "He bought most of it legally, even though the sales were forced on the previous owners by threatening their lives."

The Kid sipped his coffee. "I've already got my lawyers working on that. They'll straighten it all out and figure out who should own what. Eventually things will settle back down."

Theresa looked at him and shook her head. "You have all these lawyers working for you and a seemingly limitless amount of money. Who *are* you, Kid Morgan?"

He smiled. "Well . . . I suppose I can trust a preacher and a lady who runs an orphanage. My real name is Conrad Browning. I'd appreciate it if you'd keep that to yourselves, though."

Kellogg frowned, still baffled, but Theresa looked surprised. "Browning," she repeated. "I know that name, from when my husband worked for the railroad. Someone named Browning *owned* part of the railroad."

"My mother," The Kid said. "Now I do."

The minister leaned forward in his chair. "Then what are you doing going around like a . . . a . . ."

"Gunfighter?" The Kid asked with a smile.

"Sometimes it takes us a long time to find out who we really are. I suppose maybe I'm still learning."

"But that story about the two missing children," Theresa said. "That was true?"

"Every word of it."

She reached across the table and rested her hand on his for a moment. "Then I'm sorry you haven't found them. You're going to keep looking?"

"Of course." The Kid drank the rest of his coffee. "In fact, we've already replenished our supplies, the team is hitched up to the buckboard, and my horse is saddled. Arturo and I are ready to go."

"And even though you have a lovely town," Arturo said, "I won't be sad to leave."

Kellogg laughed. "I don't blame you. But we'll be sorry to see you go, after everything the two of you have done for us and everybody else in Powderhorn. You saved the settlement in more ways than one."

Theresa added, "I don't know how we can ever repay you."

"Just keeping making it a good place to live," The Kid said. "That'll be payment enough."

A short time later, they stood on the hotel porch and waved farewell as the rider and the buckboard left Powderhorn, heading west again. Kellogg reached over and took Theresa's right hand in his left as they continued to wave.

"Do you think he'll ever find them?" Theresa asked.

"I know he will," Kellogg said. "No matter how long it takes. And when he does, God willing, Kid Morgan won't be alone anymore."

Turn the page for an exciting preview of

MATT JENSEN, THE LAST MOUNTAIN MAN:

DAKOTA AMBUSH

by

William Johnstone
with J. A. Johnstone

Coming in February 2011
Wherever Pinnacle Books are sold.

Chapter 1

When Matt Jensen rode into Swan, Wyoming, few who knew him would have recognized him. He had a heavy beard, his hair was uncommonly long, and he looked every bit the part of a man who had not been under a roof for two months. He had said good-bye to Smoke Jensen in Fort Collins, Colorado, arranging to meet him in Swan eight weeks later. Not since then had Matt seen civilization, having spent the entire two months in the mountains prospecting for gold.

The success of Matt's two months of isolation was manifested by a canvas bag he had hanging from the saddle horn. The bag was full of color-showing ore. Prospecting wasn't new to Matt. He had learned the trade under the tutelage of his mentor, Smoke Jensen, so he knew the color in the ore was genuine. But exactly how successful he had been would depend upon the assayer's report.

Swan was a fly-blown little settlement, not served by any railroad, though there was stagecoach service to Rawlings where one could connect with the Union Pacific. The town had a single street that was lined on both sides by unpainted, rip-sawed, false-fronted buildings. It could have been any of several hundred towns in a dozen western states. As Matt rode down the street, a couple of scantily dressed soiled doves stood on a balcony and called down to him.

"Hey, cowboy, you're new to town, ain't you?" one of them shouted.

"You gotta be new 'cause I don't know you," the other one added. "And I reckon I *know* just about ever' man in town if you get my drift," she added in a ribald tone of voice.

Matt smiled, nodded, and touched the brim of his hat by way of returning their greeting.

"Come on up and keep us company. We'll give you a good welcome," the first one shouted down to him.

"Ladies, until I get a bath, I'm not even fit company for my horse," Matt called up to the two women as he rode underneath the overhanging balcony where the two women were standing.

The second soiled dove pinched her nose and, exaggerating, made a waving motion with her hand. "Oh, honey, you've got that right," she teased.

Laughing, Matt rode on down the street until he reached a small building at the far end. A sign in front of the building read, J.A. MONTGOMERY, ASSAYER.

Matt swung down from his saddle and tied his horse at the hitching rail. Hefting the canvas bag over one shoulder, he stepped inside where he was greeted by a small, thin man.

"Can I help you?" the little man asked.

"Are you the assayer?"

"I am."

Matt set the canvas bag on the counter, then took out a handful of rocks and laid them alongside the bag.

"I need you to take a look at this," Matt said.

Montgomery chuckled. "You want me to tell you if it is gold or pyrite, right?"

"No, mister," Matt said. "I know it's gold. What I want you to do is tell me how much money all this is worth."

The assayer picked up a couple of rocks and looked at them casually, before putting them back down. Then, taking a second look at one of them, he picked it up again, and he examined it through a magnifying glass.

"What do you think?" Matt asked.

"You're right," Montgomery said. "It is gold."

"You have any idea as to the value?"

"Do all the rocks have this much color?"

"I wouldn't have bothered carrying them in if they didn't," Matt replied.

"Well, then I would say you have two or three hundred dollars here. In fact, I'll give you three hundred dollars for the entire bag, right now."

Matt put the rocks back in the bag. "Would you now?"

"In cash," Montgomery said.

"You always cheat your customers like that?" Matt asked.

"What are you talking about?"

"What I have here is worth two thousand dollars

if it is worth a cent," he said. "Thank you, Mr. Montgomery, but I believe I'll take my business somewhere else."

"I'm the only assayer in town."

"Perhaps. But Swan isn't the only town," Matt said as he left the office.

Up the street from the assayer's office Matt saw a sign that read HAIRCUTS, SHAVES, BATHS.

"Tell you what, Spirit, you've had to put up with my stink long enough," Matt said, speaking to his horse. "I think I'll get myself cleaned up before I go looking for Smoke."

Dismounting in front of the building, Matt lifted his bag of ore from the horse, then went inside. Fifteen minutes later he was sitting in a tub of warm water, scrubbing himself with a big piece of lye soap.

"Don't know if there is enough lye soap in all of Wyoming to get that carcass clean," a voice teased.

"Smoke!" Matt said, a big smile spreading across his face. He started to stand.

"No, no need to stand," Smoke said, holding his hand out, palm forward, to stop him. "You think I want to see that?"

Matt laughed. "How did you know I was in here?"

"We did say we were going to meet in Swan today, didn't we?"

"Yeah."

"I saw Spirit tied up out front. Did you think I wouldn't recognize him? He used to be my horse, remember?"

"I remember," Matt said.

"How did you do?" Smoke asked.

"See that bag there? It's full of ore. At least two thousand dollars worth, I would guess."

Smoke whistled. "That is good," he said.

"Tell you what, I'll be finished here in a bit. What do you say we go get us a beer? I haven't had a beer in two months."

"Sounds good to me. I'll go get us a table, and I'll even let you buy the beer, seein' as you had such a good outing," Smoke said.

A few minutes after Smoke left, Matt was out of the tub, had his shirt and trousers on, and had just strapped on his gun belt when three men burst, unexpectedly, into the room. All three had pistols in their hands.

"We'll take that bag of ore, mister," one of them shouted.

"Who are you?" Matt asked.

"We're the folks you're goin' to give that bag of ore to," one of the three said, and they all laughed.

While the three men were laughing, Matt was drawing his pistol, and while they were reacting to him drawing his pistol, Matt was shooting.

The pistol shots sounded exceptionally loud in the closed room as Matt and the three men exchanged gunfire. When the shooting stopped Matt had not a scratch, but the three would-be robbers lay dead on the floor.

Matt was examining the bodies when four more men came bursting into the room. Three of them were carrying sawed-off shotguns. They were also wearing badges.

The fourth man with them was the assayer.

"There he is, Sheriff! He is the one who stole the bag of ore!" Montgomery shouted, pointing at Matt.

"What?" Matt asked. "What are you talking about? I didn't steal any ore from you!"

"He come into the office a little while ago," Montgomery said. "He had a bag of worthless rocks, usin' it as a way o' getting my attention. While I was looking at his rocks, he stole a bag of genuine ore. I didn't have no choice but to send my brother and two cousins to get the ore back. Didn't know it would come to this, though."

Montgomery looked down at the three dead bodies, then shook his head sadly. "If I had known they was goin' to be murdered like this, I never woulda sent 'em over here. A bag plumb full of gold nuggets isn't worth getting three good men killed."

"Come along, mister," the sheriff said, waving his shotgun menacingly at Matt. "You are about to learn that folks don't come into my town to steal and murder and get away with it."

"Sheriff, this man is lying," Matt said. "I brought some ore in for him to assay. He tried to cheat me out of it so I told him I would go somewhere else. You think I would stop to take a bath if I stole anything in this town?"

"I don't know what you would do, mister," the sheriff said. "But the thing is, I know Montgomery and I don't know you. So I reckon we'll let the judge sort it all out."

Matt looked at the three shotguns leveled at him. He was holding a pistol and he had a notion, but declined. He might be able to kill the sheriff and both his deputies before they realized what was happening, but then, he might not, either. They were carrying shotguns, which gave them an advantage. It would also mean killing innocent men and he couldn't bring himself to do that.

Matt turned the pistol around and handed it, handle first, to the sheriff.

"You are making a mistake, Sheriff," Matt said.

"You let me worry about that."

Montgomery reached for the sack of gold ore.

"Leave it," the sheriff said.

"Why should I leave it, Sheriff? This is the selfsame sack of ore he stole."

"Leave it," the sheriff said again. "We'll let the judge decide whether or not that gold ore is yours."

Montgomery glared at the sheriff, then looked over at Matt. "I'll be standin' in the crowd, watchin' you hang," Montgomery said.

"Let's go, mister," the sheriff said to Matt with a wave of his shotgun. "I got a nice jail cell for you until the judge gets here."

Matt had been in jail for three days awaiting the arrival of the circuit judge so he could be tried. Smoke sat outside his cell visiting with him.

"I shouldn't have left you," Smoke said.

"Why not? If you had stayed, you would be in jail with me right now," Matt said. "What good would that do?"

"I guess you have a point. I couldn't help you any if I were in there with you. At least, by being out here, if you can't convince the judge you are innocent, I'll take matters into my own hands. I'll get you out of here, no matter what I have to do."

Matt was about to answer when he looked up to see the sheriff coming into the jailhouse, leading Montgomery. Montgomery was in shackles.

"What is it?" Matt asked. "What is going on?"

"You're free to go," the sheriff said as he opened the door to the cell. "Mr. Montgomery here will be taking your place."

"Sheriff, I have to hand it to you for doing your job," Matt said. "You've had a good three days of investigating."

"It wasn't me," the sheriff said. "It was John Bryce."

"Who?"

"John Bryce," the sheriff repeated. "Mr. Bryce is a newspaper writer for the *Swan Journal*, and he has been doing some, he calls it, investigative journalism. Here, read this," he said, handing Matt a newspaper.

An Innocent Man in Jail!

J. A. MONTGOMERY A CROOK
SHOULD BE CALLED TO ACCOUNT

We are under obligation to report to the public in general and to Sheriff Daniels in particular, the criminal activities of J. A. Montgomery who has set himself up in Swan as an assayer. Montgomery is no such thing. Although he has hanging on the wall of his office a degree from Colorado School of Mines, this newspaper is in receipt of a letter from that institution claiming that no such person as J. A. Montgomery graduated, nor was ever a student there.

Further investigation has disclosed that Montgomery is wanted by the sheriff of Madison County, Montana where, also fraudulently passing himself off as an assayer, he murdered and robbed a prospector. The circumstances of that event are so similar to the recent event between J. A. Montgomery, his brother Clyde, two cousins, Drake and Birch, and a recent visitor to our town, Matt Jensen, that this newspaper believes Mr. Jensen, who is currently incarcerated, is innocent.

Should Matt Jensen be any longer detained, it would be a gross miscarriage of justice. Subjecting the county to a trial to establish his innocence would be a waste of time and taxpayers' money. The writer of this piece, John Bryce, is willing to stake his reputation upon the accuracy of this report, and urges Sheriff Daniels to act quickly to correct this error.

"After the paper come out I sent a telegram to the sheriff of Madison County, Montana, and he answered that Montgomery was wanted for murder, just like the newspaper article said. I went over to talk to Montgomery and found that he was tryin' to leave town."

"So I am free to go?" Matt asked.

"Yes, sir, you are free as a bird."

"Is this fella, John Bryce in town?" Matt asked.

"Yes, sir, he's over at the newspaper office right now," Sheriff Daniels said.

"I think I'll go look him up."

"Do you own this paper?" Matt asked when he and Smoke found John Bryce hard at work in the newspaper office.

"Oh, heaven's no. It takes a lot of money to own and operate your own newspaper," John said. "I just work here for Mr. Peabody as one of his journalists. Someday I expect to own my own paper, though," he said.

Matt, who had had the ore returned to him, reached down into his canvas bag and pulled out four pretty good sized rocks. "Here," Matt said, handing the rocks to the newspaper man. "Cash these in and you may have your paper sooner than you realize. If there is ever anything I can do for you, just let me know."

"Bless you, Mr. Jensen," John said, accepting the gold with a broad smile. "I'll never forget you for this."

Chapter 2

Fullerton, Dakota Territory, twelve years later

A brick had been thrown through the front window, and great jagged spears of the glass reached out from all corners of the frame. Two months earlier John Bryce had paid a professional painter to come over from Bismarck to paint the window.

FULLERTON DEFENDER
John Bryce—*Publisher*
Millie Bryce—*Office Manager*

The letters were broad and black, outlined in white and gold. That sign, once a source of pride, was now no more than a few discordant letters on the remaining shards of glass.

LLE	ON	F	DER
J	y		*lisher*

Not one letter of Millie's name remained.

At the moment, John was standing inside the office of the *Fullerton Defender*, surveying the damage. The perpetrators had done more than just break his front window, they had also trashed the office. His arm was around his wife, and he held her close to him as she sobbed quietly. Type had been scattered about the room, newsprint had been ripped and spread around, the Washington Hand Press, by which John put out his weekly paper, was lying on its side.

They had come to the newspaper office directly from their breakfast table, after City Marshal Tipton told of the break-in. More than a dozen citizens of the town had already been drawn to the scene of the crime by the time John and Millie arrived. The group stood in a little cluster on the boardwalk in front of the building.

The perpetrators had left a note.

Don't be writting no more bad artacles about Lord Denbigh or we will kum back and do more damige to you nex time.

"Who would do such a thing?" Millie asked between sobs.

"It's fairly apparent, isn't it?" John replied. "Denbigh did it."

"We don't know that," Marshal Tipton said.

"The note doesn't suggest that to you, Marshal?" John asked.

"Just the opposite," Tipton said. "Denbigh is an educated man. Now, I'm not as smart as you are, but even I know how to spell the words *come*, and *damage*."

"I don't mean Denbigh did it himself," John said. "I mean he had it done."

"Maybe there are just some people in town who got upset with you because you've been coming down pretty hard on Denbigh in your stories. Denbigh has done a lot of good for this town."

"Really? What good has he done?"

"Let's just say he does a lot of business with the town."

"Yes, by allowing only the businesses he wants to stay, and squeezing out the others. He's killing this town, Marshal Tipton. And the people in town know it, only they are too frightened to do anything about it."

"So you plan to mount a one person campaign, do you, Bryce?"

"If I am the only one willing to do anything about it, then yes, I will mount a one person campaign."

"Uh—huh," Tipton said, stroking his jaw as he surveyed the shambles of the newspaper office. "And look what it got you."

"It has set me back a bit, I'll admit," John said. "But it won't stop me. It'll take me a day to clean up. I'll have the paper out this Thursday, just as I do every Thursday."

"I'll help you pick up all the type, Mr. Bryce," a young boy of about twelve said.

"Thank you, Kenny."

"I can go get Jimmy to help too, if you want me to."

"That would be nice," John said. He turned toward the group of people still standing outside the office, and seeing Ernie Westpheling, called out to him.

"Ernie, would you help me set the printing press back up?"

"Sure thing." Ernie, who had been a colonel during the Civil War, was a local business man who owned a gun store.

A couple of other men also volunteered to help, and within a few minutes the printing press had been righted and was once again in its proper place. John surveyed it for a moment or two, then patted the press with a big smile.

"Not a scratch," he said. "It takes more than a few of Denbigh's hooligans to put ole George out of business."

"George? I thought your name was John," one of the men who had helped him said.

"It is. George is the name of my printing press."

"You've named your press?"

"Sure. It's not only a part of this newspaper, it is the heart of the newspaper."

"What are you going to do about your window?" Ernie asked.

"I'll have to order a new glass from Bismarck," John said. "In the meantime I guess I'll just board that side up."

"What are you going to do about this, Marshal?" Ernie asked.

"I'll look into it, see if I can find out who did it,"

Tipton replied. "But if I don't come up with any witnesses, I don't know what I can do."

"There has to be a witness somewhere," Millie said. "It had to make a lot of noise when they broke out the window."

"You live no more than a couple of blocks from here, Mrs. Bryce. Did you hear anything?" Tipton asked.

"No."

"The newspaper belongs to you and your husband, so you would be even more attentive, I would think. You heard nothing, but you expect others in the town did?" Tipton shook his head. "No ma'am, I don't expect I'm going to find anything."

"That's because you aren't looking in the right place," John said. "You and I both know who is behind this."

Tipton glared at John, but he said nothing.

Central Colorado

"Is the son of a bitch still following?" Cyrus Hayes asked Emmet Cruise. The two men had stopped for a moment in order for Hayes to relieve himself, and Cruise crawled up onto a rock to look back along the trail.

"Yeah, he's there," Cruise said.

"What the hell? Are we leaving bread crumbs or something?" Hayes asked as he buttoned his trousers. "Who the hell is that, and how is he staying on our trail?"

"I don't know who he is, but he's good," Cruise said.

"Yeah, well, let's go," Hayes said. "The more distance we can put between us and him, the better I will feel."

Earlier that morning, Hayes and Cruise had robbed the Rocky Mountain Bank and Trust in Pueblo, Colorado and, during the robbery, had shot down, in cold blood, a teller and two customers. The two customers, a man and his pregnant wife, had been friends of Matt Jensen. Because of that, even before the state got around to offering a reward for two bank robbers and murderers, Matt went after them.

Knowing they would be pursued, the two outlaws took great pains to cover their true trail, while leaving false trails for anyone who would follow. Reaching a stream, they rode right down the middle of it, confident they were erasing any sign that could possibly be followed.

For most trackers that might work, but not for Matt. He had learned his tracking expertise from Smoke Jensen, who had learned his own skills from an old mountain man named Preacher, arguably, the best tracker who had ever lived. Because that know-how had been passed down, Matt was almost as accomplished as Smoke or Preacher. He could follow a trail through the water by paying attention to such things as rocks dislodged against the flow of water, or silt disturbed by horse's hooves, leaving a little pattern in the water for several minutes afterward.

Matt was tracking down the streambed when a rifle boomed and a .44-40 bullet cracked through the air no more than an inch from his head.

He leaped from his horse and ran though the stream, his feet churning up silver sheets of spray as he ran. The rifle barked again. Right on top of that he heard the flatter sound of a pistol shot. Almost simultaneously two bullets plunged into the water close by.

Reaching the bank on the opposite side of the stream, Matt dived to the ground then worked his way toward a nearby outcropping of rocks. He sat with his back against the biggest of the rocks while he took a few deep breaths.

"Who are you?" one of the men called out to him.

"My name is Jensen," Matt called back.

"Jensen? Matt Jensen? Son of a bitch!" The outlaw had obviously recognized Matt's name. There was fear in his voice.

"Which one are you?" Matt called back. "Are you Hayes or Cruise?"

"What? I'm Hayes. How did you know our names?"

"Half the town saw you two boys riding away from the bank, and half the ones who saw you, knew who you were."

"What are you after us for, Jensen?" Hayes called. "I've heard of you, but I ain't never heard that you was someone who would chase a fella down for the reward. Is that why you are chasin' us?"

"I'm not after the reward."

"Then if you ain't after the reward, what the hell are you comin' after us for?"

"It seems the thing to do," Matt said, without being specific as to his reasons.

"Well, mister, you made a big mistake," Hayes shouted. "'Cause all you're goin' to do now is get yourself kilt!"

Hayes and Cruise fired again, and once more the bullets whistled by harmlessly.

"You still there?" Hayes called.

"I'm still here."

"I tell you what, mister. Me and my partner here just talked it over, and we got us an idee. We have got us near 'bout five thousand dollars that we taken from the bank. A thousand of it is your'n if'n you'll just go away," Hayes called.

"No deal."

There was a beat of silence, then Hayes called out again. "All right, how 'bout two thousand? We'll give you two thousand and all you got to do is let us ride away."

"You expect me to believe you two are willing to give me nearly half of what you took from the bank?"

"Why not? It's no big deal, we can always rob another bank," Hayes shouted back. "Two thousand dollars. You don't come across money like that very often, do you?"

"Not very often," Matt agreed.

"So, what do you think? You going to take us up on the offer?"

"Let me think about it," Matt said.

"You do that."

Matt had no intention of taking the two men up on their offer, but he responded in such a way as to enable him to stall for time until he figured out how best to handle the situation. He picked up a stick about two feet long, put his hat on top of the stick, then raised it slightly above the rock.

A rifle boomed, and the hat flew off the end of the stick.

"Ha! You got 'im, Cruise!" Hayes shouted.

"Whoa, I guess you two boys weren't really serious about giving me all that money, were you?" Matt called out.

"Son of a bitch, I missed!" Cruise said.

"Mister, you know what I said about givin' you that money? Well you can forget about it. We ain't goin' to give you nothin'," Hayes said. "Except maybe a bullet right between your eyes." His shout was punctuated with another rifle shot hitting the top of the rock, then whining off into the valley.

After that there was silence.

The silence stretched into several long minutes.

"Hayes? Cruise? You still up there?" Matt called.

Another rifle shot hit the rock just to the right of him. The one with the rifle had improved his position. As Matt scooted around to put the rock between himself and the shooter, there was a second shot.

Matt saw the puff of smoke from the rifle, so he aimed at the spot and waited. Seconds later he was rewarded by seeing Cruise's face raise up.

Matt pulled the trigger, and Cruise fell forward, sliding belly down until his face ended up in the stream. Matt watched for a moment longer to make certain Cruise was dead when suddenly he heard the sound of horses' hooves. Looking around he saw that Hayes had used the opportunity to get mounted and was galloping toward him. Hayes had his pistol in his hand, firing at Matt as he rode.

Matt fired back. A puff of dust rose from Hayes' vest, followed by a tiny spray of dust and blood. Hayes pitched backward out of his saddle but one foot hung up in the stirrup. His horse continued to run, raising a plume of water as the outlaw was dragged through the stream. When the horse reached the other side of the stream and started up the bank, Hayes' foot disconnected from the stirrup and he lay motionless, half in the water and half out, not more than ten feet from where the body of his partner lay.

Matt ran over to them, his gun still drawn, but the gun wasn't necessary. Both men were dead.

Chapter 3

Hayes and Cruise were not the first outlaws Matt had ever tracked down. He was neither a lawman nor someone who hunted other men for a reward the government paid, but he was always on the side of law and order. Sometimes, going after an outlaw just seemed to be the right thing to do.

He never sought trouble but, somehow, trouble had a way of finding him. As a result, Matt Jensen was one of a select company of men in the West whose very name evoked fear among the outlaws and evildoers.

Matt took the bag of bank money from Hayes' saddle, and started back to Pueblo, but just after noon, his horse stepped into an unseen prairie dog hole. The horse broke a leg and Matt had to shoot him. It was a hard thing to do; Spirit was only the second horse he had ever owned. Indeed, that horse had carried with him the spirit of his first horse, who was also named, not coincidentally,

Spirit. There was nothing Matt could do but take shanks mare, so, throwing his saddle, saddle bags, and the money bag over his shoulder, he began walking.

Matt Jensen dropped his saddle with a sigh of relief, then climbed up the berm to stand on the ballast between the railroad tracks. Before him the clear tracks of the Denver and New Orleans lay like twin black ribbons across the landscape, stretching north to south from horizon to horizon. For the moment they were as cold and empty as the barren sand, rocks, and mountains that surrounded him, but Matt knew a train would pass through there sometime before sundown.

Since putting his horse down, Matt had walked for two hours, carrying his saddle with him. At the moment, he was standing alongside the railroad tracks some thirty miles south of Pueblo. All that was left for him to do was catch the train, so, using his saddle as a pillow, he lay down beside the tracks to wait. As he waited, he thought of the horse he had just put down. In order to combat the grief that threatened to consume him, he turned his thoughts to his first horse named Spirit, and how he had come by him.

Right after the war, while still a boy named Matt Cavanaugh, the man known as Matt Jensen made the trip west from Missouri with his father, mother, and sister. On the trail west, their wagon was attacked by outlaws, and all were killed but Matt. He escaped, managing to kill one of the outlaws in the process. The incident left Matt an orphan and shortly thereafter he wound up in the Soda Springs Home for Wayward Boys and Girls. Rather than providing a refuge, the orphanage was so evilly run that eventually Matt escaped from the home.

A few days later Matt, nearly dead from hunger and the cold, was found in the mountains by the legendary Smoke Jensen. Smoke took the boy in and raised him to adulthood. Out of respect and appreciation, Matt Cavanaugh changed his name to Matt Jensen and though there was no blood relationship between the two men, they regarded each other as brothers. When it was time for Matt to go out on his own, Smoke surprised him with an offer.

"Why don't you go out to the corral and pick out your horse?" Smoke had asked.

"My horse?"

"Yeah, your horse. A man's got to have a horse."

"Which horse is mine?" Matt asked.

"Why don't you take the best one?" Smoke replied. "Except for that one," he added, pointing to an appaloosa in one corner of the corral. "That one is mine."

"Which horse is the best?" Matt asked.

"Uh-uh," Smoke replied, shaking his head. "I'm willing to give you the best horse in my string, but as to which horse that might be, well, you're just going to have to figure that out for yourself."

Matt walked out to the small corral that Smoke had built and, leaning on the split-rail fence, looked at the string of seven horses from which he could choose.

After looking them over very carefully, Matt smiled, and nodded.

"You've made your choice?" Smoke asked.

"Yes."

"Which one?"

"I want that one," Matt said, pointing to a bay.

"Why not the chestnut?" Smoke asked. "He looks stronger."

"Look at the chestnut's front feet," Matt said. "They are splayed. The bay's feet are just right."

"What about the black one over there?"

"Uh-uh," Matt said. "His back legs are set too far back. I want the bay."

Smoke reached out and ran his hand through Matt's hair.

"You're learning, kid, you're learning," he said. "The bay is yours."

Matt's grin spread from ear to ear. "I've never had a horse of my own before," he said. He jumped down from the rail fence and started toward the horse.

"That's all right, he's never had a rider before," Smoke said.

"What?" Matt asked, jerking around in surprise as he stared at Smoke. "Did you say he's never been ridden?"

"He's as spirited as he was the day we brought him in."

"How'm I going to ride him, if he has never been ridden?"

"Well, I reckon you are just going to have to break him," Smoke said, passing the words off as easily as if he had just suggested that Matt should wear a hat.

"Break him? I can't break a horse!"

"Sure you can. It'll be fun," Smoke suggested.

Smoke showed Matt how to saddle the horse, and gave him some pointers on riding it.

"Now, you don't want to break the horse's spirit," Smoke said. "What you want to do is make him your partner."

"How do I do that?"

"Walk him around for a bit so he gets used to his saddle, and to you. Then get on."

"He won't throw me then?"

"Oh, he'll still throw you a few times," Smoke said with a little laugh. "But at least he'll know how serious you are."

To Matt's happy surprise, he wasn't thrown even once. The horse did buck a few times, coming down on stiff legs, then sunfishing and, finally, galloping at full speed around the corral. But, after a few minutes he stopped fighting and Matt leaned over to pat him gently on the neck.

"Good job, Matt," Smoke said, clapping his hands quietly. "You've got a real touch with horses. You didn't break him, you trained him, and that's real good. He's not mean, but he still has spirit."

"Smoke, can I name him?"

"Sure, he's your horse, you can name him anything you want."

Matt continued to pat the horse on the neck as he thought of a name.

"That's it," he said, smiling broadly. "I've come up with a name."

"What are you going to call him?"

"Spirit."

* * *

As Matt lay alongside the track he continued to think about his two horses named Spirit. He had given them good lives, treated them well, always making certain they were well fed and cared for, but in the end, both had died before their time. By being his horses, they had been subjected to more danger than most.

He thought about the expression in Spirit II's eyes, just before he had pulled the trigger. It was as if Spirit II knew what was about to happen to him. Was he blaming Matt? Was he telling Matt he understood it had to be done?

Before he could sink any deeper into the morass of melancholy, he heard a distant whistle. Pushing the gloomy thoughts away, he got up from his impromptu bed and looked south, toward the train. When first he saw it, it seemed to be creeping along, though Matt knew it was doing at least twenty miles per hour. It was the distance that made it appear as if the train was going much slower. That same distance also made the train seem very small. Even the smoke pouring from its stack seemed but a tiny wisp against a sky which had now been made gold by the setting sun.

Matt could hear the reverberation of the puffing engine, sounding louder than one might think, given the distance. When the train came close enough for him to be seen, Matt stepped onto the track and began waving. After a few waves, he heard the train braking so he knew the engineer had spotted him and was going to stop. The train which had appeared so tiny before, appeared huge. It ground to a squeaking, clanking halt with black smoke pouring from its stack. Tendrils of white steam, escaping from the drive cylinders and limned in gold by the rays of the setting sun, wreathed the huge wheels.

The engineer's face appeared in the window. "What do you want, mister? Why'd you stop us?" he called down to Matt, raising his voice over the rhythmic sound of venting steam.

"My horse stepped in a prairie dog hole and I had to put him down," Matt said. "I need a ride."

The engineer stroked his chin for a moment, studying Matt as if trying to decide whether or not he should pick him up.

"What's going on here? Why did we stop?" another man asked, approaching the engine quickly and importantly from somewhere back in the train. The man was wearing the uniform of a conductor.

"This fella needs a ride," the engineer said. "His horse went down on him."

"I'm not in the habit of giving charity rides to indigents," the conductor said.

"I can pay," Matt said. "I need to get to Pueblo."

"You can pay, can you? Well let me ask you this. Does this place look like a depot to you? Do you think you can just flag down a train and board it anywhere you wish?" the conductor asked in a self-important and sarcastic voice.

"I don't know about you, Mr. Gordon, but I wouldn't feel right just leavin' him out here," the engineer said. "I mean, him losin' his horse and all, kind of makes it like an emergency, don't it?"

The conductor stroked his chin and spent a long moment studying Matt. All the while the pressure relief valve continued to vent steam, giving the engine the illusion of some great beast of burden, breathing heavily from its exertions. Some distance away a coyote barked, and closer in, a crow called.

"Hey! What's going on? Why have we stopped?" a passenger called, walking toward the engine.

"Get back in the cars, sir!" the conductor shouted

"You've got a trainload of people wondering why we stopped. We've got a right to know what is going on," the passenger said.

"Please, sir, get back in the cars," the conductor repeated. "I will take care of the situation." The conductor waited until the passenger reboarded the train, then he looked up at the engineer.

"All right, Cephus, have it your way," the conductor said. He turned to Matt. "I don't like unscheduled stops like this, but I don't want it said that I left you stranded out here. It is going to cost you two dollars to go to Pueblo."

"Thanks," Matt said, taking two dollars from the poke in his saddle bag and handing it to the conductor.

"Sorry about your horse, mister," the engineer called down from the cab window.

"Yes, he was a good horse."

In an elaborate gesture, the conductor pulled a watch from his vest pocket, popped open the cover, and examined the face. The silver watch

as attached to a gold chain making a shallow U
cross his chest.

"Cephus, we are due in Pueblo exactly one
our and twenty-seven minutes from right now,"
e conductor said to the engineer as he snapped
ie watch closed and returned it to his vest
ocket. "I do not plan to be late. That means I
xpect you to make up the time we have lost by
iis stop."

"Yes, sir, Mr. Gordon, don't worry. If Doodle
:eps the steam up, we'll be there on time."

"Don't you be worryin' none about the steam,"
oodle, the fireman said, stepping onto the plat-
rm that extended just behind the engine. "You'll
ive all the steam you need."

"Come along," the conductor said to Matt. "You
in ride in any car. There are seats in all three of
iem. They are all day coaches."

"I'd rather ride in the express car, if you don't
ind," Matt said.

"No, I'm sorry, I can't let you in there," the con-
ictor replied.

"Maybe you haven't heard," Matt said, "but the
ink in Pueblo was robbed this morning."

"Yes, I heard. What does that have to do with
iything?"

Matt held up the canvas bag he had taken from
yrus Hayes' body. "This is the money that was
ken from the bank."

"What? What the hell, mister? Are you telling
e you are the one who held up the bank?"

"No," Matt said. "I'm the one who is taking the
oney back to the bank. I would just as soon not

be riding in one of the passenger cars, while I'
carrying this."

"Oh," the conductor said.

At that moment the door to the express car sli
open, and the express messenger looked down o
them. "He can ride in here with me, Mr. Gordo
It will be all right."

"I'll let him in there, but remember, it was you
idea, not mine," Gordon replied.

"I'll remember. Hi, Matt," the messenger said

Matt smiled up at a friend with whom he ha
played cards many times. "Hi, Jerry," he greete